IN THE MIRROR, A PEACOCK DANCED

JUSTINE BOTHWICK

Uncorrected Proof

NOT FOR RESALE OR QUOTATION

22 JULY 2021
Print Edition ISBN 9781913099718
£8.99 | $15.99 | €9.99

24 JUNE 2021
Also available in eBook
Special eBook Pre-Order Price
£1.99 | $2.99 | €2.99

For publicity enquiries, please contact
publicity@agorabooks.co

For sales enquiries, please contact
hello@agorabooks.co

About the Author

Justine Bothwick grew up in Kent and Hampshire, and studied in London. In 2005, she moved to Italy and now teaches English in an international secondary school in Rome. She is married to a Roman architect. Together they have a flat in the city with a small balcony on which she grows her ever expanding collection of plants and watches the local birdlife.

Justine is a graduate of the Manchester Writing School's Creative Writing MA programme and has short stories published in *Fictive Dream, Virtual Zine, Confingo Magazine,* and forthcoming in *The Lonely Crowd,* and with *Nightjar Press.*

In the Mirror, a Peacock Danced is her debut novel.

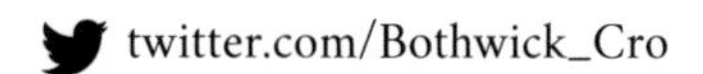

Also by Justine Bothwick

Short Stories

The Taste of Sand

Petrified

A Spotter's Guide to the Seashore

Behind Closed Eyes

Another Man's Smile

Tenderness

Life Trickles In

Static

IN THE MIRROR, A PEACOCK DANCED

JUSTINE BOTHWICK

This is a work of fiction. All characters and events in this work, other than those clearly in the public domain, are entirely fictitious. Any resemblance to any persons, living or dead, is entirely coincidental.

ISBN 978-1-913099-71-8

Proof copies printed and bound in Great Britain by Pixel Colour Imaging Ltd, 2020

Cover Design By: Emma Rogers

Cover Images © Shutterstock

First published in Great Britain in 2021 by Agora Books

Agora Books is a division of Peters Fraser + Dunlop Ltd

55 New Oxford Street, London WC1A 1BS

For Mum and Dad,
with love

PART I

Chapter One

AGRA, 1938

It was a morning for wraiths and spirits, with a swirling fog that shrouded the December sun. Florence shivered and kicked her horse into a canter down the road towards the gate of the fort. The speed of the animal, the percussion of hooves battering the dried mud, settled her thoughts.

The Red Fort was full of ghosts, or so they said, and last night she had dreamt of her mother flickering in and out of its empty rooms and courtyards. She didn't believe in ghosts, not really, but she'd awoken in the dark of her room, early on the morning of her eighteenth birthday, with a sense of longing. The dream had disturbed her, an echo of a laugh remaining as she sat up in bed. Her first thought had been the cemetery, but visits there failed to move her. The Fort, however, was full of shadows and silent corners where it might just be possible to hear her dead mother's voice once again.

The gates appeared ahead, indistinct at first, russet columns flanking a large door. At the entrance, the guard, a man she had known since she was small, raised a hand as she jumped to the ground and looped the reins over a post. She walked along the side of the wall until she came to a small door hidden behind a pillar, lifted the latch, and slipped inside.

She headed away from the residential quarter towards the far side, which had been left to crumble and decay after the sieges of the previous century. In places she had to clamber over rubble and broken walls, or squeeze through jagged gaps where, according to her father, once had stood jewelled thrones inlaid with precious stones. *Plundered the lot, we did,* her father liked to say. *And what for? A handful of private museums and exclusive exhibitions where no one will ever see them.* Florence tried to shake his voice from her head. The gloomy corridors opened out into a large, rectangular space, flanked by fine, marble screens. A thousand stars perforated the walls so they seemed as delicate as lace.

The exercise and activity, however, had erased the strangeness of the dream and lifted her mood, and Florence thought perhaps she ought to be more pragmatic about things, rather than give way to fanciful notions of communing with the dead. She sat in a corner of the courtyard, where the sunshine was beginning to filter through the mists, and raised her face to the light. Of course, it was all because of the argument with her father the night before, not even an hour after she had arrived from Simla. Two days by bullock cart, car, and train, and she had stood on the platform, gritty-eyed and in need of a bath. The rest of her pals dispersed with tearfully smiling mothers and stiff-backed fathers, but Florence had to wait until Ravi appeared, apologising that Mr Harry *Sahib* was having lunch at the Club and had taken the car.

At home, the first person to greet her had been Sita. At least there was Sita, with her gentle embrace, the familiar scent of cardamom on her skin and jasmine in her hair. 'You are grown again. Taller than me now,' she had said smiling up at her. It was true. It was the first time Florence had been aware of her height, looking down at the woman who had raised her, protected her, had always been there as a salve to the hurt of her father's moods.

'Eighteen tomorrow. Please don't tell me Papa has organised a party.'

'Ah, you know your father, my golden one.' Sita smoothed Florence's blond curls. 'Try to make him happy.'

'But it's my birthday. Shouldn't he be trying to make me happy? Not humiliate me in front of everyone, like he always does.'

Sita patted Florence's hand. '*Beti*, he just wants to show everyone what a wonderful daughter he has. He is proud of you.'

'But he's not proud of me, is he? Not of who I really am. Just an idea of who he thinks I ought to be.'

'Don't be upset now. I will run you a bath. You will feel better after.'

And Florence had felt better, for a short while, but then her father had arrived home and told her what he expected at the party tomorrow, and the usual argument had begun.

It had been the same for as long as she could remember. And so, this year, she had asked him, told him, she just wanted dinner at the Club with the few friends she had remaining in Agra, and that would be an end to it. And as always, he'd ignored her. She needed someone on her side, apart from Ravi and Sita, someone he might listen to. She needed her mother.

Florence looked around the courtyard of The Fort, the red sandstone glowing in the strengthening sun. 'How could you do it?' she said into the silence. 'Leaving me alone to be raised by him. I was just a little baby. What happened to you, Mama? What did he do to you?' She waited, feeling foolish in her faint hope that somebody might answer, but there was just the sound of a crow cawing from top of the wall. *Stupid bird*, she thought, and threw a stone in its direction. It tilted its head to one side, looking at her for a moment, then lazily flapped away over the roof. With a sudden swell of emotion, Florence raised her voice. 'Just tell him, Mama. Can't you tell him to let me be who I want to be?' But of course, no one replied.

After a few more minutes of sitting by herself, Florence began to feel a bit ridiculous. This wasn't going to help, hiding in abandoned corners of crumbling old forts. She had to be realistic. Papa wasn't going to change. There was nobody who could stand up to him on her behalf, least of all her dead mother. She'd have to handle him herself. Maybe she could convince him to respect her wishes, and if not, she would have to learn not to care.

Florence stood and looked around at the courtyard, by now filled with light. How silly she'd been, all over a little dream. She walked across the slabs of stone, thinking she should get back to her horse. She would have a good gallop across the fields to get all these ideas out of her system, and then she would start her birthday properly.

As she gathered the reins and urged Oscar into a trot, she knew, however, that there was still a question she wanted her father to answer. And she was going to ask him again today, and maybe this time he would give her a proper response.

Chapter Two

PORTSMOUTH, 1953

On the day that Robert started school, Florence also had an interview at the new factory that had opened up on the outskirts of the town. That morning, she hurried around the little house, two-up two-down, trying to make sure they both looked presentable. Riding out at sunrise to climb around old forts seemed the stuff of fairy tales these days. She arranged her son's new uniform on his bed — the one that converted into a chair in the front room — while he sat at the kitchen table, spooning porridge slowly into his mouth. When he had finished, she grabbed the bowl and pushed him towards the sink with instructions to wash his face, get dressed, and comb his hair. In the meantime, she attacked her own unruly mop, jamming in some pins to keep it from flying all over the place. She thought briefly of Sita's gentle hands, brushing her curls into shining submission, ensuring she looked her best for every special occasion — her eighteenth birthday party came to mind — but then pushed the memory away: there was no time for idle nostalgia now. She pulled on one of her precious pairs of nylons, taking care not to snag them with her nails, and smoothed her skirt back down. Then she did up the buttons on her blouse and gave an approving little twirl for nobody in particular. The clock on the mantelpiece said half-past eight.

'Robert! Quickly, please. We need to go.'

She heard the thud of feet overhead as Aunt Sarah roused herself from bed, and then the shriek of wood on damp wood as she heaved open the sash window. Aunt Sarah was a great believer in fresh air. Robert appeared in the doorway, hair slicked back darkly away from his face, socks pulled up, and shirt tucked into his shorts, which were obviously two sizes too big for him. Florence nodded and helped him into his blazer, also cut for someone several years older. He ran to the front door, buckled on his shoes, picked up his satchel, and waited with a look of bright hope on his face. With everything in order, she pushed her son out on to the street. They set off, Robert running to keep up with her long strides.

'Come on, Robert. You can't be late on your first day. Come on!'

Florence deposited Robert with the schoolteacher in the yard and kissed him on the cheek. He looked lost and very small as he waited in a line with all the other children, but she didn't have time to stay until they went inside. She waved at him and blew him another kiss, then turned and walked as quickly as possible to the bus stop down the road.

The morning shift had already started when she arrived at the factory gates, and the street outside was quiet. A watchman let her in, and she followed the path along to the office building: a fancy, red-brick affair presiding over a green lawn complete with splashing fountain. She pushed her way through the door and followed the signs along a hallway lined with plush red carpet to the reception. This wouldn't be such a bad place to work. Warm, comfortable – miles better than being at home all day in that poky house listening to Aunt Sarah lecture and moralise, that was certain. A woman sat behind a desk, hair piled high on her head and a pair of glasses shaped like wings perched on her nose.

'I'm here for the interview. For the secretarial position. Florence Greene.'

The woman leafed through a book and frowned. 'No. That was yesterday. Today is assembly-line workers. You need to go to the shop floor.'

Florence took a letter out of her bag. 'It says here, tenth of September. That's today. And here's my name, and here's where it says for the position of secretary.'

The woman sighed and adjusted her glasses to look directly at Florence. 'Well, there's been some mix-up, I'm afraid. We appointed a secretary yesterday. Like I said, today is assembly-line workers. If you're desperate for a job ...' and here she stopped to look Florence up and down in a way that made her want to check she hadn't already laddered her stockings, 'then you can go down to the shop floor and ask there. They'll probably take you. People can't get enough of our potato crisps, it seems. We've doubled our shifts. The watchman will tell you where to go.'

The conversation was at an end. Damn it. She'd been worrying about this interview all week, and now it wasn't even going to happen. At least she hadn't told Billy. Why was it so difficult to get a job? She'd just have to wait and see if anything else came up. Florence thought about the cold, small house and the long day stretching ahead with Aunt Sarah. Perhaps she could just pop along and see what the other job was like. No harm in having a look. She could always say no.

* * *

She would start the following week. The line-manager showed her out of the building. 'I'm sure I don't have to remind you of the need for punctuality, do I, Mrs Greene?' he said holding open the door.

'Don't worry, Mr Rudge, I'll be on time.' Her shift began at eight, which meant Robert would have to walk himself to school, but it was only at the end of their street, and the school-crossing patrol man would make sure he was safe. She would finish by four, so Aunt Sarah would only have to look after him for an hour or so. Walking down the hill to the bus stop, satisfied that her arrangements would work, Florence debated when, or indeed if, she should tell Billy.

* * *

She waited until he came home on Friday evening. He was always in a good mood on a Friday, looking forward to the pub, football on Saturday afternoon, a rest and a roast dinner on Sunday. Florence had been to the butcher that afternoon especially, to get the ingredients for one of his favourite meals: liver and bacon. It meant using up their rations — for Sunday there was only the very smallest piece of beef — but she wanted him to be in the right frame of mind when she broached the subject of going out to work.

At six o'clock, she heard the tick-tick of the bicycle being wheeled into the narrow entrance hall where it lived overnight, and shortly after, Billy stomped into the kitchen. As usual, he went straight to the big square sink and washed his face and hands. Florence slid the plates on the sideboard out of his way and passed him a tea towel to dry himself. He proffered her a cheek, which she kissed and then returned to prodding at the meat in the pan on the stove.

'Champion. Liver and bacon on a Friday night. What more could a man want?'

Billy settled himself at the table and looked expectantly around the room as Florence served his food. In one corner, Robert was playing with his abacus, sliding the coloured beads this way and that and slowly trying to write numbers on his little piece of slate.

'Come on, Robert. Time to eat. Sit yourself down.' She pulled out the chair for him, and he slid on to it, then made a face when he saw what was on his plate. Florence ignored him.

'Our goodly Aunt Sarah is out. Something with the church. So, it's just us this evening.'

Billy nodded as he lowered his head towards his plate, scooping large forkfuls of liver and mashed potato into his mouth. As she bit into a piece of the liver — a texture and flavour she would never get used to — Florence thought for a brief moment about Cook's famous chicken curry, then quickly dismissed this as dangerous ground — she didn't want to end up crying into her food tonight. She needed Billy on her side.

She waited until he was mopping his plate with a piece of bread. Billy wasn't much of a talker while he was eating anyway. She would be assertive, she thought. Billy had quite conservative ideas, but she didn't think he would outright deny her something she wanted. And anyway, all those years of handling her father had taught her a thing or two about difficult men.

'I went to the new factory the other day. They've given me a job there. I start next week.'

Billy continued wiping his bread around his plate, chewing and nodding. 'I see,' he said, once the plate had been entirely cleaned of gravy. 'Why's that then? Not got enough to do here?'

'It's not the quantity, Billy. It's the quality. I'm sick of being Aunt Sarah's drudge.' She checked herself, trying to keep her tone reasonable.

'I always thought a woman should be at home. Give a man something to look forward to at the end of the day. Like this.' He indicated the plate. 'A good meal, a clean house. And children need their mothers around.'

'Robert's at school now, and my shift ends at four. You'll still have food on the table when you get home in the evening, don't worry.' She should have known his biggest concern would be his stomach. 'And Aunt Sarah will be happy to get a few extra pennies each week.' She was about to add that they could use a bit of extra cash themselves, in the light of Billy's non-existent promotion and tendency to make money vanish, but she stopped herself. Injuring his pride wouldn't help her cause. Instead, she added, 'And it means we can save a bit more towards our own place. Get out of here at last.'

Billy pushed his plate towards her. 'I suppose it won't hurt then. Just until we can get a house of our own. After that I'm sure you won't want to go out to work anymore. Let's face it, who would?'

Florence took their plates to the sink, smiling to herself, excited by the prospect of her new job. At least Billy listened to her sometimes, and he never shouted. It was his easy-going nature that Florence had found attractive in the first place. When she'd arrived in England, she had been acutely aware that, as a soon-to-be divorced mother, she was not likely to be anyone's first choice of date, let alone anything more serious. At least with him she didn't feel judged. She met him at the social club tea dance, three years after she had arrived in

England on that cold, autumn morning, the ship finally pulling into the docks after those queasy weeks at sea.

* * *

The ship's horn blasted, and the gun-grey waters of the dock roiled around them. For the first time in a sick and delirious fortnight, Florence filled her lungs with fresh air. Grasping the salt-crusted rails, unsteady after so much time in bed, she marvelled at the crowds below. A smut of oil landed on the back of her right hand, and she smudged it into her skin.

Clank of huge chains, and the anchor dropped. Grind of cogs and wheels as the gangway lowered. She found herself shuffling in a tide of people towards the shore. She barely had time to say goodbye to the Hansons before they too were swept away, and she was left with her luggage by the side of the road, hailing a cab to take her to the station.

Aunt Sarah was expecting her. Her dead mother's older sister. A religious widow of reduced circumstances who had agreed to let Florence stay in her spare room for a nominal rent and help with the housework. It was another tiring journey by train and finally a cab to the narrow street of dirty-bricked terraced houses, jammed one against the other — a neighbourly invasion of privacy and space. By the time Florence arrived at the address written in her diary, she was too exhausted to pay any attention to the cold, the damp, or the lack of facilities. She ate the soup Aunt Sarah served and followed her in a trance up the stairs to the bedroom. The only thing she could think as she drifted off to sleep was how relieved she was the floor no longer heaved up and down underneath her. For a while, the sickness in her stomach abated, and she slept in chunks of oblivion and woke in moments of disorientation until Aunt Sarah's brisk knock on the door announced it was time to get up.

Florence pulled at the rough, heavy curtains, but the small patch of sky she could see above the roof of the house opposite was still dark. No peacocks dancing on the lawn here, no temple bells jingling, no Oscar waiting for her in his stable, pawing at the straw in anticipation of their morning ride. The air in the room bit sharply, and she rummaged through her case for the warmest clothes she could find.

Before she had finished dressing, the knock came again, and this time Aunt Sarah entered the room.

'Good, you're up. I don't like idle people. There's a pot of tea and some bread on the table, then we need to get started. It's Monday, and I'm sure you know what that means.'

Without waiting for a response, Aunt Sarah left. Florence had no idea what could be so significant about Mondays, but no doubt Aunt Sarah would let her know, and in great detail.

So it was that, from day one of her new life, Florence pitched into a world of domestic chores and frugality. People behaved as if the war hadn't ended: rations still in force and a sense of righteous indignation towards unnecessary luxury or waste.

'On Mondays we wash the sheets, of course,' Aunt Sarah had replied to Florence's tentative question. She finished her tea. 'I'll show you how to start up the boiler.'

The gas-fired copper vat bubbled away in the scullery. Soon the whole house began to fill with steam, until Aunt Sarah flung all the windows open. That nipping, eager air again. Florence wasn't used to it at all.

Aunt Sarah gave her a long stick and instructed her to agitate the sheets. Florence poked and prodded the cloudy water and occasionally grated flakes of Sunlight soap, watching them float like feathers then dissolve into nothing.

After what felt like hours, Aunt Sarah finally seemed satisfied. 'It's time,' she declared. 'And hanging them to dry will be so much easier with two of us.' Florence heaved the sopping whites out on to the side, and together they wrung out the excess water, then lugged them out to the washing line in the tiny brick-lined back yard.

That was her first morning in England.

The next day began in the same way — the early morning knock, a bitter cup of tea, a slab of bread, and then to work. Tuesdays were for cleaning the rugs and polishing the furniture, the brass, the few pieces of silverware.

'I have a tin where we put all our used tea leaves.'

By now, Florence had realised that a response was neither expected nor desired. Instead she nodded and continued rubbing at the base of a candlestick she'd been given to clean.

'When you've finished the silver, sprinkle the tea leaves on the rugs. It draws out the dirt. Then take the rugs outside and beat them.'

Florence hung the heavy carpets over the line and began to thwack them with the beater. Tea leaves flew about her head. Draw out the dirt, indeed. More likely it just added to the accumulated detritus in the old, faded threads. Still, she thought as she flailed at the rugs, better not to question Aunt Sarah's methods at this point. Especially as there was a difficult conversation to be had between them, and the sooner the better.

It was Sunday, after they had reconstituted the remains of the lunchtime roast into shepherd's pie and bubble and squeak as supper for the next two days. She had been allowed a bath in the old galvanised tub in front of a fire, lit especially because Aunt Sarah understood that Florence was having trouble acclimatising to her first autumn in England. Florence wrapped the borrowed flannel dressing gown tightly around her and brushed her hair in the small circle of warmth that emanated from the sparkling orange coals in the grate. She wondered how on earth she could tell Aunt Sarah she was pregnant.

In the end, she decided a practical approach might be best.

'I think I need to see a doctor.'

'Oh?' Aunt Sarah looked up from the prayer book she was squinting over. 'Something you picked up on the ship?'

'Not on the ship, no. Before I left.'

'I hear it's filthy there. I'm surprised any civilised person can survive it. Well, look at your mother.'

Florence ignored Aunt Sarah's derogatory comments about India — there had been several in the past few days — and refused to be drawn into a conversation about her mother, which she knew would only end in a litany of her father's faults. She looked at the dingy room around her, thought about the lavatory, which she had been surprised to learn was outside in the garden, with its scraps of newspaper hanging from a string for the purpose of cleaning oneself — no bucket, no water. She considered the damp and the mould on her bedroom walls, and compared it to the house in Agra — all yellow sunlight and glowing, polished wood and warmth and colour. Even Sita's village: the women's saris laid out to dry in a shimmering rainbow, children bathing in the lake, fires lit, huts swept out at dawn as the sun appeared on the horizon, and peacocks calling from the trees. This English home certainly didn't feel like the pinnacle of civilisation, that was for sure.

'I'm not sick, exactly.'

'What do you mean? What are your symptoms?'

'I've been feeling ever so queasy. Vomiting sometimes. And quite faint.'

'Well, if you're not sick ... Oh.'

Aunt Sarah put down her prayer book, then picked it up again and flicked through the pages. She wouldn't look at Florence.

'Tell me at least that it's his, your husband's. That Nick person.'

'Yes. Yes, of course.'

Aunt Sarah continued to peruse her prayers, as if searching for a message from heaven. Finally, she put the book down again.

'Well, that's it. You'll stay here. You can bring the child up here. Your cousins will be happy to give you some support. And you'll have my guidance. We can visit the doctor tomorrow.'

Florence thought about her cousins, two serious women in their thirties with a number of crying, morose children in tow who had descended earlier that day to welcome her to the family and invite her to their Bible club. She thought she wouldn't expect too much in the way of female companionship and sympathy from them. She already knew what Aunt Sarah meant by guidance. She stared into the fire and wondered if she would be allowed to throw on a few more pieces of coal.

'No point pulling that face, my dear. The Lord has decided this for you and placed you into my care, and much as I cannot even entertain the idea of a woman divorcing her husband, perhaps your circumstances allow for some leeway. After all, you couldn't have been expected to stay there.'

Aunt Sarah seemed energised as she stood, snapped her book shut, and headed towards the stairs.

'Don't stay down here too long. You need your sleep. Another busy day tomorrow.'

When she had left, Florence picked up one piece of coal and placed it on top of the embers. What on earth had happened to her life? What had happened to the girl who rode elephants through the jungle in search of tigers, or took a railroad cart down the line to watch a locomotive being inspected? On the boat she had, in her delirium and sickness, said her goodbyes to it all, in fragments and flashes. And she had vowed to hide it away, all that had happened, all that she had been, and, above all, that magical moment, barely three months before, flying high through the sky while the crowd cheered below and a rainbow appeared above. She had decided none of that would help her now. Because nobody here could possibly accept it. Not the circus, and certainly not India and all it meant to her. No, she would have to lock it away inside her forever. And yet, how could she? How could she never allow her mind to take her back, in dark, cold moments such as these, to the only place she had ever known as home? Suddenly she was afraid that it would disappear, that by not visiting those hidden rooms in her mind, she would lose it all, as if none of it had been real.

As the single piece of coal glowed in front of her, she wrapped her gown tighter around herself and shivered. No, that couldn't happen. She had to keep it alive somehow. Because if she didn't, she doubted very much she would have the strength to survive this future. The fire sparked and hissed, and across time and space she heard the crowd chanting in unison: 'Three … two … one …'

Chapter Three

PORTSMOUTH, 1948

Robert Harold was born on the thirtieth of April, nineteen-forty-eight. It was an unremarkable entry into the world, and Florence was soon back with him at Aunt Sarah's. The first weeks passed in a blur as she mastered breastfeeding and nappy changing and catching precious moments of sleep when she was able. For a month or so, Aunt Sarah let her grow accustomed to the business of looking after a baby and eased up on the demands for help with housework. Her cousins came to visit with bags of old baby clothes, for which Florence was grateful, along with plenty of advice, which was less agreeable after a while.

What she came to enjoy most were the times when she found herself alone with Robert in the house, and she was free to walk him from room to room as she told him about the house in Agra, and his Grandad Harry, and her horse, and Sita and Ravi and Ester, and all the other memories that she managed to keep locked away at all other times. For nobody wanted to hear them. Nobody here had any interest in her life before she had arrived in England. Oh, if only they knew what she had done.

One day, she swayed with him back and forth and sang to him the old children's lullaby. *Rock-a-bye baby, on the tree top.* The song conjured up other memories though: the sensation of the trapeze, the bar gripped in her palms, her body — muscular and responsive — in control of invisible forces beyond her understanding. How she missed it, that sense of power, of independence as she swung, higher and higher, and prepared to somersault through the void, down into the net far, far below.

Robert grizzled and wriggled in her arms, and she marvelled at what she had been. Then a huge sense of loss overwhelmed her. What had she done, leaving it all behind?

* * *

As Robert grew — heavier, bigger, longer, and eventually taller — the expectations for hard labour returned. Aunt Sarah began to busy herself more often with her charitable work, and Florence was left to look after the home. So, she fell into a sort of trance, hypnotised by the drudgery of her daily, only life. She learned to cook, to clean, and to eke out the money until the end of each week, making sure they used their rations and that nothing was ever wasted. Money arrived, unpredictably, from her father. It was never quite enough to put something by, but it meant she could pay a meagre rent and buy the occasional item of clothing for Robert. Her cousins continued to supplement her own wardrobe with their homely and sensible hand-me-downs. She couldn't afford to say no.

'You're looking rather wan, you know,' Aunt Sarah said over the top of her cup of tea. Florence had just sat down after a morning of boiling nappies and pegging them out on the line. Robert was banging a wooden building block on the stone of the hearth. The skin on her hands was raw and flaky. She scratched at her knuckles. 'I'm just a bit tired. And there's been no sun for weeks. It's enough to make anyone feel down.'

Aunt Sarah ignored her. She had opinions about hot weather — thought it made people lazy and feckless. Florence had heard it many times before.

'There's a tea dance at the social on Saturday afternoons. Carol at number five, her daughter attends. Why don't you go with her this week? I'll look after Robert. Won't I, Robert?' She raised an eyebrow at him. Seeing her, Robert lowered the wooden block and began to push it quietly along the floor instead.

Perhaps it was a strategic move on Aunt Sarah's part, as the available space in the house seemed to diminish day by day, while the noise and clutter grew. Or perhaps she had noticed her niece's lacklustre appearance, the creases etching themselves permanently between her eyes, and taken pity on her, knowing that it would only become more difficult to find someone to share a life with again. Whatever it was, Florence's first instinct was to refuse.

'Oh, I'm not sure I remember how to dance.' It was too hard even to imagine herself there, smiling, talking, nodding, listening to conversations, and telling her own stories. And dancing.

'Nonsense, girl. Why don't you go upstairs and see if you can find something to wear in those old suitcases of yours? I'll help you if it needs adjusting.'

So Florence found herself digging through a box of clothes that had remained untouched since her arrival in England, and found herself trying on an old dress last worn, she recollected, after her honeymoon, when they had travelled to

Simla. It was at a tea dance where Nick had sung with the band, and she had sat with the usual group of husbands and wives and tried to look as if she was a woman in the first romantic flush of marriage. The dress still fitted her now, despite having had a child; rations and housework kept her slim. She carried it down to Aunt Sarah, and together they washed it and dried it and took great care when pressing the folds of sky-blue silk that flowed out of the narrow waistband, navigating carefully with the hot iron around the row of pearly buttons that led up to the girlish collar and cap-sleeves.

* * *

'Very respectable, very … pretty.' Aunt Sarah nodded and helped Florence into her coat. 'Now, make sure you enjoy yourself. We all deserve a little fun every now and then. Even your old aunt has been known to waltz on occasion.'

Florence dismissed this unlikely scenario from her head, thanked her aunt, and bent to kiss Robert goodbye. He cuddled her knees briefly and then returned to pushing his favourite toy car around the legs of the dining table. Outside, it was a breezy spring afternoon, and as she clicked down the street in her old and only pair of good shoes, she felt her body relax, the frown lift from her brow, and a strange sense of expectation filter into her consciousness.

Inside the social club, a small band was playing old, familiar tunes. Florence joined the group of women standing along one wall, waving to the neighbour's daughter who started to move towards her but was suddenly stolen away by a short man in a badly cut, grey flannel suit. Florence waved again and found a spot where she could lean on the corner of a table next to a stack of tea cups, with a plate of biscuits also in reach. She nibbled and tapped her feet to the songs she knew so well, songs she herself had sung at another club in another time and place … and then there had been Nick, crooning. God! It didn't seem possible. She was just descending down the slope she knew she ought to avoid, that dark slope down into her memories, when a cheerful type in a navy blazer and baggy beige sports trousers swayed up to her.

'Billy's the name,' he said holding out his hand. 'Would you care to dance?'

Florence swallowed the remains of the biscuit. She hesitated for a moment. The last time she had danced with a man had been on her honeymoon. Four years ago, was it? And look at where that had got her. Was she really sure this was what she wanted?

'It's been a while,' she said.

'Don't worry about that. I'll look after you. Just follow me.'

He seemed kind and harmless, so she took his hand, and he whirled her on to the dance floor.

For a while, Florence let herself be led around the room, enjoying the sense of freedom the movement gave her. Finally, perhaps, she had found a use for all those dance lessons. The man was about her age, perhaps a little older. He had the kind of face that Florence thought might be described as apple-cheeked: two rosy globes appeared when he smiled, which he did for almost the entire time that they danced. His eyes were blue and his hair a nondescript brown, darkened with the Brylcreem that she could smell as he drew her in closer when 'Moonlight Serenade' began.

'Ooh! This is my favourite.'

Florence nodded in agreement, and they continued around the room. He guided her in an impeccable foxtrot, and she was aware of other people looking at them. It had been a long time since she'd so much enjoyed being the centre of attention.

The following Saturday, he took her out for a drink and a

walk along the prom. They sat outside a pub, looking across the flat grey expanse of the Solent towards the port. Billy placed a half a lager and lime in front of her.

'The Navy, that was my war,' he said, indicating the ships out to sea and slurping his beer. 'I had a good time of it, really. Saw places I'd never've seen otherwise. Got me away from the docks for a while, too. Mind you, a man can have too much of a good thing. I'll not travel again. You learn to appreciate your home when you've been away.'

He started to talk about his job at the docks. Florence offered a few details about her past in India, but for the most part she listened and worried if and when she should tell him about Robert. Inside the pub someone was playing a piano. The music drifted through an open window. Billy went for more drinks and came out, singing along to 'Daisy, Daisy' as he splashed the glasses down on the table. The music, the piano, the singing: it was all rather comforting. She sipped her drink and realised she was enjoying herself again. Billy talked on as they walked down the promenade, a nippy breeze blowing her hair in all directions, so that she was forced to tie her scarf around her head. Billy didn't seem to notice. He was more concerned with getting just the right amount of salt and vinegar on their haddock and chips that they took, wrapped in newspaper, to a bench facing the sea and ate with their fingers. Florence found this quite liberating after all those prim and proper meals with Aunt Sarah. When they had picked the last chunks from the bottom of the paper, Billy turned to her.

'Florence, I've had a smashing evening. What do you think? Would you agree to be my girl?'

Florence wasn't at all ready for this. Things moved fast here, it seemed. She couldn't think of a reason to say no. Except for one thing.

'I'd like to say yes, but perhaps you should know something first.'

Billy sat back and waited. Florence considered how she should start, but then the facts just fell from her lips.

'I was married, in India. But now I'm getting divorced. And I have a child by my husband. A son. Robert.'

Billy nodded, ruminating over the information she had just divulged. Then he stretched and placed an arm behind her, still looking out to sea.

'And how old is Robert?'

'He's two.'

'Ah, just a little lad then.' Billy pulled her closer to him. 'Well, you'll have to introduce me one day. Now, what would you say to one more drink before I see you home?'

Florence was so grateful for his lack of censure, that to kiss him seemed the least she could do. And that was that. They went steady for six months, and then Billy proposed to her. Later, when the divorce papers came through, they were married. Billy told her he wanted someone to make a home for him to come back to in the evenings. Florence was hardly listening, so wrapped up was she in thoughts of moving out from Aunt Sarah's and into a house of her own. But that wasn't quite how it worked out.

Three years later, when the opportunity arose, she took that offer of the job in the factory. The wages were not exactly a fortune, but she was determined to put some money by, towards their own house in the not-too-distant future. After the wedding, Billy had suggested he move in with her and Aunt Sarah, just until he got the promotion he knew was sure to come his way soon. They doubled the rent paid to Aunt Sarah, who Florence thought was secretly glad to have company she could lecture to. And so their married life began.

Still, even though Billy's job at the docks wasn't badly paid, and even though money from her father continued to arrive every couple of months or so, there never seemed to be quite enough to make ends meet. Often, she would meet Billy on a Friday afternoon after they both clocked off, so that they could wander around the open-air market, gathering up the bargain fruit and veg and picking through the factory rejects and extras for household goods. And yet he would still turn to her on a Saturday afternoon, just as he was leaving for the football, and ask her to empty her purse for him.

Chapter Four

AGRA, 1938

Back at the house, Sita and Ravi had hung coloured streamers from tree to tree, as they did every year for her party. Florence sipped her tea on the veranda. She was thinking about her tenth birthday. For some reason it seemed significant, the time when she had first started to dread this event. She thought back to the girl she had been then. She'd invited her three best friends, and Papa had promised her they would play some games and not just have to stand quietly and be good and pretend to be interested in the *conversation*. There was the new dress Papa had bought for her, creamy silk with a bright sash the blue of the sky after the rains. She'd washed quickly so that she could get dressed and practise twirling around to make the skirt puff out like a cloud before the guests arrived. But Papa had said, 'No grubbing around in the flower beds today, Florence,' and so she'd sat carefully on a chair in one corner. No going in search of emerald beetles clasped inside chrysanthemum petals, or the startled eye of a peacock feather caught on a thorn, or the twitchy, striped palm squirrels that would sometimes take food from her hand if she kept very still. Instead, she had sat and fidgeted and waited for her party to begin.

When the garden had filled up, it was mostly adults going on and on about home and news and talking about other adults who weren't there. She'd rounded up Ruthie, Katie, and Jane, and the four of them sat in large wicker chairs that Sita heaved into place for them. They all reclined like ladies at the Club, though their feet didn't quite touch the ground. Despite the nip of the December air, a young boy from the village wafted a fan in front of them.

What had they talked about? Vague memories of the conversation came back to her.

'What do you think your birthday present is? What did you ask for?'

She'd thought for a moment before answering Ruthie, who was a year older and already talked a lot about boys. It probably wouldn't do to tell her that what she wanted more than anything was the wonderful model train that she had seen in the catalogue the last time she'd been home for the holidays. But when she had shown it to Papa, he'd shouted, *'for God's sake, Florence,'* and thrown it into the bin. Florence didn't think it was a trick. He really wasn't going to get her the train.

'Probably that dress we saw in your magazine, and some new ballet shoes. And lots of books. He always gets me lots of books. Oh, and he promised to take me to the circus tomorrow.' Florence turned to Jane and Katie. 'Did you see them setting up the big top last week? You should ask if you can come with us. I saw the poster and they have dancing horses and trapeze artists and fire jugglers and everything.'

'Mama promised me pearls for my next birthday,' Ruthie said, ignoring Florence's excitement about the spectacle.

Ruthie had always managed to make her feel babyish and awkward, even then. So she'd shut up about the circus and clapped her hands, and the young boy with the fan ran back up the garden path and then returned carrying a tray of lemonades for them. He'd frowned with concentration as he walked towards them, picking his way over the uneven paving stones. She'd watched him, concerned; if he dropped them, Ruthie would never let her live it down at school. But then people had started calling her name from the other end of the garden. Her three friends jumped down from their chairs and walked past the boy, ignoring him and the tray he held out to them. Florence followed, giving an apologetic smile as she ran to catch up with them.

Then what had happened? She pictured her father standing by the table surrounded by other adults. He held a large box tied with a ribbon.

'Many happy returns, Florence.'

Cook had appeared carrying a white cake decorated with sugar flowers and coloured candles, just as she'd asked for. When he'd placed it on the table, the women nearby urged her to take a deep breath, and Florence had done as she was told. She'd managed to blow out every single flame, first time. Which meant her wish might just come true. There. That was it. Her birthday wish. Had that been the first time she'd been aware? Had felt the first resentment, the first desire to resist?

Everybody had applauded, and Papa placed the box on the ground in front of her. Florence lifted the lid and then she, too, clapped her hands. Looking up at her was a tiny white and brown puppy. Florence reached down, picked it up, and held it to her face.

'Thank you, Papa!'

'Not just any old hound. Pedigree Jack Russell, she is. Took a lot of finding.'

'Then I shall call her Jacqueline. Jackie for short.'

She saw her friends in their little group watching her. Ruthie had a disapproving set to her mouth.

'Harry, you sentimental thing, you. What a sweet gift.' One of the women standing next to her father, who always seemed to be standing next to him at parties, brought her face up close to Florence and the puppy. Florence had smiled back at her but did not offer to let her hold Jackie.

'What about diseases, Harry? You'll have to keep it inside,' said Ruthie's mother, who was staring at the first woman. 'I suppose she can take it with her when she goes back to England. When are you going to send her? Is she going to stay with her aunt?'

This was the first Florence had heard of being sent to England. She watched over the top of Jackie's tiny head as her father accepted a slice of her cake from the kitchen boy. She was desperate for a piece too, before all the sugar flowers disappeared, but she didn't want to interrupt this important item of news.

'I'm not going to send her back.'

Ruthie's mother shook her head. 'She can't stay here. It's ... unhealthy. In all sorts of ways. She'll develop all sorts of strange ideas. She needs to be back at home, finish school there. Then she can go up to London and find a nice young man. Look, Ruthie's going home at the end of next term, aren't you, Ruthie?'

The girls all turned to look at Ruthie.

'Yes, I'm going to school in Sussex and then to London to live with Aunt Helen.'

'And I'm sure you will be very happy, my dear.' Papa finished his slice of cake and passed his plate to a boy who ran away with it to the kitchen. 'Florence, however, is staying here with me. Why would I want to send her back there? Miserable place. Just endless grey clouds and bloody awful food.

Florence is all I have. And there will be plenty of eligible fellows here when the time comes.'

The women all looked at each other, but clearly it didn't do to argue with Papa. Florence looked at the cake again. It was vanishing fast, being handed out at speed by the kitchen boy to all the guests. She edged closer to the table and reached for a plate. The puppy started wriggling in her arms.

Here it was. Here was the moment when she'd felt for the first time the imposition of his will, with no regard for what she herself really needed or wanted.

'Florence. Time for some entertainment, I think.'

'Papa, I don't want to.'

'Nonsense. Come on.'

Florence put the plate down again and sighed. This was exactly what she hadn't wanted the party to be. So much for birthday wishes. Papa began yelling for everyone to follow him inside. Florence did as she was told. As she walked past, still cuddling the puppy, she caught Ruthie smirking at the other girls.

Of course, inside she'd had to stand by Papa and sing while he'd played the piano, and everyone else had to stand round and applaud after each song finished. Florence thought the audience was very polite to ignore the wrong notes on the piano and the moments when the music slowed down or sped up according to whether it was a difficult section or not. The puppy had run around the piano legs and yelped whenever Florence had to sing a high note, which had made the audience laugh. Florence knew her voice sounded weak and warbly, and she didn't always sing completely in tune. She could hear it, and her music teacher had told her many times, too. But Papa had insisted on the extra lessons and insisted she accompany him when he played at his parties. The only thing worse would be if he decided she had to put on her ballet shoes and dance too.

Her last memory of that day was going to bed. She'd placed Jackie on the covers next to her and cuddled down under the blankets. Sita had tucked a hot water bottle at the end of the bed, and Florence warmed her feet as the cold air in the room skated over her face. While the puppy slept immediately, Florence had reviewed the important events of the day. Jane and Katie had told her that she was their best friend. And Ruthie was leaving for England in five months' time. Good. She could take her pearls and her nasty, squint-eyed smile and go and live in that place of rain and grey skies that everyone was always talking about. Florence, on the other hand, was staying in India. She would grow up here and keep Papa company, and when she was older, she could help him with his work on the trains. Because surely — she'd thought — he wouldn't want her to do the singing and the dancing forever. She could live in this house and keep Jackie and have her own servants and, she'd supposed, one day a husband, too. She'd fallen asleep with her hand on the puppy's warm little body, a tiny hopeful heart beating under her fingers.

* * *

Florence shook herself out of her reverie, finished her tea, and stood up. In the garden, the servants had set out a long table, and they were hurrying backwards and forwards from the kitchen, bringing plates and cutlery and crystal glasses. The morning fog had lifted, and everything sparkled against the white tablecloth like icicles in the sun. Florence turned her back on it and went inside to find her father.

He was at his desk, frowning over the newspaper. Next to him was a pile of sheet music, and Florence could see the titles of popular tunes, including those he'd told her to learn this term in her singing lessons.

'Been galloping about on that nag of yours, have you?' he said, without looking up. 'Needs a bit of exercise. Where'd you go, the village?'

'The Fort, actually.'

He nodded without appearing to have heard. After a silence, during which Florence stood and looked out of the window and her father tutted several times at whatever he was reading, there came the sound of breaking glass from the garden, and it was this that finally stirred him from his paper.

'Hope you've forgotten all that nonsense from last night,' he said, looking at her at last. 'Got the music here. We should have a practice beforehand. You are going to get changed out of those awful jodhpurs, aren't you?'

Florence breathed out slowly. She was eighteen. She was a woman. She wasn't going to put up with this any longer. 'Do you think Mama would have approved of the way you treat me? Is this what she would have wanted for me, to be your little entertainer, your little monkey dancing away in front of everyone?'

'The way you move, I'd say it's more like one of those dancing bears.'

Oh, he was insufferable, she thought. He knew just how to make her feel completely inadequate. She wasn't going to cry though. Not this time. 'I dreamt about Mama last night, that she was wandering around the Red Fort, not at rest because of something you'd done. What did you do to her? You've never told me what happened. Why?' Florence was aware that she was letting her emotions take over. Her father laughed.

'Oh, so you're angry with me now because of a dream? Honestly, pull yourself together. You know what? I don't see how I'm the villain in all of this. After she died, I could have sent you off to England to some miserable boarding school, or to live with one of my awful relatives. But I kept you here. I raised you. You've had a charmed life so far, and I think the least you could do is humour me by accompanying me in a bit of music every now and then.'

'Why can't you let me be who I want to be?' She was close to tears, and she gripped the desk, daring to look him in the eyes, demanding that he answer, but her father just sat back in his chair, clasped his hands over his head and exhaled loudly.

'Listen, Florence. I don't want to have this argument again. Not on your birthday. I have to go to the office. Why don't you come with me, help tidy up some papers, answer the telephone when I'm in the meeting? I know how much you like that. And then perhaps you can put all this silly drama to one side and indulge your old man when we get back. It's just a couple of songs, for heaven's sake.'

It was true, she did love to go with Papa when he went to the station, and she could pretend she belonged in that world of meetings and telephones and documents, not to mention the trains themselves. A world of logic and systems and cause and effect, where what you did seemed to matter.

Her father stood and stuffed some papers into his case. 'See you at the car in five minutes.'

Chapter Five

AGRA, 1938

Florence wasn't ignorant of her father's story and all that he had been through. She knew that since her mother's death all those years ago, her father had continued to do the job he had been sent to India to do. And it was true, he had resisted the advice of his colleagues and their wives to pack Florence off to England to live with her mother's sister. In the end, he had decided on a good boarding school up in the hills, where she could escape the heat and dust and breathe clean air, at least during term time. He continued to have her back at home during the holidays, though.

When she was younger, he had told her stories of his youth. How he had always found numbers and mathematical problems easy, and so had fallen naturally into the same path his father had followed, working for the railway company. His engineering abilities had kept him safe during the war, enlisted with the Royal Engineers to oversee the construction and repair of those lines vital for moving men, munitions, and supplies, first at the centre in Hampshire and later on in France. He'd impressed the right people, because as soon as the war was over, the government called him up and offered him a management position preparing the line for the Grand Trunk Express. He wasn't sure about India, or even if he wanted the job, but with a new wife to keep — and the expectations of his father to live up to — he accepted.

So it was that every morning at eight o'clock, in the fogs of winter, or the heat hazes of summer, or the deluge of monsoon rains, he left his refuge and descended the steps to the waiting car so that Ravi could charge across to the other side of the city and deposit him at his office behind the station. Florence also knew that he was increasingly disillusioned by his job, where he would spend eight hours a day, in his words, 'imprisoned' by charts and plans and long, frustrating telephone conversations with his superior in Delhi. What he really wanted to be was a musician, but he'd come to all that far too late, and besides, it wouldn't really pay the bills.

They sat together in the back of the car, her father humming a tune, one that Florence was supposed to have practised for the party. She tried to distract him. 'Wasn't today your day off? For the party?'

He continued looking out of the window. 'You mean the party you suddenly don't want? Honestly, Florence, you become more of a mystery to me each time you come home.'

She decided to ignore this. 'Is it Mr Hanson again?' She knew his boss could be difficult and liked to remind his employees who was who by keeping them at his beck and call. The car pulled up outside the station and, without answering, her father jumped out and made his way through the people, tongas, rickshaws, and street stalls that crowded the steps in front. Florence hurried after him.

Inside, however, the office was empty. Her father tutted. 'Meeting finished already, is it? Bloody Kit Hanson.' He paced around the room. Florence followed him, looking at charts on the wall, unrolling diagrams of engines on the desk, arranging pencils in a line. 'What do you want me to do?'

He looked at her, as if he had forgotten she was there. 'Leave all that. Come on, let's get out of here. When was the last time you saw Prakash?'

They walked into the station, dodging through the crowds until her father looked up and waved at the window of the signal box. Prakash peered down, grinned, and indicated they should join him.

Florence slipped in after her father. The eleven o'clock to Delhi had just arrived, and Prakash carefully slotted the metal token into the machine that would allow the clunking signal to lower, then he recorded the details in tiny handwriting in his logbook. It was work that required concentration, and she knew better than to interrupt the man while he was doing his job. Instead, she gazed out over the lines running away from the station, joining and disappearing towards the edge of the city. On the platform, crowds surged towards the train: *chai wallahs* holding cups of tea up to the windows; porters with towering stacks of luggage, trundling towards the exit; beggars swaddled in filthy rags, hoping to catch a rupee thrown from the piteous purses of the English ladies staring down from the heights of their first-class carriage. Bells clanged, and Prakash talked briefly on the telephone, then, with a grinding of wheels and the scream of metal on metal, the beast slowly steamed out of the station. Hands protruded from open windows to bat away the clinging children who dropped one by one to the platform floor as the train picked up speed. Prakash turned to them with a large smile.

'Mr Harry-Sir. Miss Florence. Just in time for tiffin.'

He held out a greasy paper bag. Florence picked out something that looked like a ball of fried onion and stuck it in her mouth. Her father did the same and nodded at Prakash as he chewed.

'How is the piano, Mr Harry? When are you going to be giving us a concert again?'

Her father waved his hands. 'I think concert is too grand a word. It's just a hobby.'

Florence knew how much her father liked visiting Prakash, exactly for this reason. He'd often said to her that Prakash 'might work on the railways, but he has the soul of an artist'. Although Florence suspected her father just loved being flattered, and Prakash was very good at it.

'Nonsense, Sir. It is quite clearly your vocation.'

'I do wish I had taken it up earlier, Prakash. I think I could have been very good, you know.'

'But Sir is very good now. We were very much enjoying the music at the party last Christmas.'

'Well, I'll be doing it again this year. After the Christmas camp. You will come again, won't you?'

'I wouldn't be missing it for the world. Will Sir be having another band this year?'

'Yes, I've found a rather good jazz outfit up from Bombay. Trying to get them in at the Club. Very talented, they are. Just need someone decent to manage them.' This was the first Florence had heard of her father managing a band. Honestly, why couldn't he just do his job and be normal, like her friends' fathers? None of them insisted on playing piano on stage at the Club.

Prakash nodded. 'And Miss Florence. Another year at school finished?'

Florence declined the offer of another snack. 'I arrived yesterday. It's my eighteenth birthday today.'

'Can't quite believe where the time goes,' said her father, stuffing another bhaji into his mouth.

Prakash continued to nod and put the now-empty greasy paper bag into a drawer. 'Children are our greatest blessing, Sir.'

'Of course they are.' Her father nodded. 'Of course they are.'

* * *

'You don't really think I'm much of a blessing, do you?' Florence said as they sat in the back of the car while Ravi negotiated the roads filled with people, animals, and potholes.

'Of course you're a bloody blessing,' her father replied, though the irritation in his voice suggested otherwise.

Florence slumped in her seat. Out of the window, she saw a row of posters, peeling and ragged on a wall, for the circus. How funny, when she'd just been thinking of it earlier. In the end, all those years ago, her father had forgotten to take her, and so the dancing horses and acrobats and jugglers had only ever performed in her imagination. Perhaps she could go this time. But as they drove past the last poster, she saw it was too late — it had come and gone a month ago. She sighed, and her father looked at her and relented.

'Sorry, Florence. I suppose you've kept me sane, probably, all these years working in that place, surrounded by idiots.'

'Then what is it? Why do you always seem so disappointed with me?'

'I'm not disappointed. Just a bit ... let down, I suppose. Let's face it. I've showered you with every opportunity to become something special. You've had dancing lessons, singing lessons, piano, painting. And none of it cheap, either. And yet, you just seem so ... average at it all.'

Florence closed her eyes, the familiar feelings of hurt and inadequacy rising through her body.

'Come now, don't get upset,' her father said, patting her on the shoulder. 'You're a lovely girl and a loving daughter. I can't complain about that. It just that you're not at all what I imagined you'd turn out to be.'

* * *

Ravi parked the car, and Florence and her father walked up the garden path. She glanced at the table laid with a white cloth, white napkins, and vases of white lilies.

'Looks wonderful as ever,' she said, trying to show her appreciation.

Her father rubbed at his temples. 'Can't say I'm in the mood for this now. I'll have to spend most of the afternoon talking to Kit Hanson. So would you try and enjoy it at least?' He looked at his watch. 'Still, inviting Prakash should get right up Kit's nose. And there's a new chap from Ajmer who's just started working for us. Kit will loathe having to socialise with him.' He smiled. 'Just time to get washed up and have a quick drink before the guests arrive. I'll see you down here at two.'

Chapter Six

PORTSMOUTH, 1953

That first day at the factory, Florence kept her mouth shut and her eyes open. She was assigned to work with a large woman called Ruby who had no problem heaving the drums of peeled potatoes into the top of the large hopper where they were chipped and ejected into a vat of boiling oil.

'You have to watch the timer like a hawk.' Ruby crossed her arms and eyed Florence with a stern expression. 'Make sure you lift that tray out of the oil at exactly the right time, mind you. Even a couple of seconds late, and the whole batch will be burnt, and that'll come off my wages for today, so you'd better pay attention, or else.'

Ruby heaved her large bosom upwards for a moment, resting it on her arms, then let it fall, as if to underline her words. She bustled off to load the hopper, and Florence waited for the moment when the chips fell and she had to start the timer. A few minutes later, she lifted a tray of perfectly golden crisps out of the oil and tipped them on to the conveyor belt. She admired them as they sailed towards the next station to be bagged up, together with that special little blue packet of salt. It was a strangely satisfying experience.

'Oi! Florence!'

Ruby was glaring at her, waiting to pour another heavy load of potatoes into the hopper. Florence turned back to the fryer, ready for her moment once again.

* * *

After two months, Mr Rudge the floor manager came to find Florence when she was on her morning break. She stood up from the table where she'd been sitting, dunking a biscuit into her tea. She smoothed down her cotton overalls and adjusted the white turban all the line workers had to wear.

'Morning, Mrs Greene.' Mr Rudge picked at the corner of his moustache and looked down at the clipboard he was carrying. Florence recognised her own handwriting on the application form she had filled in before she got the job. 'Good news, I hope. I'd like you to take over as line manager — vacancy just came up. Bit more administration, less standing around on the line. I see you have quite a lot of experience. In India — railways, was it? Quite some responsibility, too, driving all those supplies around in the war. I'm sure you'll find the line a piece of cake in comparison. Have to keep your people in order though — no slacking. Got to keep the figures up, that's your number one priority.'

Florence nodded and shook his hand, reassuring him she would certainly make sure productivity stayed high. Mr Rudge marched off, and Florence sat down to her tea and biscuits again.

What followed were good times that she would always remember with fondness: the jokes, the camaraderie, the sense of being useful. The company's profits continued to climb, and

Florence and her team felt glad to be a part of something, contributing to rebuilding the country and helping people to surface from the darkness of the previous decade. And as the months lightened, so did Florence's load, until finally she found herself settled in those plush, carpeted offices she had visited just over a year ago on the wrong day.

Systems and logistics: that was her area. Well, of course it was. To Florence, the factory seemed one giant engine under her control. She visualised the supplies being fed into the engine of the production line, combusting into a new product that in turn transformed into money — driving the whole operation, and their lives, forward, and at the same time feeding back into the system in a beautiful, fluid flow circuit. Once upon a time, a young man had explained it all to her, on the back of a napkin. But that was another life.

Florence hurried down the street towards home. It had been a busy day in the office, and she was tired, but she knew Aunt Sarah had limited reserves of patience when it came to Robert's noisy, after-school exuberance. She pictured the toys scattered across the floor of the front room, his shoes and coat left in a pile by the door as he played at being a pilot or a fireman or whatever his latest obsession was. Instead, as she neared the house, she saw his little figure sitting on the kerb, head in hands. She approached him slowly, wondering if it was just one of his odd games, but then she saw the tears falling and mingling with the dust in the road.

'Robert, darling. What's the matter?'

Without a word, he leaned in against her as she too squatted in the street. After a while, she took him by the hand, and he consented to follow her, little shoulders heaving with sobs. Inside the house, she removed his coat and gasped at the rips in his school shirt. On his arms, she found red marks starting to darken. Aunt Sarah brought him a glass of milk and left them alone. After a while, he calmed his sobs and slowly the words came out.

'The other boys… they say I'm dirty. They pushed me over in the playground. They said I needed a bath, and I said I have one every week and a wash every morning, but they just laughed. They tried to take off my shirt, but I wouldn't let them, so they twisted my arms and wrists and rubbed my skin and it felt like it was burning. Why don't they like me, Mummy?'

Florence felt her heart pierced, and she gathered him in her arms and hugged him hard to her. Robert pulled away and looked up at her again.

'Mummy, what's a golliwog?'

Oh, Christ. It was true that Robert had inherited his father's dark skin and curly black hair, and the flecks of green in his hazel eyes certainly gave him an exotic look, but Florence had never once imagined it would lead to this.

'They are just nasty, ignorant little boys, Robert. You can't listen to them. Stay away from them at playtime. Stay where the teacher can see you. You understand?'

Robert nodded silently and then threw his heaving weight at Florence again. She held him and stroked his head until, sometime later, he seemed calmed. She offered him his abacus, and he began to slide the beads forward and back, counting in a sing-song voice, and soon he was absorbed in a game of shopkeeper. Florence went into the kitchen where Aunt Sarah pushed a cup of tea across the table and read her a passage from Psalms, which Florence knew was her way of giving comfort. Florence looked at the clock on the wall above Aunt Sarah's head. Billy would be home in an hour.

She hoped he might have something more pragmatic to offer.

* * *

The next evening, there was the usual sound of the front door bursting open, boots stamping on the doormat, and the bicycle being wheeled inside. Florence was in the kitchen keeping an eye on the stew. As always, she made sure the sink was clear and laid out Billy's flannel and a bar of Lifebuoy soap on the side, ready for his wash. After a few minutes, he still hadn't appeared, and Florence, hearing some unaccustomed shouts and thuds from the other room, went to see what was happening.

Billy was kneeling on the floor opposite Robert, who was standing, skinny little arms raised, as if in defence. On the end of each skinny little arm was a large red boxing glove. Billy, flushed in the cheek, grinned up at her.

'This should show 'em, those little blighters. Come on, Robert, 'ave a swing at me hands, see what you can do.'

Robert, a doubtful look on his face, slowly moved his right hand back and then thrust it clumsily towards Billy. The weight of the glove unbalanced him, and he overshot the mark, toppling forwards. Billy caught him before he hit the floor and pushed him upright again.

'Got to do better than that, my lad. Come on, try again.'

Again, the scene was repeated, and again, and each time Robert's little arm wavered around, shot forward, and he nearly fell. Florence watched one more time, seeing Robert's face growing redder and Billy more serious, until she'd had enough.

'Dinner's nearly ready, you two. Time to wash up.'

Later that evening, when Robert had fallen asleep and Aunt

Sarah had retired upstairs to say her prayers, Florence felt compelled to raise the subject of the gloves.

'Very generous of you to buy him those. Weren't they expensive?'

'Don't worry yourself, my love. I've been doing all right recently.'

Florence didn't know what this meant, exactly. That promotion at the docks had never happened, and if they were doing all right, it was thanks to her wages at the factory.

'Do you think he's big enough? I mean, isn't he going to get himself hurt? I don't think he should take them to school. He'll just get himself into trouble. He's so much smaller than all those other boys. I'm not sure teaching him to fight is the answer, Billy.'

'Nonsense. Lad needs to toughen up a bit. This isn't your fancy life in India now. Things are different here. He's going to have to learn to look after himself. Especially looking like he does. I mean, there's not much you can do about the colour of his skin, can you?'

Florence took a sharp breath. Billy had never said it out loud before. When they'd first started courting, he'd asked a few questions about Robert's father, and Florence had filled him on a number of details — Nick's family and background, his work, and a brief mention of the problems that had caused the divorce. Aunt Sarah had always changed the subject whenever the question of Florence's past marriage came up. Nobody had ever said anything directly to her about colour or race. But now, these boys at Robert's school ... She felt sickened, and unforgivably naive. She'd taken so much for granted, both here and in India. Yes, there'd been glances and mutterings in Agra when the engagement was announced, but hadn't everyone at the Club swooned over Nick and his handsome looks? They couldn't get enough of his voice, singing their favourite songs, night after night. Hadn't they accepted him, more or less? And then, she'd been raised by Sita, and Ravi. They were as much family to her as her father had ever been. Of course, she'd seen fellow English men and women treating Indian people with disdain and contempt. She knew there'd been prejudice and exploitation, and worse. But this with Robert? This was ugly, blind hatred — and out of the mouths of children, too. In India, she'd felt insulated in her home, had felt exempt from blame. Suddenly, she began to doubt herself. All those years she'd presumed Sita had been happy with them, but maybe calling Sita part of the family had been nothing more than convenient self-deception. Perhaps it wasn't what Sita had wanted at all.

Florence was tired. She couldn't think how to respond to Billy right now. She resolved to sleep on it and come back to it tomorrow. Except that, with everything that happened the next day, the gloves got forgotten, along with Robert's problems at school.

As soon as she stepped off the bus the next morning, Florence sensed something was different. It was a ten-minute walk up the hill and, as she went, she became aware of an unusual noise up ahead, distant bells and shouts. The air, too, had a tang to it, and as she turned the corner, she saw people crowded outside the factory gates. A widow's veil of black smoke drifted gauzily in the air above. She hurried up behind everyone and stood on her tiptoes to see what was happening. In front of her was Mr Rudge. She tapped on his shoulder.

'Mr Rudge. What's happening? Why can't we go in?'

Mr Rudge frowned over his shoulder, then lightened his expression at seeing Florence. 'Ah, Mrs Greene. Terrible, terrible events. A fire in the night. Burnt to the ground. The engines have only just managed to extinguish the last of the flames.'

Florence felt a wave of shock surge through her body. This couldn't be true. 'Oh, heavens! How … Was anybody …?'

Mr Rudge looked sombre, casting his gaze down. 'Two night watchmen are missing, I'm afraid. Terrible, it is. Terrible.'

He turned away from her as a policeman with a loud-hailer stood in front of the gates now and began to ask the crowd to go home. Florence looked around for anyone she knew from the office, but all she could see were the stupefied and uncertain faces of the line-workers as they started to move away.

Then it came to her, what they had already understood: no factory, no job.

It wasn't the money. Well, it wasn't just the money. Over the next week or so, Florence waited at home, telling herself and Aunt Sarah that Mr Rudge was sure to call round and let her know what she could do to help get things back up and running again. The office hadn't burnt down, after all. But the days passed, and there was no word. The newspaper reported that there had been some kind of electrical fault, and that the bodies of the two watchmen had been recovered. Florence thought perhaps she ought to go to the funerals but never quite managed to find out when they took place.

In the meantime, Aunt Sarah seemed rather too pleased to have her help around the house again. It didn't take long for the callouses to reappear on her hands and the frown lines to re-double on her face. When Robert returned home after school every day, she found herself impatient with his silences, with his reluctance to answer her questions and, at the same time, pushed away his unpredictable little hugs, those clinging arms.

Then, one morning, Florence found a letter on the doormat as she bustled Robert outside and sent him on his way to school. Sitting down at the kitchen table, she opened it, hoping that this was her summons back — back to that light, plush, busy world where she was more than just a drudge forever cleaning and preparing food: where she got to *matter*. She unfolded the pieces of cream paper and read, with an expressionless face, the termination of her contract. Apparently, she would receive a small severance payment of a month's wages. And that was that. She folded the papers again, placed them back in the envelope, and put it in the drawer with all the household accounts, receipts, and bills.

Then she poured a cup of tea and stood at the window, watching the rain fall on roofs of all the other little houses around them. She would give anything now to saddle up Oscar and gallop him through fields of mustard flowers, to feel the exertion in her body and the rhythm of the animal underneath her. To be free to roam, to make her own decisions. How had she not realised the possibilities she'd once had? How could she have given up on it all so easily? And what on earth could she do to get that life back?

* * *

Florence grew quiet, and thin. The energy that had borne her out of the house every morning, on a wave of activity and ideas, vanished, leaving behind only a sense of dissatisfaction and resentment as she went about the endless loop of daily chores. Billy told her he didn't understand why she was so down-in-the-mouth, and she said it was because of the money, and the house, which it was. But not only.

Then, some weeks after, Billy stamped into the house much later than usual on a Friday evening. As he drew nearer to Florence to kiss her cheek while she stirred at the pot on the stove, she could smell the alcohol on his breath. She pulled away from the arm around her waist.

'I see you've already been celebrating the weekend.'

After a moment's silence, when she turned around, she saw him sprawled on a chair at the table, grinning at her.

'Celebrating more than the weekend, my love.' With that, he reached into his pocket and smacked a thick wad of notes on to the table.

Florence gasped. She reached for it and held it up high. 'What on earth have you done, Billy?'

'Let's just say my luck finally came in.'

* * *

It was luck enough for both of them, enough for a deposit on one of the new prefabricated houses that had been built on the hill above the city. Still small, still cold, but with an indoor lavatory and bathroom, and a small grassy garden at the back, it felt like luxury after the years at Aunt Sarah's. And Billy had even promised her one of those new twin-tub washing machines. As long as Florence never let herself think back to the house in Agra, then perhaps she could be happy there.

A week after they moved in, the three of them stood in the tiny front room, looking out of the window at the view across the city. Billy squeezed her to him and kissed her ear. His breath was loud and damp.

'Here we are, my love. See, I told you. Our own house. And after all that, you never needed to go out to work. Now you can stay at home and look after us, and maybe we could think about a little brother for Robert. What do you reckon?'

Florence wasn't sure what she thought. The house was one thing, but another child?

Over the city, rainclouds were gathering, and shortly the view blurred to grey and vanished. Water coursed down the windows and hammered at the flat roof over their heads. To the right and to the left, the road was empty. Nobody hurrying with an umbrella flapping and tugging in the wind, nobody dodging muddy puddles, and nobody running along the street, keys in hand to get home and out of the weather.

She turned away from the gloom and went to the kitchen, where she began to prepare their special housewarming meal of a steak and kidney pudding, rinsing the offal and kneading the dough, and pleading with every push that tomorrow would be a bright new day.

Chapter Seven

AGRA, 1938

The garden was filled with people eating and drinking, and the murmur of conversation floated up into the pastel blooms of the frangipani trees above and in through the window of Florence's room. She was sitting on her bed with Jane and Katie, discussing the latest letter from Ruthie. London was apparently a constant round of parties and a queue of men lining up to take her out. Florence didn't entirely trust that this was the whole truth, but Katie was so taken with the romance of it all that she kept her opinions to herself.

'It will be me next year,' said Katie. 'Finally, away from this place and out in society. I imagine my wardrobe's going to cost a fortune. What a pity you two won't be there.'

'You know, there's all sorts of things happening in Europe at the moment,' said Jane, suddenly serious. 'It all might be very different a year from now.'

'Don't be dull. Anyway, people won't stop having romances and getting married, will they?' Katie said and made a face at Florence that suggested Jane was always a bit of a killjoy.

'Well, they will if all the men have to go away to fight,' said Jane.

'Oh, Florence, tell her not to be such a spoilsport. On your birthday, too.'

Florence smiled at them both. She would miss Katie, despite — perhaps even because of — her frivolous take on life. At least Jane was staying, for the time being. The Hansons had come out the year before Harry, so she had known them her whole life. While her father was often to be heard muttering complaints about how Kit Hanson treated him in the office, Florence had always liked spending time with Jane and her family. They just seemed so much more sensible than Papa.

'Shouldn't we go down?' said Katie, looking out of the window. 'All the food will be gone, and I'm starving.'

Florence checked her reflection in the mirror. Her face looked different these days. Older, having lost that kittenish quality as her features began to choose and settle into the proportions and angles of adulthood. She touched her hair. Sita had styled it earlier, but its thick, curly texture meant it was already escaping from the pins and combs. Florence tutted, and started repositioning the hair grips. She gave Jane a hand-mirror so she could see the back.

'I don't know why you bother.' Jane lowered the mirror. 'Anyway, it looks fine.'

Florence hoicked Jane's arm back up and continued fiddling with the pins. 'If you had my mop, you'd understand. If it gets out of control, even for an afternoon, well then, I might as well cut the whole lot off. And anyway, you know how Papa is.'

'Who cares what you look like?' said Katie, obviously anxious to get to the banquet laid out in the garden below before it disappeared. Florence knew her father had ordered tinned truffles and caviar, a whole stilton, and lobster mayonnaise, among other delicacies. The table would be dominated by Florence's favourite, though: a spectacular haunch of mutton, marinated in Cook's secret recipe of herbs and spices and baked for a day in the clay oven, until it fell from the bone and melted in your mouth. 'It's only boring old Agra,' Katie continued. 'Same as boring old school. Same old, boring old people.'

Florence thought about the coming holidays and all the parties that her father would be giving, not just this one. She wondered why people still came. Why weren't they sick of the same thing every year? Her father's uneven piano playing. Florence being forced to sing — or worse, dance — in front of everyone. Katie was right. Same boring people in the same boring places.

Agra was small. You just about knew everyone. It would be different in Delhi or Bombay. Papa wouldn't be able to get away with it in a big city like that, she was sure. In Agra though, he was eccentric, which she supposed people must find charming. That and the fact that he'd never married again. That's what kept all the women coming back, no doubt. Desperate to fix him up with someone. Or have him for themselves. For Florence was no fool when it came to seeing through the intentions of the women surrounding her father. Even if she didn't know the precise details, she understood in abstract terms the idea of desire.

Jane lowered the mirror again. As if she'd read Florence's thoughts, she said, 'Hope you've been practising your songs, Flo. I'm sure everyone can't wait to hear the new repertoire. What was it last time? *Ooooh, it's only a …*' Jane started to sing in a tuneless falsetto.

Florence smiled. She knew her friend's teasing was really a show of solidarity. 'Oh, don't worry, Jane. I've got a new one all lined up, especially for you. It's called "These Foolish Things Remind Me of You".'

'Oh funny, Flo.' Jane was quiet for a moment, then continued. 'Really though. Why does he make you do it?'

Florence patted her hair down one last time and stood up. 'Come on. Time to face the music, so to speak. Hope you brought your ear plugs.'

* * *

Her father was standing with the Hansons in the garden. Here, the topic of conversation was also London and events back home, but somewhat more informed. The gin and limes had been flowing freely, it seemed.

'Of course, now it's a refugee problem,' said Mr Hanson, rather forcefully. 'Thousands of them flooding the country every year since 1933. We can't just keep on taking them in. We've got our own problems, too: unemployment rising.'

'Those thousands have employed thousands more Brits, so your argument doesn't stand up,' said Florence's father. He looked a bit red in the face, and she wondered just how many gin and limes he'd drunk so far. 'Anyway, that's hardly the point. Hoare's right. It's an international problem, not one that can be solved by a single country. In the meantime, persecution continues, and they're ramping up operations into Czechoslovakia.'

'There was an awful account of the happenings in Vienna in the paper. Did you read it?' Mrs Hanson said. Mrs Hanson was not usually one to keep quiet, even around the men. She had quite progressive ideas about women — and in Florence's opinion, she was usually right. A bit like Jane, really. 'Horrifying. And all completely orchestrated by the government. Not at all spontaneous as they'd have us believe.' Mrs Hanson stopped and looked at Florence, then smiled. 'We shouldn't be talking about this now. Not on your birthday. Has Cook done one of his special cakes for you again this year? No one is ever too old for a cake on their birthday.'

Florence wanted to say that Mrs Hanson should carry on, because no one ever really talked properly to her about what was happening in the world. Now that she was eighteen, she felt she ought to be more knowledgeable, like Jane was, but before Florence could answer, her father stood up, not altogether steady on his feet, and thumped the table. 'Yes, time for cake and then some music.'

Florence felt a sharp pain in her stomach, as if all her fear had concentrated itself there for a second. 'Papa, please. I said I don't want to.'

Her father's face grew even redder, and his expression changed to something that made Florence afraid of what might happen next. By her side, she felt Jane put a hand on her arm. Mrs Hanson, looking concerned, tried to intervene. 'Perhaps she's too old for all that now. I mean, it's always been wonderful,' and here she gave Florence a glance to show she was on her side, 'but she's a woman now. Shouldn't she decide? Of course, we'd still love to hear you play, Harry.'

'Nonsense,' said her father. 'Fuss about nothing. Just a few tunes to keep an old man happy. It's not much to ask.'

And so her father summoned everyone inside with all his false modesty, as he always did, and she was hauled up alongside him to regale them all with some popular hits of the moment. She tried to blank out the faces staring at her, which seemed to be so close she could hardly breathe. She felt exposed and ridiculous. What were they all thinking? It was the worst performance so far; her throat seemed to be constricting as if someone had their hands there strangling her. Perhaps it was the collective wishes of the crowd working a spell. Her voice became weaker with each new phrase and bar. It was a particular form of torture and felt like the longest twenty minutes of her life.

She was released after five songs and, while the audience clapped and smiled, she fled into the garden and round the back of the house to the stables. The only one to follow her was Jackie, wagging her tail in excitement that she might be taken out on a walk. Florence bent to pick her up, and the little dog licked her ears in happiness at the attention.

She walked past Bikram, the *syce,* who was sleeping in the shade, clearly not expecting any visitors when there was a party going on. She didn't wake him. She didn't want any human company right now.

Oscar had his head over the stable door. He snorted and stamped when he saw her. Florence placed Jackie back on the ground, then stepped inside the stable. There, she picked up a brush and comb and began to groom the chestnut flanks with long, even strokes. Dust and hairs flew around, settling on her new dress, which she didn't give two hoots about, though she knew Sita would be cross with her later. The rhythm of the action soothed her, and after a while she laid her head against the animal's strong, smooth neck and felt released from the humiliation of the afternoon.

In the yard, Jackie began to yap, and Florence looked out to see what the matter was. She saw somebody leading a horse up the path towards her. She stepped outside, shielding her eyes against the sun, and called out. 'Can I help you?' The figure stopped and, leaving his horse, walked towards her, hand outstretched.

'Good afternoon. I'm looking for Harry Hunt. Is this the right place?'

Florence put out her hand and let the stranger shake it. 'I'm his daughter, Florence.'

The man's expression changed. 'Ah, Florence, is it? Your father has told me all about you. Jayachandra Lal, by the way. Or Jay, if you prefer. Pleased to make your acquaintance.'

Florence stared at the man, taking in his smart cream jacket and tie, immaculate riding breeches, and polished boots. She suddenly felt conscious of the streaks of dust on her silk dress and the incongruous picture she must have made, standing there in her party outfit, holding her grooming kit. Who was this man, anyway? She'd never heard Papa talk about a Jayachandra, but apparently he knew who she was.

'Oh. Well, you must tell me everything he has said, so I can correct you.' Florence hoped that this was the sort of answer one gave to men who claimed to know things about you – just the right amount of cleverness to keep them in their place, without killing the conversation completely. Ruthie would have approved. She walked back towards the stable door.

'Your *syce* doesn't happen to be around, does he? I think my horse has gone lame,' he called after her.

Florence leant against the wooden slats of the stable. 'You're hardly on time, you know. The food's all gone, and the entertainment started a while ago. Do you always turn up this late to a party? It's not altogether polite.'

Jay looked confused. 'What party? Harry told me to pop over for a drink this afternoon. I thought he wanted to talk about the meeting this morning. I would have arrived earlier, but Charlie-boy here seems to have picked something up in his hoof. Any chance someone could look at it?'

Although she resented this unknown man intruding upon her moment of seclusion, Florence couldn't ignore an animal in pain. She walked over and ran her hand down its near front leg. 'It's my birthday party. I'm eighteen today.' As soon as she said it, Florence felt a rush of embarrassment. What a thing to say. Adults didn't go around telling each other how old they were. He must think she was such a baby. The horse lifted his hoof for her, and she inspected it carefully.

'Are you now? Well many happy returns.' He indicated her dress. 'Watch out. You'll ruin your birthday frock.'

Florence wondered if he was mocking her. She lifted the other hoof and looked carefully. There was a sharp stone wedged in under the frog. 'Oh, no wonder he's not walking properly.' She called for Bikram, who appeared, yawning, and told him to take the horse away and attend to it.

'Your Hindi isn't bad. Better than a lot of the *memsahibs*,' Jay said.

There was something about the way he said *memsahib* that made it sound as if he were insulting her. As if being a British woman was something almost laughable. Florence gave him what she hoped was a withering look. 'And your English is excellent,' she said. They stood facing each other on the path. He looked like he was smirking at her.

'Sorry, I have to ask. Why are you here, grooming your horse, dressed in a long silk dress and sandals, when it's your birthday party?'

'I really don't think that's any of your business.' The exchange was beginning to make Florence feel a little heady. She gathered herself together. She ought to remember her manners, even if this man was exceedingly irritating. 'If you want, I can show you up to the house. Bikram will look after your horse.' She didn't wait for him to answer but set off up the path in front of him. When they reached the veranda, her father, who had finished playing the piano, thankfully, and instead was winding up the gramophone, gave a big wave and yelled for Jay to join them. Florence watched as the young man stepped easily inside the house, accepted a drink from her father and assimilated himself into the circle of people surrounding him.

Florence looked around for Katie and Jane. She spotted them searching through the pile of records on top of the piano. Katie was obviously saying something about the new arrival, giggling into her hand and fluttering her eyelashes in his direction. Florence joined them and shook her head at Katie. 'Don't bother, Katie. He's a bit of a prig.'

Katie continued snickering. 'But immaculate in those riding breeches and jacket.'

Florence looked at Jay again. He did stand out among the other men, and not just because he was Indian. 'His manners don't match, unfortunately,' she said, picking up a record and studying the sleeve. 'Let's put this one on next. I suppose you want to dance, Katie.'

The three moved away to the other side of the room, and Florence deliberately did not look back. Jay was just another thing about this afternoon she wanted to forget as soon as possible.

Chapter Eight

PORTSMOUTH, 1955

Moving out of Aunt Sarah's house did not prove to be the escape she had hoped for. Instead it brought the shortcomings of her marriage into sharp relief.

Now Billy often stopped at the pub on his way home from work, and after dinner he mostly fell asleep in his chair or studied the racing results in the paper with a large glass of rum in his hand. On Saturdays, she hardly saw him at all, what with the football and the ensuing celebrations or commiserations that usually lasted until closing time. On Sundays she cooked lunch and helped Robert with his homework.

Occasionally, Billy could be persuaded to go with them to the seafront, though Robert didn't like the funfair; the strange noises and screams of the people on the rollercoaster upset him. He did, however, love the Rock Gardens, and the three of them would sometimes walk in the late afternoon along its twisting paths through the arrangements of boulders and shrubs and exotic plants. Then Florence played hide and seek with Robert while Billy sat, smoking a cigarette, on a bench.

Robert's favourite place was the lily pond, where he could

spot fat goldfish. Florence instead always found herself by the fountain at dusk, waiting for the coloured lights to come on, turning the place into an enchanted wonderland. She would sit and, just for a moment, let herself be transported back to the wobbling, metal platform above the circus ring, the spotlights painting coloured circles on the sawdust of the arena far below. She would hear the cheer of the crowd as she flipped herself over the side of the net, landed and turned to each side, arms raised in an athlete's salute, and she would stare into the falling rainbows of the fountain and remember another life. Then she and Robert would wander back to find Billy, their way lit up by the lights hidden in foliage, glowing softly in green and pink.

But on Mondays, Florence's week loomed ahead, empty and grey, which was how she herself started to feel after a while. Once Billy and Robert had left the house, she would clean, and there was the shopping to be done. But no matter how hard she scrubbed surfaces or how many times she went out to buy provisions, she felt more and more as if the walls were closing in on her and she was stuck in birdlime, unable to move — unable, sometimes, to breathe. One day, she reached for the bottle of rum that Billy kept in the cupboard and poured herself a glass, and the warmth comforted her like an embrace from the inside.

* * *

And then there was Robert, with his peculiar games and odd obsessions, which Florence was sure didn't help matters at school. She'd asked the teachers to keep an eye on him, not that they had seemed very interested, and there had been no more tears in the afternoon or reports of any incidents. Florence, her instincts deadened by the fog of her own despair, allowed herself to think he was no longer suffering. Well, mud and rips and bruises — every boy came home with those, didn't they?

Each day Robert slammed the door and kicked off his shoes as she raised herself from the armchair and went to greet him on her way to the kitchen.

'How was it today?'

She would try to pat his hair down, to tame the wild black curls standing out around his sun-darkened face. He would shrug and slide off into his bedroom, leaving her to start on the cooking. Sometimes he would bring her an offering, sitting to do his homework at the table and asking her for help while she clattered around.

'You're so good at it, you could *teach* maths,' he said to her once, and she felt an enormous compliment had been paid.

'I'm sure I couldn't, darling. By next week you'll be cleverer than me. Then what would I do?'

At the bottom of the hill there was a wall that separated the road from the embankment that led down to a train track. Trains ran regularly from Portsmouth Harbour to London, via Southampton. Sometimes Florence would walk down there to watch them, to feel the old thrill as the bricks of the wall under her hands trembled when the engine rumbled by. She closed her eyes and inhaled the smell of oil and smoke, wiping away the smuts from her face afterwards with the back of her hand. And sometimes, on a Saturday afternoon, when Billy had gone to the football and left her alone, she would take Robert down there, too. She sat him on the wall and murmured to him her memories of the station at Agra, and train journeys to school in the mountains, and the day she had watched a locomotive being inspected. She told him how her friend had climbed inside the firebox of a train and disappeared, and then how she herself had once climbed inside a cannon and disappeared, too. Robert gazed in wonder at her stories and then cheered and clapped as the three o'clock from Portsmouth Harbour to London sped by below.

Then there was a signal box, not too far away, that she also loved to visit. She'd go on her own sometimes, taking a detour on her way back from the shops in the mornings, to watch the trains where the track ran right next to the road. She liked to lean over the fence and listen for the bell codes, trying to remember what Prakash had once taught her on the rare occasions when, as a little girl, her father had taken her to the station and she had been allowed up there to sit next to the signalman as a treat. Now she'd crane forward to see if the signal arm lowered or not, and if it didn't, then she'd wait with increasing anticipation for the distant rumble to grow and rush towards her, and for a moment, as it passed, she'd be transported back to the days when her life had been punctuated by travel and trains, and the world had seemed vast and full of possibility.

She took Robert there one day after school, meeting him at the bus stop. A group of other boys ran up the hill, shouting and whooping, but Robert didn't say goodbye. He was in one of his quiet moods, humming songs to himself that only he knew. Florence knew better than to question him. Instead she walked quickly down the road, knowing he would scurry after her, and perhaps the exercise would bring him out of himself.

From the open window of the signal box, a series of sharp rings came down to them where they stood by the fence next to the track. 'Listen, Robert. Count the bells.' Robert looked up but refused to join in. 'Five taps. One tap,' continued Florence encouragingly. 'And three taps. I think that means the man in the other box is asking if the line is clear.' They waited, and shortly came the reply. Robert looked at Florence with one of his silent questions. 'I don't know, darling. Watch the signal arm.' They watched, but the arm remained raised. Robert began to hop from foot to foot, and sure enough they soon heard a whistle and the canter of wheels as it powered down the line. As it passed, Robert screamed then buried his head in Florence's skirt. She laughed and stroked him. 'It's all right, Robbie. I thought you liked it.' Robert extracted himself from her arms and laughed too.

'I do,' he said. 'I really do. How long until the next one? Can we stay?'

Florence checked her watch. 'I don't know. It depends. Billy will be home soon.'

'Next train is in ten minutes.' A voice behind them made Florence turn, and what she saw made her catch her breath, just for a second. For he had the same sweep of hair, the same wiry build, the same dimple in his chin as Jay. Florence stared.

'I'm sorry, I didn't mean to startle you.' His voice was familiar, somehow, those cadences, that tone. And yet, of course it wasn't him. This man was young, younger than her perhaps, and he certainly had not suffered as a prisoner of war. There was too much verve and shine about him for that.

'No, sorry … You just … Ten minutes, you say? Well, I think we could stay for that, don't you, Robert?' Her son turned away, and Florence patted his curls. 'He's shy.'

'So am I, usually,' the man said. 'But if I meet a fellow enthusiast, then I don't mind talking.'

Florence looked at the man again. He was wearing a dark signalman's uniform and carrying a leather case. 'Do you work here?' she asked.

'I do, yes. Shift starts in ten minutes, after the next engine. I'm evenings and weekends usually, but Donald up there needs a favour.'

'I'm sorry, can I ask, where do you come from?'

'Ajmer, madam.' He seemed to stiffen as he said this.

Florence gasped. 'Not the Railway Institute — the Inster?'

'Yes, exactly. Do you know it?'

'Not personally, but I knew somebody else from there. I grew up in Agra.' From the window above, the series of bells started again. 'How long have you been here? Wasn't it hard to become a signalman?' The bells stopped.

'Agra? Really? I always wanted to go there, and Delhi, too, but my parents sent me away in '48. I had a degree already, but I also studied at the technical college here, and then got an apprenticeship.'

'Oh? What did you study?'

'Maths, in India, then engineering here. Very good courses. Very good teachers. Although not everyone was so open minded, if you understand,' and at this he looked down at Robert, 'which I think you probably do.'

Florence checked herself for a moment. The conversation felt so normal, so easy. She'd almost forgotten where she was. Then the bell rang again and the man looked at the signal. 'She'll be here in a couple of minutes. Are you ready, young fellow?' This time, Robert looked at him and gave him a slow smile. Seeing the two of them, both with dark skin and dark hair, Florence imagined how it might have been if her son had had a father like him, had grown up somewhere he didn't always seem so different.

After the train had screamed past, Florence took Robert's hand. 'Come on, darling. We'd better get home.' She turned to the man. 'It was nice to meet you. My name's Florence.'

The man picked up his case and nodded at them both. 'It was my pleasure. I'm Haresh. Pleased to meet you.' He paused, and she thought he might ask them to stay, or invite them up to see the controls, but then he turned, let himself through the gate with a key, and began to climb the steep stairs that led up to the box above.

Back at home, preparing dinner, Florence couldn't stop thinking about their conversation. Frankly, she was amazed at seeing an Indian man working on the railway. She was even surprised he'd been accepted into the college. Well, perhaps times were changing. As she chopped the carrots and mashed the potato, an idea took hold that felt like a tiny beam of light shining through the darkness. As she served up dinner and took her seat at the table, she continued to think, and by the time her plate was clean, she knew what she was going to do.

On Monday, she rose early, keen to make herself look presentable. She'd spent Sunday afternoon rummaging through her clothes, trying to pick the right outfit. She wasn't quite sure which note she should strike. She could go for something practical, to show she could pull her weight. She took out a couple of pairs of her favourite wide-legged trousers. When she was at home on her own, she loved wearing these with a loose cotton shirt, Katharine Hepburn-style. Dressing like this reminded her of the girl she had been, in her jodhpurs at dawn, or even driving that truck in the war. She laid them on the bed and looked for a moment. Inside, however, she knew that it would be too shocking, too informal. No, she didn't want to frighten them away with first impressions.

There was a new cotton sundress she'd bought on Commercial Road last week. Blue with white spots and very feminine, it showed off her waist when she cinched in the belt. She certainly wouldn't seem a threat in that, and if the professors were old-fashioned, she might be able to use it to her advantage. No. She shook her head, tutting at herself for even thinking it. That's not what this was about. There was nothing for it — it would have to be the suit with the pencil skirt in sensible tweed and her brown brogues, which needed a polish. That outfit had served her well in the offices at the factory, and it would do the same again for her now.

When she arrived at reception, a woman took her name and told her she'd have to wait to speak to someone in admissions. The woman had been friendly until Florence had mentioned the course she was interested in, at which point her face had taken on a slight cast of disapproval. She handed her a selection of reading material about the college. Florence noticed that a leaflet for the Art School had been placed on top. There was nothing about engineering.

It was nearly an hour before the receptionist told her she could make her way to the office on the second floor, where Mr Mason would see her. After two flights of stairs and a long, gloomy corridor, she paused outside the door to catch her breath, brushed herself down, checked her shoes were still well-polished, then knocked three times, loud and clear.

After five minutes of social niceties, Mr Mason lounged back in his chair, hands behind his head. 'But what actual qualifications in the field do you have, Mrs Greene?' he asked.

Florence pushed several pieces of paper towards him across the desk for the second time. 'Here's my college report, which shows I had the highest scores in maths in school. Then there's the letter of reference from the railway offices in Agra, my services during the war — both in the offices in Delhi and driving the supply trucks from Calcutta — and finally my letter of recommendation from the factory, where I worked as line manager and then in logistics.' Florence waited while he glanced at the documents in front of him then reached for a cigarette and lit it.

'Smoke?' he offered. Florence shook her head. 'Listen, Mrs Greene. You undoubtedly did an impressive job during the war, as did many women, and it must have been a fascinating experience growing up in India. And this is indeed a very good school report. I imagine Auckland House school in … Where?' He looked down at the piece of paper again. 'Simla?' He obviously had no idea where Simla was and had no intention of finding out. Florence smiled and said nothing. 'Well, I'm sure it gave you a good grounding in many artistic subjects and knowledge of the social graces,' he continued. 'But I see no mention of the scientific subjects, for example. I'd be doing you a disservice if I led you to think that this qualifies you to study for a certificate in engineering here. And besides, what would you do with it afterwards? There just isn't the demand for women in the workplace now. I'm sure your husband would tell you the same thing.'

Florence knew she had to remain calm and polite, and preferably pretty, too. She smiled at Mr Mason. 'But what about the factory job? That must count for something.'

'Well, yes, indeed. Have you thought about trying to find something similar again?'

'But that's not the point. I want to do something different. I thought this place was becoming more open-minded, taking on people from different backgrounds.'

Mr Mason frowned as he finished his cigarette. 'That's as may be, Mrs Greene. But it doesn't change the fact that even if you were able to complete this course successfully, despite your lack of previous qualifications, what on earth would you do with it? Are you going to take your own husband's job down at the docks?' He laughed, a nasty little laugh, at his joke.

'Not at the docks, no.' Florence could barely contain her frustration. 'What if I took the qualifications that I need here first? I'm sure I could do maths and science in a year.'

'Mrs Greene, I think we should call this a day.' He stood up and turned to the shelf behind him. 'Why don't you take some of these leaflets away with you and have a read. If you are so set on coming to our college, I'm sure we can find something more appropriate for you.' He passed her a bundle of folded papers. 'I don't know if you're any good with a paint brush, but our Art School has an excellent reputation. I know lots of ladies enjoy taking classes there. You really should consider it.'

Down in reception, Florence signed out in the visitors' book, under the patronising smile of the same woman who had spoken to her before.

'Do you have a bin?' Florence asked before she left. The woman indicated one at the side of the desk. Florence stood over it and raised her hand. 'I won't be needing those,' she said, and dropped the bundle of leaflets from a height. She walked out of the building and didn't look back.

She rode home on the bus and a wave of anger and indignation that carried her up the hill and in the front door of her house. But by the time Robert came home from school, her high emotions had dispersed, leaving her only with a sense of hopelessness and despair. The rum bottle came down from the top shelf again. It was the only thing that would get her through another family meal and another tedious, silent evening with Billy, trying to find a way back to the memories that were becoming more nebulous now, harder to hold on to. Sometimes even she herself began to doubt the truth about her past.

Fingers of guilt about Robert poked around her gut as she drank, and so she drank more, and thought of her own mother. Dorothy. Was this how she had felt about her life in India with Harry? Florence wished now she had tried harder to make her father talk about her mother. But he had always changed the subject. There was only the letter, which Florence suddenly wanted to read again.

Underneath the bed there was a box that contained the ephemera of another life. Now, she pulled it out into the light, removed the lid, and peered in. Just a bunch of odds and sods, as Billy would say. She dug underneath sheaves of papers, certificates, and photographs. A diary. A journal. An old mouldy ledger. She ignored a bundle of silk scarves and pushed to one side a set of wooden elephants, until she could feel the smooth edges of a sandalwood box. She pulled it out and opened it. Inside was a sheaf of letters, bound with a red ribbon, and a fragile, heart-shaped leaf, but it was another letter, written on paper stamped with the Agra Railway Office address, that she was looking for. She unfolded it carefully and began to read.

20th September 1947

Dear Florence,

I hope you are reading this safe and comfortable in your cabin on the ship. I trust the Hansons are looking after you, and I hope you are looking forward to your new life in England.

Since you agreed to leave, I have been thinking about our relationship, how I was as a father. And I know you always had many questions about your mother — I should have been more open with you.

It was your eighteenth birthday, if I recall correctly, that you stormed into my study, demanding to know what happened to her (and berating me for making you sing and dance at your party. It was only a couple of songs. Honestly!). I didn't talk about her when you were growing up, and it became a habit. It was painful and complicated. But you deserve to know about her, and about how I was with her. I hope you won't blame me too much after you have read this. I am going to try to be honest.

When I took you, my firstborn, in my arms and carried you up the wooden stairs from the garden into the shuttered-down cool of our house in Agra, I was unimaginably proud. This is where everything changes, *I thought. And then you began to cry, and you looked me in the eye like a tiny tigress, challenging me, as if to say you wouldn't let me get away with anything. Your mother was exhausted, and after five days in 'that awful hospital', as she always called it, had already gone up to bed. We'd just appointed Sita, and, I remember, before I handed you over, I hoisted you skyward, left you momentarily in suspension under the slow, chopping blade of the ceiling fan. Then Sita took you, swaddled you, and nestled you in the cot, and peace descended once more.*

I hadn't known quite how much everything would change, however, and how quickly. Six months later, Dorothy was hardly eating anything, so I had to intervene. She had never been especially robust. Even in England she had complained about the heat in summer, the damp in winter, the smells up in town and in the countryside, sickness on trains, on boats, and even in a certain type of hansom cab. All this had increased a hundredfold since we'd come to India, and by another magnitude since pregnancy and the birth. So I was taking her lunch on a tray to her room. I remember it being dark and airless because she insisted on keeping everything closed against the outside world.

She'd been like it for so long, I'd lost my patience. I probably shouted and opened the window. When I look back now, I can see she was ill not only in her body. She was so afraid of everything.

It was a beautiful day outside. Sita was sitting on the lawn underneath the window, bouncing you — six months' old already — up and down on her knees. But Dorothy was so unhappy. She picked at the food I'd made for her — just a couple of eggs. Even now, I don't know any other husbands who would do the same. And then this ridiculous argument started. She was flapping her hands, complaining about a fly, telling me to close the window. And of course, I refused. Said something along the lines of, if she wanted to rot in there in the dark and with no air to breathe, then she could get up and close it herself. Well, of course there was a bloody fly. We were in India!

Later, I sat in the shade in my favourite spot in the garden, you know, under the frangipani trees. I remember feeling relaxed for once; Ravi was chopping wood somewhere with those slow, methodical thuds, and I had just finished lunch and a beer. I always wanted my days off from the station to be a time when I could read, and play the piano, and generally be another person to the man everyone else expected me to be — especially Dorothy. She wasn't the slightest bit interested in any of that though. I think that's why I was determined you were going to be different.

There was a peacock shrieking — remember when Sita used to tell us that meant the rains were coming? Perhaps this one was an omen, a warning. Perhaps I should have paid more attention.

Anyway, at some point I was dozing off and your mother woke me, shouting from the window above, demanding I come up and see her. I can't say I was happy at being summoned again, and no doubt I was more than a little grumpy. And all she wanted to show me were a couple of mosquito bites on her arm. Of course I told her she should have tucked the netting under the bed properly, and she told me she'd been saying there was a hole in it, as if she expected me to repair it. After a few more minutes of arguing, she stormed off to have a bath. I sat on the bed, under strict instructions to kill the ravening beast, not that there was any sign of it. Not quite sure what she expected me to do — take one of my antique scimitars and issue a challenge, perhaps.

Turns out she was right to be worried. Not even a couple of weeks later the doctor was there, telling me she was very unwell, telling me I should have called him before. Anaemia after the birth, an infection of the kidneys, and now malaria. She needed to be in hospital, and I knew how much she hated that place. But she needed treatment, intensive care, and fast.

It all happened rather quickly after that. She went downhill over the next few days and by the end of the week, she was gone.

The church was crowded for the funeral, which surprised me. I hadn't realised so many people had liked her. I was glad they were there. It made me feel less guilty. People passed you around while I read the eulogy, all the women looking at me as if there's nothing worse (or more enticing, maybe) than a man left to cope with middle-age and a child alone.

I didn't know what to do when everyone had gone. I walked from room to room, lighting candles and lamps until the whole place glowed like a tomb. You know, I love this house, always have. And I walked it, thinking about the past and trying to imagine the future without Dorothy. I stood in the salon and looked at its precious wall hangings woven by the hands of local women a hundred years ago. I paid a fair sum for those. Gave them to Dorothy on our third wedding anniversary. Not that she liked them particularly.

And of course, I moved on to the library: my refuge. Filled with the plays of Oscar Wilde and Shakespeare, the novels of Henry James: I promised to read them all to you. Then I sat at my piano, played Chopin and Satie. Perhaps you'll never understand this, but the feeling of being transported, of time suddenly becoming meaningless at the keys — it's the place I feel at once most alive and almost, at times, obliterated.

So, you were left to grow up without a mother. And I to grow old without a wife, without someone to share the memories of the ordinary and the extraordinary. And what is a life if it is not shared? Not a day goes past that I don't feel guilt at what happened. At the fact that I should have been kinder.

Forgive me, Florence, for it all. For not taking better care of your mother. For letting you down when you needed me most. For not protecting you as a father should always protect a daughter, however young or old. Go make a life for yourself in England, find somebody to share it with, and know that I shall always regret how it all ended for you here.

With deepest affection,
Your loving father

Florence folded the letter again and placed it back in the box. If only her father could have found the words and the courage to tell her this before she had left. Perhaps she would have stayed, taken care of him. A quiet life, but at least one of independence, where she had roots and an understanding of how to do more than merely exist.

For what had been the purpose of travelling halfway across the globe, to end up once more in a miserable marriage, in a country where she would never belong and where her son would always be different? A country where her only option was to spend lonely, endless days dreaming of the past and dreading the future.

Chapter Nine

AGRA, 1938

It had become a tradition over the years for Florence and Harry to spend Christmas week at the governor's annual festive camp, up-country on the edge of the jungle. There were elephant drives and big-game hunts during the day, and dinners and dances at night to keep everyone entertained. VIPs from miles around attended, so of course Harry had used his charms and his influence with his superiors in Agra and Delhi to make sure he was invited.

That year's Christmas camp was the most lavish Florence had ever seen, as though everyone knew something terrible was coming and had determined to celebrate this one last time in style before the world detonated. There were perhaps a hundred tents for guests. The governor's accommodation, vast swathes of canvas festooned with ribbons, was set back a short distance away from the main group, and all day long servants ran backwards and forwards between the VIP tents and the kitchens in the guest house.

Florence's more modest tent was nearer the camp pond, and she tried to put thoughts of crocodiles out of her head in the evenings as she prepared for bed. She was grateful that Sita slept near her, in a cot behind a curtain, always there to protect her should she need it. It wasn't only crocodiles that crept into her dreams. On occasion, she had woken to hear a gruff *cough-cough* that seemed only a few yards from her head, and in the morning Ravi had shown her the pugmarks left by a tiger and her cubs in the mud by the pool's edge. Once, when she was little, a leopard had walked through the camp, unconcerned by the shouts and screams, disappearing with a twitch of its tail into the jungle before anyone could do anything about it.

On Christmas morning, Florence woke in the dark as Sita brought in the tray of tea and biscuits that the boys had left outside the tent. Florence sat up and held out her hand, grabbing Sita's arm.

'What is it, *beti*?' Sita said, setting down the tray and sitting on the edge of the bed. 'Didn't you sleep? Bad dreams again?'

Florence nodded. 'I just have this feeling that something terrible is going to happen. My stomach is all in knots.'

Sita patted her hand. 'I think you are reading your father's newspaper too often. I've seen you. Every evening now. All this talk, of war and of killing. You are too young.'

It was true that since her birthday Florence had taken to picking up the papers when her father had finished with them, hiding them in her room and reading them at night before she fell asleep. But she didn't think she was too young to inform herself about the world. Jane and her mother talked about current affairs, and it was all her father and his friends ever discussed. She just wished it didn't have to be quite so relentlessly awful. Assassinations, persecution, concentration camps, pogroms (she'd had to look that word up in the dictionary), military invasions, refugees. And that was just in Europe. Sometimes at night her mind was little more than a flickering procession of images formed of everything she'd read. She yawned. 'Perhaps you're right, *amah*. And it is Christmas after all.'

'All my life there has been violence and bloodshed in this land. Terrible events which are the children of other terrible events in the past. And yet,' Sita kissed Florence's hand and stood up, 'we are here, and in this moment, we are happy, no?' She walked to the door of the tent. 'Drink your tea. It's time to get up.'

Florence lay for a while, enjoying the sounds of the lamps being lit and the warmth of the bed with its heavy blankets insulating her against the cold. She waited until Sita returned with a jug of hot water, then slipped out from under the sheets, hauled on her clothes, and washed her face at the basin. Then she took her tea and a couple of biscuits and stepped outside. It was still dark, and in the tents around the camp the shadows of the other waking guests loomed large, like nightmarish puppets against the glowing, yellow canvas walls, as they too prepared for the morning ride out. Her father's tent remained unlit. He would rise at the last minute and arrive as the party set off, to avoid being stuck with the shooters at the front of the hunt. How he hated to shoot at the wildlife.

Spoons tinkled in chai glasses, servants murmured in Hindi, water splashed into basins accompanied by a brief refrain of vigorous throat clearing and coughing. Down the slope, on the road, she heard the elephants huffing and shuffling, whispering down their trunks and chinking their chains in expectation of activity and food. Behind the percussion of all these slight and surface sounds, however, remained the huge silence of the jungle, dense and absorbing.

Half an hour later, as the sky paled, most of the group had assembled by the gate and the first elephants had already left. The governor led the way, followed by the officers and the men in charge from Delhi, all keen to advance their careers, all in pressed khaki and all with rifles gleaming and regulation topees set firmly on their heads. Florence, feeling better with so much to distract her, watched them disappearing down the road. Sure enough, once they had gone, her father appeared by her side.

'Missed the vanguard, have I? Pity. Looks like we'll be bringing up the rear as usual. Just as well. Something wrong with my rifle anyway.'

Her father walked towards one of the elephants being unshackled by its mahout. Florence was about to follow him when she heard a voice calling his name. She turned to see someone jogging towards them. As he neared, she recognised him as the irksome man who had arrived late to her party the week before.

'Completely overslept,' he said. 'Set an alarm, but I must have gone off again. Have I missed the boat, so to speak?'

'I'm afraid you've missed your chance with the Delhi lot,' said her father. 'You'll have to put up with me and Florence instead. I wouldn't worry too much about that gun. The beaters have long gone. We won't be seeing many tigers from where we are, I shouldn't think.'

The man looked at the gun and then tucked it under his arm. He held out a hand to Florence. 'A pleasure to meet you again.'

'I didn't know you were invited to the camp,' said Florence, allowing him to grasp her hand for a moment. 'I'm sorry, I can't remember your name.' Before he could answer, the mahouts started calling them. Florence walked away, towards the elephants.

Once they had dispensed with the awkward business of getting on to the elephants and into the howdahs, and the beasts had heaved themselves back up and were heading down the road after the rest of the party, Florence told the boy to bring the elephants alongside each other. Her father was a little way in front, and she could hear him singing loudly from underneath his hat.

'Jayachandra Lal.' The man leaned towards her across the back of his elephant and smiled. 'But I think you knew that, really.'

'Why would I say I didn't, if I did?' Florence felt she had a right to be indignant, even if what he said was true. Jay was a very easy name to remember.

Jay looked ahead again. 'Your father is quite an interesting character.'

'Yes, that's one way to describe him. How long have you worked with him?'

'I came up from Ajmer last month. I'm helping him with the express line.'

'Are you an engineer, too?'

'Yes, but don't worry. I won't go on about trains and motors and dull stuff like that.' At this, the reserve that Florence thought she had been maintaining so well, and her mild sense of irritation with this man who seemed a bit too over-confident in her opinion, disappeared in an instant.

'Actually, I'm rather interested in all of that dull stuff,' she said, turning sideways in her howdah to face him. 'I'm hoping Papa will let me help him in the office during the holidays. I love seeing how it all works.' As she said it, she wondered what on earth he must think of her. She was fairly sure Ruthie would not list railways and trains and engines among her interests when she struck up a conversation with a man.

Jay gave her a look that she couldn't interpret; Florence stopped talking and fiddled with the pins in her hair instead.

They continued along for a while in silence as the road became a path and the path snaked into the forest and the forest eased itself ever closer around them. When they reached the old temple, Jay told his mahout to stop. Florence watched him as he took it all in: the carved pillars crumbling into the verdure; the grey tendrils of the banyan tree cascading earthwards over the relics of statues of dancing gods; a screen of pierced latticework filtering the early morning light into intricate shapes on the ground in front of them. She had seen it all many times before, but somehow his scrutiny made it appear a newly discovered treasure. She pointed at the monkeys, seated on a nearby wall — their soft, pale fur shining, tails interlinked behind them — as they basked in the warmth of the rising sun. He laughed, and Florence felt a pleasant sensation of satisfaction at having caused this reaction in him.

'What a truly beautiful place this is,' he said.

He continued to gaze around, and Florence thought about doing something daring.

'What would you say if we were to ditch the hunt and go and see the lake instead? It's lovely at this time of day.'

'Sounds wonderful, but what about your father?'

'Oh, don't worry about Papa. He'll have caught up with the officers' wives by now and will be entertaining them with his silly stories. He'll just think we're being a bit slow.'

'If you think he won't mind, then let's go. I blew any chance of impressing the bosses when I overslept anyway.'

So Florence instructed the mahouts to take the path that ran in the opposite direction from the hunt. They plodded through the forest for another fifteen minutes until the trees and bushes began to thin out and they came to the edge of a small lake. The elephants stopped, lowered their trunks and drank.

Florence looked out over the water, wanting to see it through Jay's eyes, suddenly hoping he would approve of the place she had brought him to. The sun reflected off the silvered surface pricked by the dark spearheads of reeds. A small heron poked its way around the weeds in the shallows, then moved in large, careful steps on to a log. She was trying to think of something interesting to say, when she heard Jay whisper her name. She looked, and he was pointing in the opposite direction to the lake, at the raised bank a few yards away, and there, among the tall grasses, she saw the enormous, extended body of a sleeping tiger.

Florence took a deep breath. Around the tiger lay the bloody parts of a dismembered deer: a shinbone, a fleshy haunch, a hoof. Florence gazed at the beast, at its plush fur, vivid orange, black and white, and the rhythmic lift and fall of its ribs as it slept on, sated for now by its kill.

A thought occurred to her, and she turned to look at Jay, ready to condemn him with her outrage if he so much as raised his gun. But Jay was staring at the tiger too, a slight and endearing smile on his face. After another minute, he whispered again.

'Bloody amazing animal. Huge.'

They continued to sit and watch in silence until the mahouts began to signal that they should get the elephants away before the big cat awoke. Florence thought it looked like it would sleep for days yet, but the boys became more agitated, and so she finally gave them the sign to move off. They turned back to the path and walked through the trees until they felt far enough away to talk.

Florence didn't bother to hide her excitement. 'I've never seen one that close before! Did you see all the body parts strewn around?'

'Looked like enough for several Christmas lunches.' Jay seemed equally roused. 'Hope you don't think I'm a coward for not taking a shot. Would have been unsporting, don't you think? It was just too damn beautiful to kill.'

'Absolutely! Papa and I hate it when they bring back the bodies to camp after the hunt. It's too sad. I'm so glad you didn't shoot.'

On the return journey, the elephants walked side by side, and now Florence chatted with no inhibitions, pointing out the birds and the plants around them, repeating the names that Sita had once taught her in English and Hindi, making him laugh and compliment her on her knowledge of the jungle. She felt a little wild herself, but when they arrived back at the tents, the place was still quiet, save for the servants arranging the tables for lunch. Only the smell of chicken curry and wood smoke drifted out to meet them. Now they were back on the ground and back in the camp, the feeling between them faltered, and Florence fell silent. Walking by his side, she felt young and graceless again. They stopped and he looked around. She waited for him to speak.

'Think I'll go and wash up. I imagine the others will be back within the hour. Thank you, Florrie, for an enchanting morning. See you at lunch, I suppose.'

He walked off, rifle under his arm, and Florence stood for a moment, unsure of what to do, unsure of what to think. He had called her Florrie! No one called her Florrie. Was that a good thing? Or was it a name you gave to little girls? She didn't want him to think of her as a little girl, of that much she was now certain. She waited a moment longer, watching him walk over to the other side of the camp. His shirt, striped by the sun and shadows, had a tigerish look to it, she thought. Then she took off her hat and ran to find Sita, to make sure her most elegant dress was ready for her to wear at lunch.

* * *

The Christmas camp was declared by all who attended to be an overwhelming success. The Governor shot a tiger, the roasted Christmas peafowl was only slightly dry and, above all, Harry's band from Bombay kept the guests stomping and spinning until the early hours every night.

They accompanied him back to Agra for the New Year celebrations at the Club, and by the time January chimed into town, Harry's star had risen alongside that of his crowd-pleasing quintet. After midnight, Florence, who had spent the evening with Katie and Jane, pretending to look bored at even the idea of dancing, fled from the ballroom when she saw her father take the stage and sit down at the piano. She was standing on the veranda, looking out over the inky darkness of the polo field and wondering when it might be safe to return inside, when a figure stepped up beside her.

'Florrie? What are you doing out here?'

Jay was standing on the step below her, brindled with shadows. Florence felt the night shift around her, felt herself shed one skin and find a new one to try on for size.

'Actually, I'm hiding. Papa's in there on the piano.'

'He's not that bad, is he?'

Florence giggled at this. Jay understood. The complicity was intoxicating.

'No. I mean, he can be a bit… hit and miss. But I'm hiding to protect my own dignity.'

'A woman's dignity is very important. You should do everything to protect it. What is it that is threatening it, exactly?'

He'd called her a woman. For a moment, Florence felt her face redden in the dark. She wanted to confide in him, to tell him her secrets.

'He always insists that I sing with him. And I'm afraid I'm as good at singing as he is at playing the piano.'

Jay nodded at this and looked serious. 'Well, I can see that would be a grave threat to your standing in public life. What can I do to help?'

'I'm not sure there is anything you can do. You can't go in there, can you?'

Jay didn't answer, and Florence hoped he didn't think she was trying to put him in his place, because that was not what she intended at all. She tried to lighten the mood again. 'Just don't tell anyone I'm here, and don't let anyone try to drag me up on to that stage.'

'I think I can manage that.'

They continued to stand and look out into the night, while the band — and her father — played on. It was a moment that Florence would revisit many times in her imagination, for a long time to come.

* * *

On the second day of the new year, Florence accompanied her father to the office. They set off at his usual time, and Florence enjoyed the rare ride in a motor car — she was more used to horseback or bullock carts up in the hills. She was determined she would learn to drive one day.

She watched the misty, dawn-time streets slide past the window, the larger bungalows turning to smaller tenements, until they crossed the river and skirted the bazaar. The smell of spices and street food frying in hot oil filtered into the interior of the car, and a wandering cow put its nose up to the window, expecting to be fed.

Arriving at the station, Florence felt a sudden twinge of nerves, and she faltered behind as they stepped inside the building.

Jay wasn't there. Her father cleared a space for her at the

end of his desk and dumped a pile of papers in front of her. As far as Florence could tell, he seemed to spend most of his time either staring at the same large chart of boxes — arrows and data written in minuscule hand — or barely concealing his irritation in long telephone calls to the office in Delhi.

She kept quiet and made a good start on the filing he'd asked her to do, all the time conscious of the empty desk where she assumed Jay worked.

It was after midday when he finally appeared. Florence watched him as he removed the dark-grey, single-breasted suit jacket he was wearing, carefully undoing its three buttons and brushing it down before he hung it on a peg by the door. His shirt underneath was crisply starched, and his trousers had a sharp crease. Even his black Oxford shoes were polished and free of dust.

'Problem with the electrics down the line.' He stood in front of her father who was on the phone and gestured Jay out of his line of vision. Jay sat down and started shifting papers across the desk, then looked up and seemed to notice her for the first time. 'Hello, Florence. So, you've been roped in to help. Sorry about that.'

Under her father's eye, Florence blushed. 'No, I'm enjoying it. It was my idea. It's fascinating, all this.' She realised her father had finished his call and was staring at her. He didn't look happy.

'Girl's mad, don't you think, Jay? Could be doing bloody anything, and instead she wants to come to this hellhole. Buggered if I can understand why.'

'Just grateful someone is doing the filing, sir.'

'Suppose so. Anyway, isn't it about lunchtime? Take her out, would you. Get some food. It'll be a long afternoon otherwise.'

They walked out into the confusion of the station. A goods

train was passing through, rumbling by only a yard away from her on the platform. Metal rods pushed and pulled, and wheels clanked on rails. There was an occasional cascade of sparks, pretty as a firework, and Florence stood transfixed, feeling the ground tremor and shake beneath her. When it had gone, she became aware again of the press of people around them, and Jay, who was laughing at her.

'You weren't lying when you said you liked trains. I thought I was going to have to stop you jumping on.'

'It's not just trains. It's machines, it's engines — any kind of contraption really. I just want to know how it works. Don't you think it's fascinating, the cause and effect? How one thing leads to another and there's a reaction, and if we are clever we can use that reaction to make something work for us? Move us, control us, organise us, propel us ...' Florence faltered, wondering again if this was the sort of thing she, a young woman, ought to be saying, or whether she was making a fool of herself. Jay gave her that look she already recognised, something between amusement and appraisal, so that she felt self-conscious and gauche.

After a moment he replied. 'You're right. It is fascinating.'

He smiled at her, and they started walking along the platform, Jay gently guiding her by the elbow, brushing away the beggars and the vendors when they stood in her way. She waved up at Prakash in the signal box. They reached another building and went into a small canteen, sat down opposite each other, and ordered the chicken curry.

Florence watched him as he began to eat, delicate and precise, deboning the pieces of meat with his knife and fork, dabbing at his mouth from time to time with his napkin. She did the same, though she knew the best way to eat it really was to use your hands — something that only Sita allowed, and only when they were alone together. Florence was conscious of the noise of other people talking around them. Was she supposed to be the one to strike up a conversation?

When he had cleared half his plate, he paused and sat back. 'I'm sorry. I was very hungry. I didn't have time for breakfast this morning. There was a bit of an emergency down the line.'

'What is it that you do, exactly?'

He didn't answer for a moment. 'I'm from Ajmer,' he finally replied. 'I grew up in the railway colony there. The Railway Institute. Do you know it?'

Florence shook her head.

'Oh, it's wonderful. Ajmer itself, it's a bit of a pit, you know? Next to the desert, fly-blown, crowded with beggars, unbearably hot. But the Railway Institute — the Inster — it's like a vision. Green lawns and fields for tennis and cricket, hockey and bowling. A veritable piece of England.'

'I wouldn't know. I've never been to England.' Florence felt a little resentful that Jay seemed to know so much more than her about the place. Still, his enthusiasm was engaging.

'You must — you surely will, in the future. I studied there, you see, and one day I hope to return.' He started eating again and then looked up. 'But I was talking about the Institute. There are dances every week. But the best are at Christmas and Easter. The Easter ball. You can't imagine.'

'We do have our own club here. Dances aren't exactly unknown.'

Jay waved a finger at her. 'No, I'm sorry but your club doesn't compare. You can't understand unless you see it. Maybe I'll take you one day.' He seemed amused by this idea, and Florence felt a twinge of excitement at the thought of it — being escorted to a magnificent ball by this man who intrigued and perplexed her in turn.

'Maybe I'll let you,' she said.

Jay let out a roar of laughter, and Florence couldn't help joining in. 'What?' she said, lowering her eyes. 'What did I say?'

But Jay just shook his head and carried on eating. Even so, their shared moment made her feel brave — and suddenly as if he'd accepted her. She wanted to know more. 'You studied in England. Isn't that quite—'

'Unusual? Difficult? For an Indian? Yes, it is.' He ate a last mouthful of rice, pushed the chicken bones to the side of his plate in a neat pile, and laid his knife and fork next to them. 'My father was a foreman, so from an early age I was around the British and around trains. I had a talent for mathematics. But it was when my father became ill that suddenly I knew I wanted to honour him, everything he had done for us. So I studied and I studied, and I passed the exams, and they took me on as a special class apprentice.'

Florence shook her head. 'I don't know what that is.'

'Thousands apply, but maybe only ten per year are selected. And I was one of them.' He looked down at the table.

'And your father?'

'Ah, well, he died. The year I was sent to London to get my engineering degree. Four years of college, first in Ajmer, and then England.'

Florence tried to take it all in, adjusting her idea of him. Apparently, he was something exceptional. 'Sounds like you should be running the show in the office. What work do you do for my father?'

'My official title is assistant mechanical engineer.' He stopped and seemed to shrink into himself, a hint of a frown across his brow, and Florence thought it strange. After all, mechanical engineer was something to be proud of. What she would give to be able to call herself that one day. This prompted a thought, something she'd been wanting to ask her father, but hadn't dared.

'In that case,' she said, 'perhaps you can explain how a combustion engine works.'

Jay leaned forward. 'External or internal?'

'I don't know. Both.'

'Do you drive?'

'Not yet, but I will.'

At this Jay smiled again and reached across the table for her knife and fork. He thought for a moment then folded his napkin and placed that beside the cutlery. Then he looked around and took a salt cellar from the next table.

'As you are so in love with trains, let's start with a steam engine, an external combustion engine.' He took a pen from the pocket of his shirt and started sketching on his napkin. 'Here we have the box where you load the coal. And here is the boiler. In an engine, you are transforming energy — from heat to mechanical. So you use the energy in the coal to heat up the water inside the boiler, creating a lot of pressure, because of the steam. Imagine you heat up a pan of water with a lid on. When it starts to boil that lid is rattling away, all that pressure building up wanting to escape. Understand?'

Florence nodded, very much taken with the delicate line of his sketches. His hands and fingers were delicate, too.

'The smaller and stronger the boiler, the higher the pressure, and we can use this pressure. So the steam flows from the boiler to a cylinder, like so.' Here, Jay picked up the salt cellar and sprinkled salt along the tubes of his drawing. 'And then—'

'Sorry, where does the water come from?' Florence interrupted, frowning at the napkin.

'Ah, yes. Good question. Here.' Jay set his glass on the napkin. 'Water tanks, mounted on the side of the engine. The water passes through a set of small tubes inside the boiler.'

'So when the steam gets to the cylinder, then what happens?'

'Good, very good. The cylinder contains a piston. It's like a bicycle pump, you know? And this is connected to the wheels of the locomotive via a crank and rod, which make this kind of circular movement possible.' Here, Jay began to imitate the action with his arm. 'Just like my shoulder, arm, and elbow. See?'

'Yes, just about,' said Florence. 'Except for one thing. I can see how the steam pushes the piston to one end of the cylinder,' she said, placing a fork on the napkin and pushing it forward, 'but how does it move back to the starting point again?'

Jay nodded. 'Very good indeed. It's an elegant solution. The rotational motion of the crank is used to drive the reciprocal — and by that I mean backwards and forwards, you know? — motion of the piston. The train's momentum carries it forward, the crank rotates and pushes the piston back again.'

Florence thought hard for a moment, then sat back, delighted. 'It's so simple!'

'It's exactly what you said earlier,' said Jay, adding a few last details and some shading to his sketch. 'Cause and effect. Using a reaction to make something work for us. Propel us. Pushing us forward. Always forward. Always forward.'

Florence thought again. 'Pressure causes change. All that energy building up. Something has to happen.'

They sat in silence for a minute, contemplating the table. Jay put his pen back in his pocket and looked at her, and this time she met his gaze. His expression was gentle and pensive, and he was nothing like the man she thought she had met not so long before on the day of her birthday party. Then something else occurred to her.

'So what is an internal combustion engine?'

But then she realised her father was standing next to the table.

'They want you on the phone, Jay. You better finish up.'

Jay stood and, with a quick look of apology at Florence, left the table. Her father watched him go and then sat down.

'You not eating that?' he said, pointing to her half-finished food. 'Shame to waste it.' He took her plate and the fork that had been serving as a piston in their engine and began to eat the cold curry. He was still frowning. 'Club tonight, Florence. I'm playing with the band, and I want you with me, please.'

'Yes, Papa.'

'And don't go bothering Jay. He's got work to do.'

'I should have the filing finished by the end of the afternoon. Papa, you look so tired these days.' She placed her hand on his for a moment.

Her father cleaned the plate with a piece of roti, sat with his eyes closed for a few seconds, then pushed his chair back and stood up. 'Very well. Anyway, back to the grindstone. Come on.'

As she left, Florence slid the napkin from the table into her pocket. She would study its pistons and valves and cranks and rods later, in the privacy of her own room, when she was finally able to escape the humiliations of her evening at the Club.

* * *

The next morning, Florence sat on the veranda with a book on her lap, but the pages fluttered in the breeze while she tried to recall every word of her conversation with Jay the previous day. When she saw him walking up the path to the house, her expression changed from distraction to surprise. What was he doing here? She watched as he brushed the sleeves of his jacket and adjusted his tie, then stood at the bottom of the steps.

'This is unexpected. Did Papa send you with some filing after all? He was adamant he didn't need me in the office today.' She put her book down and beckoned him up, hoping that her hair looked presentable and wishing she hadn't chosen to put on her oldest slacks and blouse after her ride that morning.

'Your father has gone to Delhi. He asked me to call in and let you know.'

'If that's the case, then he won't be back until tomorrow. I better tell Cook.' She turned to enter the house then stopped. 'Would you like to stay to lunch?'

Jay looked uncomfortable, and Florence could understand why. Being inside his boss's house, eating his food in his absence, with his daughter. Not at all proper.

'I'm afraid I can't stay. I have a job to do down the line. Boilersmith's gone AWOL, and there's a locomotive stuck in the shed.'

Florence laughed. 'Down the line. You men are always off "down the line". It sounds awfully mysterious. What do you get up to when you're there?'

He stared at her for a moment, and she hoped she hadn't said something wrong. 'Why don't you come with me?' he said, finally. 'See for yourself.'

She didn't answer, and maybe a minute passed. Every part of her wanted to say yes, but then again … It would be wrong, terribly wrong. And if anyone were to find out, tell her father or Kit Hanson, then Jay's job could very well vanish in an instant. Back to Ajmer and life as a foreman, if he was lucky. She didn't want to be responsible for that.

Then, in the quiet space between them, came the cry of a peacock, and she saw a glimpse of green and blue sweeping the shadows of the shrubs at the side of the house. Jay looked too, perhaps grateful for the distraction. Finally, she said, 'It wouldn't be right. Not proper.' She was silent again. Now the peacock returned and, finding a patch of sunlight under the trees, fanned open its tail feathers in front of them – a card trick achieved with the flick of a hand. A shower of emeralds and sapphires.

They turned to each other, smiling. Jay said, 'He wants you to go. It's a sign.'

'It's only a bird,' she replied. Then, as it continued to pose and shudder before them, she said, 'Let me just get my hat.'

Florence laughed as Jay handled the car with an expert's disdain for caution, swerving to avoid potholes at the last minute, taking the corners at a decent speed. They were talking about the peacock, Florence mocking his insistence that the bird had appeared for a reason.

'But you know why he sounds so sad when he calls, even with his marvellous tail,' said Jay, accelerating along a straight expanse of road between fields lined with tangled walls of prickly pears, those green plates with their tufts of needles angled uncomfortably close to the open sides of the car.

Florence shook her head. 'Is this like one of those stories Kipling wrote? Papa used to read them to me when I was little. Was there one about a peacock? I don't remember.'

'No, no, this is a Hindu tale.' Jay settled himself down into the seat. 'Having wished to be the loveliest bird of all, the peacock is showing off as usual, with his long train of brightly coloured feathers that everyone admires. But then he sees a crane, all white and plain, and insults him for being so colourless. The crane, however, just laughs at him and flies off. Up, up, up, higher and higher, and the peacock tries to follow and realises he can't, because his train — his pride and glory — drags him down. He can no longer fly any higher than the lowest branches of a tree. So that's why he sounds so mournful, perched there a few feet above the ground. He's wishing he could be up in the sky.'

'Stupid bird,' said Florence. 'Sacrificing his freedom just to be admired. Just to be loved.' She trailed her hand over the side of the car and lay her head back on the seat.

'Watch out for the prickly pears,' he said.

* * *

Some time later, they turned off down a dusty path, scarcely wider than the car itself. Florence looked at him but said nothing. Jay remained silent, too, until he pulled in and parked on a patch of grass.

Ahead of them ran a single narrow rail track. Next to the track was a small wooden shed. Jay told Florence to wait in the car then went over to the shed. He called inside and entered. A few minutes later, she saw him come out again with a man. Together, they walked out behind the hut where three other young men, not much more than boys, were waiting beside a push-trolley — a wooden bench fixed to a wheeled platform. With a lot of shoving and straining to begin with, they manoeuvred the contraption over to the rails. It took another few minutes to get it lifted on to the track, then Jay paid the man and came back to Florence.

'You didn't think we'd continue in luxury all the way there, did you?' he said. 'I'm not the Viceroy, you know.' He opened the door for her, and she slid out, adjusting her hat against the sun. Jay reached inside the car, retrieved his topee and walked over to the trolley. Florence followed, and he attempted to help her on to the platform, but she ignored him, stepping up with a neat, swift jump, much as she might mount her horse. Then she settled herself on the chair that was attached on top of the platform. 'Aren't you coming too?' she said.

Jay sat next to her, and the four men gave a shout and started to push. The trolley began to move and gather momentum. Once it was on its way, the men jumped up too, and settled themselves on the wooden slats behind the chair. The trolley gained speed and rolled along the little tracks, sometimes surrounded by fields of rocks and grass, sometimes overhung by the branches of trees. Occasionally it rounded a corner, and Florence grabbed Jay's arm for balance, holding on to her hat with her other hand. He steadied her, reassuring her she wouldn't fall. Her whoops and giggles in turn made him laugh. She had never imagined a trolley ride would be so much fun.

'And what happens if we meet another trolley coming the other way?' she said as they trundled on, occasionally helped by a push from the men sitting behind them.

'We toss a coin, and who ever loses has to lift their trolley off the tracks and let the other pass.'

'Well, let's hope we're lucky.'

Then, ahead, there appeared some buildings, and behind those ran the main train tracks. The men began shouting and heaved on the brake lever. The trolley slowed to a halt next to a large wooden shed.

'Are you finally going to reveal to me the mysteries of down the line?' said Florence as she stepped on to an area of dried mud littered with the rusted parts of old engines. There was an overwhelming smell of oil and smoke, and she coughed a few times. Suddenly Jay looked worried.

'What was I thinking, bringing you out here? This is no place for a young woman, and Harry's daughter, too.'

'Oh, nonsense,' she said, coughing again. 'I'm absolutely fine. And don't worry about Papa. He's not really like the rest of them, you know.' She leaned against the trolley, waiting for him to tell her what to do. Under the toe of her boot was a piece of metal and she toyed at it, releasing it from the earth as if it were some archaeological treasure.

A man approached them, a scowl on his face and a clip-board in his hand. 'About time. She's been in there for over eighteen hours. The schedule is going to be a complete mess.'

This man was obviously Jay's inferior, and the lack of deference he showed was, in Florence's opinion, pretty ugly.

Jay looked at the report the man had handed to him. 'McDonald, is it? Boilersmith's mate? You're right. Let's get this done as quickly as possible.' He indicated that Florence should follow him inside the shed.

The locomotive sat there in the gloom, dripping water that mingled on the ground with the sludge of ashes and scale that had been raked and blasted out of its tubes and pipes. Florence side-stepped the puddles and walked up to the engine. Tentatively, she laid her hands on the curved and riveted metal. The mate gave her a look.

'McDonald,' Jay said. 'I'm going to need overalls if you want this inspection completed.' Florence saw the mate's disparaging gaze turn on him.

'Only got these ones,' McDonald said, walking to a corner of the shed and picking something up from the floor. 'They're a bit oily, mind. You'll have to strip, if you don't want to get that lovely suit of yours ruined.'

Florence called over to him. 'What is it you have to do?'

Jay didn't answer. Florence watched as Jay, ignoring the smirk on the mate's face, took off his jacket and put it in his filthy hands. Next was his shirt, and then, without a pause, his trousers, so that he was left standing in a pair of white shorts.

The mate rolled the clothes into a bundle. 'I'll just put them down here, shall I?' he said, looking at the dank floor.

'I'll hold on to those, I think.' Florence stepped up and took them from the mate. 'Messy work, is it?' she said to Jay. 'Don't tell me you actually have to get inside?'

Jay buttoned up the soiled, greasy overalls that McDonald had passed to him and took a flashlight and a hammer from the ground in front of the engine. 'Come on,' he said to Florence. 'Now you can see how it works first-hand.' He jumped up on to the tread plate, turned around, and began to reverse himself inside the firebox. The hatch was only just big enough to allow him to pull his head and shoulders through. He smiled at Florence, who was craning to look inside, still holding on to his clothes as he disappeared from her view.

There must barely be room in there to turn himself around, she thought. She imagined how close the air would be, the grit in his mouth when he swallowed. Then a series of clangs sounded. It was loud enough outside; inside the box it would make your ears ring. There was a pause, and Jay's face appeared at the hatch. He took several deep breaths. 'What on earth are you doing in there?' she asked.

He wiped the back of his hand over his mouth. 'Testing the firebox stays. There are rows and rows. You have to hit each one to see if it rings true.' He disappeared again, and the clang of metal on metal began again. She wasn't sure how long it was before the noise stopped and Jay pulled himself up through the trapdoor again. He scratched at the dirt and sweat that covered his body.

'None of them broken,' he announced.

'Must be hot in there. Here.' She gave him a handkerchief. 'Want me to find you some water?'

'What I need is the mirror to check inside the boiler. Where's McDonald gone? He knows we're behind schedule.'

McDonald had wandered off to have a smoke by the entrance to the shed.

'Yes,' said Florence. 'Almost as if he wants you to fail.'

Jay passed her back the handkerchief and shouted, 'McDonald. Where's the bloody inspection mirror?'

Florence watched for another hour as Jay vanished inside the machine again, then came out to pronounce that the network of tubes had been sighted and were all clear. He explained that all forty-one of the washout plugs had been replaced, and that meant the water could be turned on to fill the boiler, to prepare the engine for steam raising. Jay worked quickly, despite the attitude of the mate, and Florence followed his actions intently, fascinated by the intricate, invisible workings of this sleeping dragon.

Finally, Jay gave the order to load the coal into the firebox, and they both watched as McDonald lowered in the firelighters.

'Is that it ready then?' she asked.

'Oh no. It will be another eleven hours before enough pressure is built up to send the locomotive on its way.' Jay slapped the metal sides. 'But now, at least I can sign the report. And,' he said, walking over to a hose that had been left on the ground, 'at last I can take off these revolting overalls.' The hose gushed water, and he lifted it over his head, washing away the oil and soot that looked like an extra layer of skin, and probably felt like it, too, Florence thought.

He started to undress, and Florence, all at once conscious of who she was and what they were doing, went outside to wait for him by the trolley car. He came to join her, seemingly unabashed in his shorts, and she pretended it was the most normal thing in the world as he stood beside her and dried in the late afternoon sun. Not wanting to look at him, she studied his clothes instead. 'Nice suit this. Where did you get it?'

Jay took the trousers from her. 'This one is from London. I have another similar. The London tailors are very good. I had the tailor here make copies, but the quality is nowhere near the same.' He buttoned his shirt. 'Still, a damn sight better than the collarless jacket Gopal persists in wearing, though I have persuaded him against the red silk trousers he wore on his first day at the station. The boy will never get on otherwise.'

Florence laughed. 'Who is Gopal?'

'Another young engineer, come up recently from Jamalpur. A good Hindu boy. Temple twice a day. I share my lodgings with him.'

'And you? Do you go to the temple twice a day?'

'I cannot remember the last time I went. My mother would be horrified. Just, after London, it wasn't a priority anymore.'

Florence sighed. 'London, London. I have a friend who moved to London. Her letters are full of how much she loves the city. Is it really such a special place?'

Jay knotted his tie and put on his jacket. He brushed himself down several times, picking at invisible threads or specks of dirt with a frown on his face. 'You cannot imagine unless you go. Although, the girls are as sharp as knives. Another species.' He smiled at her, apparently content that his outfit was in order. 'Not a patch on you, though. Can't imagine any of them sticking around a stinking old locomotive shed for the afternoon.'

Jay turned and jumped up into the trolley car, then offered his hand to help her up, and this time she accepted. The men behind them gave a shove and the trolley started on its way back along the track.

Florence sat, not speaking, lost in thoughts of engines and fireboxes and washout plugs and steam raising. And of Jay, disappearing through the hatch. She knew it wouldn't be only McDonald who treated Jay with such ignorance and insolence. She supposed that British and Indian workers alike might resent the idea of an Indian boss. And yet he was highly qualified.

Then there was Papa — and Kit Hanson. She'd seen a little of how they treated him yesterday. Telling him to push all those bits of paper around, answer the telephone. And now this. Down the line to clean out an engine. She didn't have to be told that he'd been sent to do something demeaning, something they would never have done, or been asked to do, even when they were young. The attitude of that awful McDonald only confirmed it. Jay must wonder at times what on earth all his education had been for.

The trolley gained speed, and Florence continued to sit there in silence until Jay said, 'I'm sorry. I shouldn't have brought you. McDonald, the clothes, the dirt … I hadn't realised how squalid it is here. I sincerely hope you are not offended.'

'Offended? Oh, for heaven's sake. It was fascinating. Just wish I could have got in there myself. Is it awfully small inside that firebox?'

The trolley trundled on, and Jay stretched his arm along the seat behind her. After a minute or two, she moved closer and twisted the weight of her body against him.

* * *

It was dusk, and the air was cool as they drove down the path away from the track. Florence sat in the passenger seat, grateful for the comfort of upholstered leather after the bone-shaking ride back in the trolley.

'You must be tired,' Jay said. 'It's a long journey, and not an easy one. Just another hour and I'll have you home.'

'Not at all. I feel quite lively. You're the one who is tired, I imagine. Quite a physical job. Is that really the sort of thing a mechanical engineer is supposed to do?'

Jay didn't reply, and Florence thought she saw that expression of discomfort pass over his face again.

'We can't have a locomotive stuck there out of action. I suppose there was no one else who could sign the report, so ...' Jay stared at the road ahead. 'I don't mind physical labour, you know.'

'Still, I wish I could do something. I should have brought some food at least.' The fields on either side of the road were empty. People had returned to their dwellings, and the scent of wood smoke from the fires in a nearby village drifted in the air. Florence watched as Jay stifled a yawn. 'If only I could drive, that would give you a break.'

There was a pause, then Jay said, 'Why don't you?'

Florence wondered if he was being serious, but he slowed the car to a halt, turned off the engine and got out of the car. 'Go on then, shove over,' he said, walking around to her side.

Florence slid along the seat and took the wheel in her hands. She couldn't believe she was actually going to do this. She looked at the panel in front of her with its dials and levers and switches. 'How do I start it?'

Jay began pointing at the space around her. 'Key, throttle, spark advance, choke. Down here: starter, there: clutch, reverse, brake.' Florence repeated the words after him, relishing their hard and practical sounds. Jay continued. 'The engine is warm, so just a little choke.'

'Extra fuel, right?' Florence had always listened to her father and Ravi when they talked in the car. Even the first time she'd ridden in one, nine years old and more excited than she could possibly let on, she'd watched and imagined herself at the wheel.

'Exactly. So, hand on the throttle, that's right, and step on the starter, and there you go.'

The engine chugged back into action, a little uneven to Florence's ear. She adjusted the spark advance until it ran smoothly. Jay looked impressed. 'Are you sure you haven't done this before?' he asked.

'Only in my dreams. Papa would never hear of it, and he never has the time to teach me — let alone the patience. Shall we go?'

Florence pressed the clutch and moved into gear. The car pulled away, a little bouncy at first, but she soon brought it under control. Steering took some concentration, however, and every now and then Jay would put a hand on the wheel to bring her back if the prickly pears along the side of the road came too close.

'Getting a bit dark, don't you think?' Florence tried to look at the panel in front of her, but as she did so, the car swerved.

'One thing at a time,' said Jay, reaching across to switch on the headlights. 'Look further ahead, where you want to go, not at the road just in front.'

She followed his advice, and soon she began to relax. How wonderful it was, to be motoring along, in charge of this incredible machine, deciding where to go, propelling them both forward into the future. 'I feel like the peacock being given back his flight,' she said, and Jay laughed.

'But unlike the peacock,' he said, 'you have your beauty *and* your freedom, Florrie.'

Heat rose in her face. She couldn't think of a reply, so she continued on, staring at the road, but now, as well as the sensation of the car and the engine, she was intensely aware of his presence beside her.

In the trolley car, rattling along in the sunlight, to lean against him had seemed an innocent action. She recalled the smooth cotton of his shirt pulled taut over the hard muscles of his chest. And she recalled his body, glistening with water as he walked out of the shed towards her, natural and proud in only his shorts. How he had dressed himself after, and she had pretended not to watch, but had stolen glimpses of the act: a man concealing his animal self so he could present an acceptable face to the world. The easy movement as he pulled up his trousers, the concentration as he fastened the buttons of his shirt, hiding away skin and hair and form and texture.

It was night now, but ahead in the distance she could see the lights of Agra. As they drew closer, she thought of the house and its suffocating hold, even without her father there. Sita would be worried, too. The extraordinary events of the day seemed to recede. She pulled in to the side of the road and turned off the engine. 'Perhaps you should take it from here,' she said, turning to open the door.

Then she felt his hand on her arm. She looked at him, and they moved closer to each other, and for a moment everything around her — the night, the air — slowed to a stop. Then something inside her broke and she was away and outside, where creatures rustled in the bushes and an owl, disturbed from its roost, floated overhead with a mournful hoot.

* * *

She ran down the path and up the stairs to the veranda, as if this would make up for the hours she had been absent, knowing Sita would be watching and waiting. Sure enough, as she eased the door open, her ayah emerged from the shadows, the ends of her shawl winding around her hands, her face creased with concern.

'*Beti*! Where have you been? Who were you with in that car? It's so late.'

'I'm fine. I was just out, with friends. At the Club. I'm sorry I forgot to tell you. But you mustn't worry so. It's perfectly all right.' The lie slipped out easily, and Florence stepped forward and put her arms around Sita, feeling the sense of calm that she always seemed to radiate. After the strangeness of the day, it was a welcome relief to hold the cherished figure close. A moment, however, was enough. Florence affected a yawn. 'I think I'll go up. No need for you to bother though. See you in the morning.' She pulled away and ran up the stairs, not wanting to see the disappointment she knew would be painted across Sita's face.

She closed her bedroom door and sat at her dressing table. In the mirror she saw someone she hardly recognised. Everything had changed, and somehow in the past week she had become another person, someone who might dare to take rides on a trolley car, and climb inside locomotives, and drive a car — and perhaps kiss a man. A man who was at best out of bounds. And at worst?

She undressed, letting the clothes drop to the floor, allowing the chill of the night air to settle on her body. She ran her hands over her breasts and down the curve of her belly, down between her legs and then along the inside of her thighs. For a moment she tensed, thinking of his body, his chest, his belly, and his thighs. Then, catching sight of herself in the mirror again, she grabbed her nightdress, pulled it over her head and shifted quickly under the bed sheets, both excited and ashamed at what she had imagined.

Chapter Ten

AGRA, 1939

In the days that followed, Florence tried to tidy away her time with Jay inside a neat box in her mind. It had been an adventure, a *Girl's Own* story to sit alongside those of kidnapped princesses and boarding-school midnight feasts. After all, what had actually happened?

Still, she wished she could see him again, just to make sure that everything between them was fine and proper. But even though she sat on the veranda every morning with her book, as she had that day, he didn't appear. Every evening she went to bed early, feeling the need for solitude. Not even Sita's presence was tolerated.

In the end, she persuaded her father to take her to the office again. She braced herself as she walked in, but Jay's desk was empty, and she learned later that he'd been called away to Delhi.

So there were no more opportunities for her to ask him how the newer design of engines produced steam at much higher pressure (she'd stolen her father's engineering magazines to read illicitly in bed), or how much energy exactly a combustion engine saved compared to steam. Instead she filed as many of her father's papers as possible and, in the end, was happy to keep an eye on him, making sure he ate properly and didn't spend too much time ranting on about what other people expected him to do. She worried he would make himself ill if he spent every day in such a state of impotent rage.

In this way, the holidays came almost to an end, but on the day before she had to leave, to return to college up in the hills, she decided to take an early morning ride out across the fields to visit Sita's old village.

It was cold, and mist hung low, like remnants of dreams in the sky, obscuring the sun. Florence walked down the steps from the veranda and through the dew-soaked grass at the back of the house where Bikram had tacked up Oscar, ready and waiting for her. As she sprung up into the saddle and leant to adjust the stirrups, Jackie appeared around the corner of the stables, tail wagging and ready for an excursion. She tried to follow them out of the gate, but Florence managed to shoo her back in. Jackie was no match for the village dogs, louche Lotharios that they were, and then there was always rabies to worry about. Florence trotted off down the road on her handsome chestnut horse, trying to ignore the little dog watching them go with her head tipped to one side and whining quietly.

After a few minutes, when Oscar had used up some of his excess energy, Florence slowed the pace. As the sun rose higher, and the temperature with it, plumes of dust started to float up around her, swirling into the air as the horse clopped down the backstreets past the entrance to the Taj Mahal. It wasn't a place that had impressed itself upon her life thus far, remaining simply a spot she went sometimes for a walk on Sundays after church with her father. Today, however, she felt moved for the first time, thinking about this monument built to love. And for the first time, as she rode past the gates and saw the translucent glow of the domes in the early morning light, it seemed wonderfully, almost unbearably, romantic.

Soon she left the outskirts of the town behind and turned on to the path that led across the fields — miles of yellow mustard flowers, their scent mingling with that of the dust and a stray puff of wood smoke, to create a strange sense of longing in her chest. Perhaps this was what people meant by nostalgia. Nostalgia for what exactly, she wasn't sure. She was only leaving to go back to school. She'd return again, soon enough.

A little way off, among the stems of yellow, a peacock danced, shivering its fan of feathers in salutation to the sun and an unimpressed peahen nearby. Florence relaxed and, now she was safe from interruption, allowed herself to think about Jay. She tried to picture him, but it was difficult to get a sense of the whole man in her mind's eye. If she focused on details, then she could conjure him up: the shining, jet hair dripping water in the sunshine; his hands, strong yet delicate as he sketched his design; the look he gave her, amused but surprised, when she asked him about his work; the press of his thighs against his trousers when he sat down in the car next to her. She tried to recall their exact conversations atop the elephants, their lunch together at the station, driving back in the car. She should have asked him more about himself. A whole day together and really, she still knew so little about him. And what did he think of her? Was she simply a diversion, an oddity — or worse, just the boss's daughter, and all that implied? Or could there possibly be something more?

She gathered up the reins and was about to nudge Oscar into a canter, when she saw another horse and rider jump the low fence from the adjacent field up ahead and join the path in front of them. She looked carefully. Then in some disbelief, then with a lurch of excitement — it seemed her magic had summoned Jay before her. She waved and then trotted to catch up with him.

'Florrie!' He pulled his horse around. 'Where are you headed?'

'To the village. My ayah comes from there. I usually visit when I'm home. Take some sweets for the children.'

'Mind if I tag along? I'm just aimlessly trotting about, trying to get some exercise. It would be good to have a guide.'

'There's not much to see, really. But it is quite beautiful there.' She added the last part in case he changed his mind. 'And the children are sweet.'

Having said this, Florence pulled her horse around and kicked it into a canter along the path. She rode fast for a couple of minutes and then slowed to let him catch up.

He cantered to a halt behind her. 'I let you win, of course.'

She laughed. 'I didn't know we were racing.'

Later, they came to a pond, and Jay suggested they give the horses a rest and a drink. While the animals snorted into the water and flicked their tails in constant war against the flies, Jay and Florence sat on the ground in the shade of a peepal tree. He bent his legs, arms resting on his knees, which splayed out, almost touching hers. He reached up and pulled a leaf from a branch trailing next to him.

Without thinking, Florence put her hand on his arm and, suddenly conscious of his warm skin underneath her touch, let it remain there a moment. 'Careful. This is a very special tree. Don't let the villagers see you do that. In fact ...' She got up and ran to the pond, scooped up some water in her hands and ran back to deposit it at the tree's roots.

Jay laughed. 'Going to take you a long time like that. I'd use a watering can at least.'

'You should know. You have to give it *jal* — water — in the morning. To honour it. This tree can solve all sorts of problems for you.'

'Oh yes, the peepal tree. It's a bit like Aladdin's lamp, right?' He rubbed the bark of the trunk. 'Can I have three wishes?'

'That depends what the wishes are.'

Jay didn't answer. He turned the leaf over and over in his hands, then held it up.

'It's heart-shaped.' He passed it to her. 'You keep it. Press it or something.' He stood up. 'Don't tell the villagers though.'

He walked back to the horses. Florence held the leaf for a moment and then tucked it inside her shirt.

At the village, they were surrounded. The women offered milk and oranges while the older children stood a little way off, grinning toothily and pointing at Jay, who was performing magic tricks, making a coin appear and disappear, much to the children's amazement. A small boy tottered out of his mother's grasp and latched on instead to Florence's hair as she sat with the women, twining his fingers around the sun-bleached ends. Florence tried not to wince as he pulled hard. The women laughed, and Florence finished her milk.

'I suppose we ought to be getting back. I have to pack for tomorrow.'

'Yes, and I said I'd stop by the office.'

Before they left, Florence distributed the sweets among the children and Jay gave a few annas to the men. Then they mounted their horses and began to ride away. Florence looked over her shoulder once more, and when she did the whole village began to wave, big, generous, arm-flinging waves, and the children jumped in the air and shouted *goodbyeee* in their best English.

They took the path by the pond again, and as they rode past, Jay leaned over and grabbed Oscar's reins. 'Wait,' he said, as the horses stamped and fidgeted at being made to stand still. 'You can't leave without saying goodbye to your tree.' He jumped down, and Florence, bemused, did the same. They led the horses over to the shade under its branches. He looked up into its tangle of twigs and leaves for a moment, then said, 'I want my three wishes.'

Florence felt a heat rising up through her body. 'I think you can only have one at a time.' She leaned back against the tree, feeling the rough bark through the material of her shirt on her back. Jay stepped closer and put his hands on the trunk either side of her, then slowly, very slowly, brought his lips to hers.

Florence's head swam, and her limbs felt weightless even as she wrapped her arms around him, pressing closer to him, hot and full of want. She wasn't sure how long it lasted — long enough that her legs began to jitter, but not long enough to douse the desire that had awoken inside her. Then suddenly, they were apart. He ran his thumb across the profile of her cheekbone. 'Where is the leaf I gave you?' he said.

Florence placed her hand on her breast. 'Here.'

He leaned forward again and placed his forehead against hers, pressed his body into hers for a moment. Then he said, 'We should go,' pulling away. 'It's best that we go.'

The horses had wandered to the edge of the pool. Florence mounted Oscar, turned him around, and kicked him into a canter. Behind, she could hear Jay following, and the beats of the hooves on the ground echoed the clattering of her heart inside her chest.

* * *

The next day, Florence hugged Sita goodbye on the veranda and made her promise to look after her father. Sita nodded and wiped away her tears with the ends of her scarf. 'Come back soon, *beti*. And make sure you eat properly at that school. You are becoming far too skinny.'

'That's never a problem with all the puddings they feed us, *amah*. You know they look after us there.' They embraced one more time. 'This is my last year. Be happy for me.'

At the station, Florence waited with her father on the platform for the train that would start her journey back to school in the hills. Katie and Jane were there, too, their mothers dabbing eyes with silk handkerchiefs. Every year the group of returning girls had grown smaller, as one by one they were sent off to England instead, to be finished and finessed and made ready for a good marriage, she supposed. Now it was just the three of them, and one more year of school left.

Her father had his arm around her shoulders and was tapping his foot and humming. He'd insisted on bringing Jackie, who sat looking up at them, beating her tail in counterpoint to his rhythm.

'Great night at the Club yesterday. Pity you missed it.'

'I'm sorry, Papa. But I had such a headache after the ride. And I still had to pack.'

'Well, keep practising the songs, anyway. We'll make an artiste of you yet.'

* * *

After she had ridden away from the peepal tree the day before, and had found the main road, she had slowed the pace. Jogging comfortably along side by side, Jay had opened up to her. He told her tales from university — of raucous boating parties, and the formal dinners, and cramming all night for his final exams. Of walking the London streets, the shops, the fashions, and the attitudes of those he met — the stares, the pointed fingers.

She in turn described her life at school and in the hills, her friends and her studies. During this time, she didn't once feel young or stupid or clumsy. They simply talked and listened to each other, and it seemed like the easiest place to be in the world. When they reached her house, they both jumped down and stood next to the horses. Florence busied herself running up the stirrups, then with nothing left to distract them, and conscious of the eyes of the servants, they had said their goodbyes.

'Will you write to me, Florence?' he'd said as she started to lead Oscar away down the path to the back of the house. 'Tell me more about what you get up to.' He smiled. 'And perhaps give me some advice about dealing with your father?'

She stopped, agitated, unsure how to respond.

'Yes, I think I can do that. Shall I send it to the office?'

He nodded.

'Will you write back? Tell me some more about your work?'

He nodded again. 'Take care, Florrie.'

It had been almost perfect, and Florence had felt ecstatic all afternoon as she and Sita packed her cases. Her father had tried to insist on one last evening at the Club, but for the first time, Florence had found the strength to refuse.

'I don't think so, Papa. You go ahead and have a lovely time. I'll see you in the morning. You are coming to the station, aren't you?'

Her father had gone out without any kind of scene, and she had been free to spend her last evening in the soft candle flame of Sita's love. Later in bed, she lay instead in a blaze of her own ardour as she pictured herself once again pressed against the peepal tree.

* * *

Autumn arrived, and for the first time in years, Florence was excited about the imminent holidays in Agra. When she had returned to school, she hadn't dared to hope that Jay would really write to her, though she always felt a surge of anticipation whenever the post was brought around at the breakfast table. Then, one morning, there it was.

Since then, Jay had written to her once a month, letters that she had read and re-read until she had committed every sentence to heart. They were chatty and amusing and always apologetic when he described what he was doing at work. Florence, of course, wrote back urging him to tell her more, and in particular if he could explain what horsepower was, and what on earth it had to do with engines. She would also appreciate it if he could explain once again what a propulsion system was. She hoped he would include one of his detailed little diagrams — he was only too happy to oblige.

So their correspondence continued — harmless, informative conversations that no one could really have found anything to frown over. For Florence though, these letters — waiting for them, answering them — kept her in a fervid state during those months, living an intense life inside her head while she drifted through the demands of college like a sleepwalker. Hockey, lacrosse, horse riding; piano and singing and dance; literature, history, housekeeping, and accounts — even her usual keen joy in her mathematics lessons — all seemed muffled and distant compared to the emotions tumbling around inside.

Katie and Jane knew something was up and had managed to needle her into confessing she had feelings for a man. But when she showed them the contents of one of the letters, they had done nothing but laugh. For weeks after, Katie kept enquiring how Jay's rod and piston were doing, and Florence finally pretended she had ended the correspondence, just to shut them up.

As the year progressed, Florence learned to keep her composure, with a repertoire of the correct expressions for any given conversation outlined on her face, while inside her thoughts of Jay and the months ahead in Agra could storm away, unchecked. Still, it took all her new-found skills of deceit to hide her feelings when the headmistress called Florence into her office, a week before the end of term.

'I've just been on the telephone to your father. You know what the situation in Europe is. Your father thinks he might have to go to Delhi for a few months, or they might even send him back to England for a while.'

Florence came out of her reverie one word at a time. Europe. Delhi. England.

'But don't worry. We're arranging for you to go with the Hansons to Udaipur for the holidays. I'm sure you girls will have a very amusing time — all the parties, the picnics, the sport. I've heard the floating palace is a dream. Anything you wanted to ask, dear?'

Florence shook her head, not trusting herself to speak. She forced her face into a sketch of someone who was looking forward to spending months going to parties in floating palaces with her best friend, thanked the headmistress, and left, closing the door behind her. Then she ran to her room, praying it would be empty as she pressed the tears from her eyes.

Chapter Eleven

PORTSMOUTH, 1955

The drink became a habit that calcified over time, though she refused to think it was a problem. Not until that particular Saturday when yet again the day loomed long and uneventful in front of her; when Billy had gone to the pub for lunch before the match, and she had walked, listless and bored, around the house, not in the mood for the radio and unable to settle to her book.

She tried. She tried not to get the bottle down from the top shelf where she'd hidden it the evening before, telling herself she would have a day off tomorrow. She tried not to get the glass and put a dash of water in it to take the edge off. And yet, there she was, drink in hand and wondering whether a ham sandwich would be enough for her permanently hungry son when Robert came running in from the garden.

'Mummy, please can we go down to watch the trains today?'

She looked down and saw he had trodden mud into the kitchen. She turned away from him and gulped down her drink.

'Not now that I'm going to have to clean the floor again. Look what you've done.'

Robert looked down at his shoes and then back up at her. 'Sorry, Mummy.' He looked guilty for a moment then brightened again. 'Is it lunch time yet?'

Florence poured herself another drink and began to hack at a loaf of bread.

Sandwiches in hand, Robert went back out into the garden. 'And you can stay out there until tea time,' she shouted after him. Well, it was a sunny afternoon. The fresh air would do him good. And she could do the cleaning undisturbed, once she'd had a lie down.

Upstairs, she watched him from the window as he dug a hole in her flowerbed, broke the stem of one of her dahlias, and then tried to plant it back into the earth. After that, he lay down on the grass, staring at the sky.

Florence felt a tiny twinge of guilt — after all, he didn't have any friends to play with — but what could she do? She couldn't force the other children, and most of the time he seemed quite content.

Oh, it was too much to think about right now. She pulled at the curtains in the bedroom and placed the glass on the bedside table. Closing her eyes, she tried to take herself back again to Agra before the war, to the house and Sita — and Jay, by now just an impression of a man, just the faintest memory of his face and his hands, and she could hardly believe it had been the same life. The rum did its work and sent her to her dreams, but it also released the tears which streamed down her face on to her pillow.

* * *

The temple bell rang out, calling the people to *puja*. Monkeys chittered around the entrance and scampered away up on to the roof as she approached. She had an armful of marigold wreaths, but they seemed to be alive somehow, entwining themselves around her like snakes, and she struggled to get them away from her. The temple bell rang again and again, and she knew she was late, that there was something she had to do, but the serpents were writhing and multiplying now, hissing in her face. The priest was singing, and she could smell the incense in the air. The monkeys returned, pressing closer around her, screeching at her, louder and louder, and then the scene began to dissolve, and she woke up in her darkened room and realised it was just a crow in the tree outside.

She sat up and pressed her palms to her eyes, as if to press the dream away, aware of a pain at her temples. She needed some air. She dragged herself over to the window and flung it open, took a few deep breaths and looked for Robert. She couldn't see him. She tutted. So he'd come inside after all. Probably made a mess of the kitchen again, or there would be toys all over the dining room for her to pick up.

Downstairs she went from room to room. The house was silent, and there was no mess in the kitchen, no toys on the dining room floor. 'Robbie?' she called, more irritated than puzzled. 'Robert, don't play games, please. I'm not in the mood.' There was no answer.

She checked the cupboard under the stairs and behind the curtains in the front room, but there was no little boy looking up at her and giggling at his own cleverness. Now, worry began to seep into her thoughts. What had he asked her earlier? To go and watch the trains. She recalled the times they had gone down to the line together, where she would lift him up on to the wall and hold him steady. They would listen to the bells of the church clock chime as they waited for the three o'clock to London to charge past, Robert with his fingers crossed for his favourite red and black engine.

She looked up at the clock on the wall — just gone half past two. She stepped out into the garden, then walked back through the house and put her head out of the front door. Nobody. Looking across the road, she remembered a time when, walking back up the hill together, Robert had insisted on crossing away from the entrance to an alleyway that ran between the houses there. When she'd asked why, he said it was where Andrew Leach lived, and that Andrew Leach was a bad boy who he didn't want to see. Florence had thought perhaps he was just embarrassed to be seen with her in front of the boys from school and hadn't asked him anything else about it. Now, however, an uneasy sensation came to her. She thought about the frown on Robert's face as he'd hurried away from the house, run on ahead and hadn't stopped until he'd reached their front door. There was a group of boys on the bus from school — she'd seen them when she met Robert sometimes. Noisy and boisterous, but the worst they did was ignore Robert, wasn't it? And anyway, he wouldn't have gone down to watch the trains on his own, would he? Surely he knew he wasn't allowed to do that.

The street was quiet. Most of the boys and their fathers would be at the football. Robert didn't like football much, though Billy sometimes offered to take him to the match. They'd been once, but the noise and the crowds of people around them had upset him and they'd had to leave early, which, as Florence recalled, Billy hadn't been happy about.

A robin flew on to the hedge in the front garden and sang for a moment. Florence bit a fingernail and wondered how long Robert had been gone while she had slept on, made oblivious by the drink. Not bothering to find her shoes, she began to walk down the hill. From the alleyway she heard the sound of someone running — that curious echoing bounce that footsteps made in the long, narrow space. She looked around, but the road was still empty. She walked faster, still biting at her nail, thinking of the wall at the top of the embankment where they went to watch the trains, wondering if it were possible for Robert to climb it by himself. To fall from it. Footsteps again, and this time a shout. She turned and saw a young boy, who she thought she recognised, running towards her.

'Wait, Missus, wait!' The boy ran up to her.

What was his name? David? David Poole, was it? He was breathing heavily and saying words that she couldn't understand.

'It weren't me, it were Leach. It were Leach what done it. You have to come, you have to come.'

Florence shook her head, fear suddenly flooding her veins. 'What are you talking about?'

'On the tracks, Missus. Your Robert is stuck on the train track!'

Florence ran as fast as she could, bare feet on tarmac and paving slabs. She heard the church clock strike quarter to the hour. The boy ran behind her, babbling words about Andrew Leach and the gang of other boys. About finding Robert sitting on the wall and holding him down and giving him a spit bath. She heard the phrase golliwog and how Robert had tried to escape. That Leach had let go and Robert had fallen.

In her mind's eye she saw him, rolling forwards down the bank towards the tracks. She heard the shouts of the others grow louder, more hysterical, then stop as Robert's body bounced off a rock and finished the last part of the slope in a trajectory that hurled him on to the tracks. But stuck? What did the boy mean, stuck on the tracks? At the bottom of the hill, opposite the wall, a car came along, and Florence stopped in front of it so it had to slam on its brakes. A man leaned out of the window, prepared to shout, but Florence was there first.

'Go to the signal box. Find the signalman. Tell him to stop the train. There's a boy on the tracks. Please!'

The man looked confused for a moment until Florence shouted, 'Please, the signalman,' once more, then he understood and drove away, revving the engine and disappearing around the corner. Florence threw herself over the wall, hearing the screams now, and scrambled down the slope towards the little body that was lying far too close to the tracks, leg outstretched in front of him. When she reached him, he grabbed at her, and she tried to pull him away, but then he yelped in pain and she saw his foot, stuck under one of the metal struts, where the moving, automatic points must have closed on it.

He clutched at her arm. 'What time is it, Mummy? The train's coming, isn't it? It's coming any minute now. Help me, Mummy, please.'

Florence looked at her watch. Five to three. It would be pulling out of Portsmouth and Southsea any moment now, and then after that it was a matter of a few minutes before it came steaming up the track and around the corner towards them. She prayed the man in the car had reached the signal box, and she prayed the signalman would believe him and stop the train. She pulled at the laces on Robert's shoe, trying to release his foot, but it was jammed too far under the iron bar. Instead she scrabbled at the stones underneath, hoping she could free him that way, but as she did so she felt the faintest tremor on the ground beneath her. She stopped, and Robert froze, too.

'Mummy?'

Florence renewed her efforts, scraping at the ground and

pulling at his leg. He too heaved and squirmed, and the ground began to shake.

'Please make them stop the train,' Florence moaned as Robert began to scream again in terror. 'Please, please, please …'

'It's coming, Mummy. It's coming!'

The ground shook harder, and Florence gave another heave. Robert screeched in pain and buried his head into her side. Florence gathered him to her, and – helpless now – put her arms around him.

'No. No!' she screamed, and pulled again, and knew it was too late. That the roar of the beast was about to arrive.

Except that nothing happened. The ground stilled, and there was a silence that fell around them. Florence looked up. Nothing. A robin flew down and eyed her from the opposite side of the track. They sat there for a while in the quiet, Robert shivering in her arms. Then in the distance she heard sirens, and a few moments later voices, as men in uniforms clambered down the bank towards them.

'The train?' she said, hardly able to get the words out.

'Stopped up the line, don't worry, Madam. Let's just get you both out of here, shall we?'

* * *

The policeman sipped at the cup of tea she had made him. The clock on the mantelpiece ticked. Billy would be home soon. She hoped he would be relatively sober. She hugged Robert to her. He was still crying, though his tremors were diminishing now. She smoothed his hair and kissed the top of his head. The policeman put his cup down and picked up his notebook from the table.

'So are you going to do something to those boys?' Florence asked.

'Mrs Greene, what I suggest is that you keep a closer eye on your son. Children should not be playing around on railway embankments.'

'He was only watching the trains. That's not why this happened.'

'He fell off a wall he shouldn't have been sitting on.'

'He was pushed.'

'Now, Mrs Greene. We don't know it was done deliberately. Just boys being boys.'

Florence hugged Robert closer to her and tried not to think of him, on his own, being attacked by the other boys while she had been numbed by the rum and asleep in her bed.

'This isn't the first time, you know. It's because of his looks, where we are from. It's racism, pure and simple.'

The policeman stood up and jammed his cap back on his head. 'Now, now. Let's not go throwing around those sorts of accusations. I'll have a word with the boys' parents.' The policeman walked towards the door. 'And you, young man,' he said, pointing at Robert. 'You stay away from those tracks, now. Do you hear?'

Florence closed the door behind him and turned back to Robert, who was sitting on the sofa staring at her. His foot and ankle were bandaged, and he had streaks of mud down his legs, arms, and face.

'What were you thinking, going down there on your own?'

'You wouldn't come. I asked you.'

'I had things to do.'

'You were sleeping. You're always sleeping. I didn't have anyone to play with. I never have anyone to play with. It's all your fault.' He flung himself down into the cushions and started sobbing again. 'I hate you!'

'Robert, please.' She approached him, sat down beside him, tried to put her arms around him again, but this time he shrank away from her into the corner of the sofa.

'No, no, no!' he shouted. 'I hate you, and I hate Billy, and I hate school, and I hate everything.'

And as she touched him, he started to scream — wild, animal sounds that cut through her to the bone. 'Stop it,' she cried. 'Stop it!' But he just screamed louder and longer.

And then, in the middle of all this cacophony, the doorbell rang. Florence, reeling from the noise and the emotion, thinking bloody Billy had forgotten his key once again, opened the door and looked in disbelief at the figure standing there.

PART II

Dehradun Training Camp
June 1941

Dear Florrie,

I am so sorry that I missed you in Delhi. We were there until just last month, but then your father pulled some strings and got me the interview for officer training school. I have to say, it was a rather ridiculous process. The chap looked me up and down and asked if I could play cricket. We had a long conversation about bowling techniques, and then he said he hoped I would get to play plenty of matches in the Army. And that was that. I was in.

Training has been tough at times – gruelling route marches are the worst, but we are also building up a sense of camaraderie. Gopal is here, too. He is very passionate about joining the Corps (the Corps of Indian Engineers, that is), and he's made me want to join them, too. So after these six months are over, I hope we'll be off together to one of the transportation units up on the northwest frontier. I can't write too much (even though I know you would find it fascinating), but it involves construction – gun pits and supply depots, and generally providing support to the Indian Army. Funny about Gopal. He was always such a good, quiet Hindu boy, but he seems to have found his calling here at Dehradun.

As for me, well ... I miss you. I had so looked forward to seeing you at last in Delhi. It's been such a long time since you went off to Udaipur, and then, of course, I was transferred away from Agra before you came back. We've never talked about your work in the railway offices there. I'm sure you were in your element. Still, your letters have been a delight to read, a flame of hope in the darkness. I'm sorry I haven't written more often.

I try to imagine you now in Delhi, working in the offices. Make sure they are putting that brain of yours to good use. Cryptology at the very least. And who knows, perhaps our paths might cross one of these days, though let us wish for a swift resolution to all of this.

I have to finish now, but before I go, I wanted to tell you there was a peacock outside the barracks this morning, dancing in the sunlight, and I couldn't help but think of you, of our (too brief) time together. Keep dancing in the sunlight, dear Florrie, and keep flying high. Beauty and freedom. That, after all, is what we are fighting for, isn't it?

Be happy,

Jay

Dehradun Training Camp
December 1941

Dearest Florrie,

Your last letter gave me a serene sense of joy. Being among all these men for so long – the mess and the stink of it, the occasional brutality, the necessary thick skin – and then to be reminded of your grace and intelligence, your kindness and sensitivity. It makes it all worthwhile. I was thinking about that awful man McDonald at the train depot. And how you rescued my clothes from being dumped in oil. I never thanked you for your quiet understanding that day. My only regret is that I didn't kiss you at the end of it all. Then I would have had two moments to treasure. Still, you seemed to enjoy driving the car (and didn't you do it well). At least I could give you that.

Here, instead, it's all up in the air. We were supposed to be departing for the northwest frontier (I think I mentioned it before), but now it's obvious that the threat will come from the East. Everything is being diverted, and us along with it. Now it's all about the lines of communication. There's talk of Malaya and Singapore, but that's as much as I can say here, I'm afraid. Gopal and I continue to help each other out. We're both officers now and I hope we'll be posted to the same place. Unfortunately the poor chap is not a very good shot. I have had to help him out of hours with his weapons training. He's passed it now, but it was touch and go for a while. Still, what he lacks in marksmanship, he certainly makes up for in loyalty and zeal. He almost makes me feel a little indifferent in comparison. He's a good boost to morale, especially when we hear stories of the disparity in pay between us and the British officers. Not to mention the inequality in conditions in the barracks. I suppose I will have to discover for myself whether any of that is true. And I suppose I will discover it quite soon. We will know about our postings in a few days. I hope I will still be able to write to you, and you to me — if you still have it in you.

My dearest Florrie, I regret now that I did not say more to you when we parted that last day, after our ride to the village. And I wish that I had kissed you one last time, regardless of what the servants might have seen. I think of our peepal tree very often. I can still feel the heat of you under my hands, the softness of you against my cheek. Do you still have the leaf I gave to you that day? Of course I know there is a chasm of difference between us, and perhaps we never had a hope. But allow me to think — at least for now — that in some kind of world, we could be together. Perhaps, in the end, that is what all this is about.

My love, be clever and passionate forever.

Yours,

Jay

HMS Encounter
January 1942

Dear Florrie,

I am penning these lines to you from the deck of the ship that is taking us to Singapore. It's night and the sea around is as black as oil. There's no moon, and I'm writing this by the light of a lamp hanging on the wall behind me. The men are asleep below, but I've crept up here alone, as who knows when I'll be able to write to you again after this.

After my last letter, we were eventually deployed, but not as expected. Instead, we arrived in Bombay and immediately joined the ship together with the Eighteenth Division of the Royal Engineers, who put to sea from Liverpool in October. They were expecting to go to the Middle East, just as we were supposed to be heading up to the border in the Punjab. None of us have the right kit for the jungles of Malaya. On board, the conditions for the Royal Engineers are much more tolerable than ours: more space, proper bunks, even a porthole or two. Us Indians, instead, are crammed into different quarters, on a lower deck, hammocks only and not a hint of fresh air. I'm sure I don't need to describe it any further. Needless to say, that's why I'm up here, where a man can breathe, and think of the woman he wishes were here to talk to, laugh with ... hold.

I'm continuing this letter the day after. Last night, Gopal came up on deck to find me. He certainly looks out for me, that boy. We fell to talking about our hopes and fears, though neither of us actually mentioned fighting. He worries for his family and wants to make them proud. I suppose at the end of it all he might get an officer's pension, if we make it out the other side, that is.

Love, by the time you receive this letter, who knows where I shall be or what I will have done. The ship is now approaching Singapore, and I sit here on my kit bag awaiting orders. The sky over the land ahead is dark with clouds — or is it smoke? I'm sure you have heard that the Japanese have destroyed almost all of the RAF planes there, leaving us utterly vulnerable to an air attack. And of course they sunk the battleship Prince of Wales last month — we are all uneasy and on edge, with the thought that we might be struck at any point, even as we disembark, which will be very soon by the look of things. I can see lines of people on the quayside — civilians, I suppose, waiting to get off the island, and here we are arriving. I can't help but feel afraid. I hope you don't think less of me for it.

Do you remember the tiger we saw together? I couldn't bring myself to shoot, even though it would have meant a great deal of glory for me. But to take a life, be it animal or human, is something I cannot at all envisage. I do recall how pleased you were that I didn't take a shot. What will you think of me now, as I enter into battle, fighting for something that I'm not sure I even understand.

I will end this now, as the ship draws closer to the docks. I hope you, too, are safe, and happy, even. What a strange world it is that brought us together for so short a time, and from such different sides of the tracks, so to speak, and now has us fighting for the same side, only thousands of miles apart.

You are forever in my thoughts.

With love,

Jay

Chapter Twelve

CALCUTTA, SEPTEMBER 1945

Florence took the three letters out of her drawer and arranged them in a line on the desk in front of her. Then she re-read the telegram that had arrived the previous day: she was leaving for Agra tomorrow. The few possessions she kept in the office at work were in a box on the floor beside her. The letters were the only items that remained unpacked.

Three years since she had heard from Jay. Nothing since his arrival in Singapore. In the end, she'd had to assume he'd been killed in the fighting or taken to a prisoner of war camp. From some of the stories she'd been hearing about those places, she wasn't sure if a death on the battlefield might not have been a kinder way to go.

For the past two years, she'd been overseeing the transfer of supplies from the ships in Calcutta to the rail wagons bound for the Ledo Road. As time passed, she'd locked away her feelings for Jay, had stopped reading his letters every night. She'd met an officer — a handsome man called Gerald — who had been impressed by her efficiency in the field. He'd chatted her up as she lounged in the shade of her truck and checked off the barrels and bales from her list, unperturbed by the noise and the heavy machinery that surrounded them. They'd met again when he was on leave and had promised that, when it was all over, the first thing they would do would be to see the Taj Mahal by moonlight together. Of course, she hadn't heard from him again after that.

She picked up the letters that were still arranged on the desk in front of her and tucked them into her bag. She sat for a while, until the light began to fade. It was over. All those years of hard work and stoicism in the face of the most terrible events, suppressing the fear, the exhaustion. But it had also allowed her to become something different, and to see another way of living.

And now it was time to go home. Her father was there. Sita was returning from the village. There'd be Ravi and even Cook, hopefully. Florence stood and went to the window. Outside on the street, trucks and tongas and bicycles flowed ceaselessly past, and she smiled as she thought of Oscar. She missed peace and solitude and riding out into the fields at sunrise. Yes, it was time. She collected her belongings and left, kicking the door shut behind her.

* * *

The long train ride back to Agra gave Florence ample opportunity to imagine what could have been: her triumphant return home. Once, she had pictured herself driving in at the wheel of one of the auxiliary service trucks she'd been in charge of, tooting the horn as she pulled up outside the Club. Jumping out and peeling off her driving gloves as she greeted old familiar faces with a hearty wave and a shout of recognition before striding into the bar to order a gin and lime.

People looking at her and understanding: she had worked hard and done her bit, she had seen terrible things, she had suffered, but she had survived.

Instead, she returned as she had left – on a crowded train. It pulled into the station and she struggled with her luggage on to the platform until she could find a porter. She edged through the mass of bodies pressing against her, trying not to lose sight of her cases, feeling limp and tired after a long journey of stops and starts, demonstrations on the line and signal failures outside just about every station. They might have been celebrating the end of the war, but travelling through India, it seemed that trouble had yet to pack its bags and leave.

Her father had been back since May and, judging by the couple of telephone conversations she'd managed with him, was much relieved to be out of the teeming sprawl of the major cities and back where he could get along mostly unobserved and left to his own devices. He'd done what he'd had to do, overseeing the conversion of locomotive workshops into ammunitions plants, and the destruction of much of what he'd worked for all his career out here, as they cannibalised the railways, dismantled tracks, and sent the rolling stock to the East. Now he had to start over, making the system work once more. It hadn't done much for his temper, but on the other hand, it meant he could begin managing the band again.

Her father. It had been so long since she had been under his influence, since she had felt the anxiety that only he could induce when he refused to listen, refused to let her have her own opinion. She'd thought all that was behind her. But now, sitting next to her bags and cases in the back of the car as it wound through the familiar streets, she felt the skin of emancipation she had worn these past six years, start to shift and shrink. The closer she came to home, the more it wrinkled and flaked. Scales peeled away from her legs and arms, quivering in the breeze for a moment before they detached and flew out of the window. By the time she reached the house and walked up the old path to the veranda, the last of it slivered away and fell, forgotten, among the weeds of the overgrown lawn.

* * *

'It's been non-stop since VJ day. We partied all through the night when we heard Chungking on the radio say Japan had surrendered. A few red faces the next morning when we realised there'd been no official announcement. We had to wait three days before we could do it all again for real. Got to love Agra.'

Florence watched her father as he gestured to the waiter for more drinks and continued to shovel down his food without even a glance at what he was putting in his mouth. He looked much older – the years of travel hadn't agreed with him, she knew – but he certainly hadn't lost his lust for life. He continued to enthuse about the endless banquets and dances and feasts and festivities that he'd attended in the weeks since victory.

'So you can look forward to some fun again at last, Florence. Looks like you need a bit of cheering up.'

The band finished a song on stage and everyone clapped. Florence tried to broach the subject that had been gnawing away at her sense of well-being for weeks now. 'Have you seen the newsreels, Papa? What was going on? What was done, both them and us? Victory, yes, but at what cost?'

'Don't start that, Florence. I won't have one of your depressing conversations again. Have another drink and eat your food, and then you are going to dance and bloody well enjoy yourself.'

And that was that, as far as her father was concerned. Either he didn't think it was worth discussing such a subject with her, or his hedonistic appetite, starved these past years, had risen like a monster to consume his conscience. Or, she supposed, she could give him the benefit of the doubt, and say that he had no stomach left for atrocity. God knew she could understand that.

Florence picked up the gin and lime that the waiter had just placed in front of her and drank it down. Her father nodded and excused himself from the table.

'Back in a moment. There's someone I want you to meet.'

Florence did not pay much attention to this last comment, distracted as she was by sudden thoughts of times past, of memories that seemed much clearer now she was here again — Jay, with his serious expression as he stood on the steps outside and listened to her explain why she was hiding. Jay with his gentle smile as he watched a sleeping tiger in the jungle. Jay with his pensive frown as he sketched a diagram on a napkin, his delicate hand holding the pen. His delicate hand guiding hers on the steering wheel of a car.

'Florence, I'd like you to meet Nick Criado, the new singer in the band. Nick, this is my daughter, Florence.'

Surprised from her thoughts, Florence looked up to see her father with a man in a tuxedo standing next to the table. The stranger was dark-eyed, and his dark hair flowed back in oiled waves from his brow. He looked like he'd stepped from the set of a Hollywood movie.

Later, the band played, and Florence danced with her father. She was immensely relieved that he didn't mention the piano or singing, which meant she could start to relax and enjoy the music.

The band really were good, and Nick brought a certain suave elegance to the stage — something that had been lacking in their performances before the war. The Club filled with people and the evening went on and on until it became a blur of song and dance and drink. It was around two in the morning when Florence realised she was exhausted and pleaded to be taken home.

'Worn you out, have we? Ah well, you had a long journey.'

Florence retrieved her stole, and her father found the car.

As they drove home, Florence, sleepy and unguarded, asked her father the question that had been a constant in her mind since she'd stepped off the train at the station, looking hopefully around her, but seeing no one she knew. 'Has Jayachandra come back, too? Is he working with you again?'

Her father looked confused for a moment. 'Jayachandra? Oh, Jay. No. Afraid we never heard from him after he left the training camp.'

It was what she'd been expecting him to say, but until she'd heard the words, there had been a chance. Instead, she would have to forget her hopes, forget what could have been.

Her father added, 'Anyway, I've invited Nick for lunch tomorrow. Find something nice to wear. Try and enjoy yourself.'

Florence, head bumping gently against the window, disappointment bitter in her mouth, assured her father she would absolutely find something nice to wear. When they arrived home, she went straight to her room, noticing in a daze the garlands of marigolds on her dresser and desk. She smiled. '*Amah*? Are you there?' She knew Sita would be outside the door waiting until the room was silent. '*Amah*, come in. We hardly had time to say two words earlier.'

The door opened and Sita peered around the side. 'My little *beti*. You must be so tired.'

Florence slipped under the sheets and then patted the bed beside her.

'Please. It's been so long.'

Sita hurried to the bed and looped her arms around Florence. 'Tell me, then, my golden one. Tell me where you have been these years. Who did you meet? Who have you become?'

Florence lay her head on Sita's shoulder and breathed a long sigh of relief, of unburdening, of love. 'I don't know where to start. It's been so much. You begin. Tell me what happened when you went back to the village. How is your family? Your sister?'

Sita sighed. 'You know, the other women, they will not talk to me. They say I think I am above them. Nobody helps me.'

Florence knew some of Sita's story. Leaving the village as a young widow, full of milk for the child that had died of the same awful disease as her husband. That Sita had ceased to belong, that the women made up lies about her whenever she visited, or simply, mostly, excluded her. She knew that Sita had instead suckled her as a baby, called her golden one, loved her as her own after her mother had died. Even when Florence had gone away to school, Sita had remained, with Harry's blessing, attending to the house and awaiting her return in the holidays. Always, until the war, that was. Florence had known all this for years, but it was only now that the reality, the enormity of what Sita had done, came to her. 'And your sister? Her husband?'

'Three children in five years of marriage, and just at the moment when everything changed. You know, the prices in the markets, everything cost so much. Too much for a family of five. I had to give my food to the young ones. My sister gave hers to her husband.'

Florence looked closely at Sita, took in the jut of her

cheekbones, hard in her face. The thinness of her arms. 'And living, all together, in that tiny hut?'

'*Beti*, you know for us this is normal. I stay quiet in the evening when he comes home, and at night there is a screen. And a blanket over the ears can stop many sounds.'

Sita smiled, but Florence saw the pain in her eyes, and imagined the evenings, sitting in the shadows, silent and ignored. Blocking out the noise of another man's pleasure in the darkness. She thought of the leaking roof in the monsoon rains, the constant cries of a baby. 'How will your sister manage without you?'

'Now your father is home, now I am here, I can send her money again. If she can eat, then the baby will be better. Her husband will have food and be strong working in the fields. Really, it is very good for everyone that you are finally returned.' Sita embraced her again. 'Now, come on, *beti*. Tell me. What have you been doing these long years? Have you been in Delhi all this time? Did you fall in love? You know, it's about time you found a husband. Then I can be ayah to your child, too.'

Florence laughed. 'Oh, slow down, please. Too many questions. No, I spent time in Calcutta after Delhi, and no, I didn't fall in love.' Here she stopped, thinking again of the letters, of the hope that had faded with every passing month and year. Then she thought again of what Sita had been through. This wasn't the time for self-pity. And if the war had taught her anything, it was how to put her feelings away inside a box, separate from the chaos and demands of the world around her. 'But I did learn to drive, *amah*. You should have seen me in my truck. I was the fastest supply driver on the road.'

Sita flicked the corner of her dupatta at Florence. 'Always so reckless. First that horse, and now a truck.' Then she relented and drew Florence close again. 'And what else? What did you see? How did you change? I need to know it all.'

They stayed there, murmuring, whispering, sometimes laughing, sometimes crying, while Florence recounted in fragments and shards her life over the six past years. She wasn't sure how late it was when her eyes finally closed and her ayah turned out the lamp and crept out of the room.

Chapter Thirteen

AGRA, DECEMBER 1945

Nick proposed on her twenty-fifth birthday. Harry was elated and pressed glass after glass of champagne upon his guests once Nick had made the announcement in the garden. Florence stood by Nick's side and accepted the flow of best wishes, as well as the comments from the women on the good looks of her husband-to-be. Florence suspected these wishes and endorsements weren't entirely genuine. She was marrying a British-Goan musician – not quite the match that any of the women standing around the garden would have desired for their own daughters, she was sure.

He was handsome though, and there was a certain thrill when he sang to her from the stage in front of everyone. He'd started to take her out for dinners, which she discovered later had been paid for by her father. Still, she supposed, musicians didn't worry too much about money, and if her father had enough to go round, then that was fine. Nick refused to get on a horse but was quite happy for her to drive him out to the countryside for a picnic. Her father wasn't bothered about organising chaperones, not after she'd been away so long during the war, but Nick never went beyond holding her hand. He gave her so many compliments, she almost started to believe them, paying more attention to her looks and clothes than she ever had before.

Their conversations were inconsequential for the most part, but he was easy company. She only had to ask him a question about himself and he would happily talk on for an age without needing her input at all. It meant she could continue to live undisturbed with her thoughts and dreams of the other life she'd lived these past years.

Often, Jay came to her in these moments, racing her across the fields on horseback or commending her understanding of the inner workings of a locomotive engine, and for a while she would forget that she was engaged to the man sitting opposite her, analysing his latest performance.

When the talking finally stopped, she would come back to reality with a fleeting sense of disappointment, before taking herself in hand. Jay was gone. Nick was here. Nick had asked her to marry him, and she had agreed. This was her life now, and she needed to embrace it.

* * *

The war had seen the end of the Christmas camps, so that year Florence and her father spent the week at home. They held a small dinner party for some of Harry's friends, who were excited to have finally seen the film *Honolulu*, starring Eleanor Powell. The next day, she went with her father and Nick to watch it at the small cinema in the town. Hawaiian tunes had been popular in the past few years, and Harry became determined to add a bit of the exotic to the stage. It was shortly after this that her father and her fiancé decided she should become a hula dancer for the band.

Nick liked her to attend rehearsals, and, one day in early January, Florence was at the side of the rehearsal room, stroking a tired and grizzled old Jackie, who was resting her muzzle on the foot of her beloved mistress and gazing up at her with anxious brown eyes. Slowly, Florence became aware her father and Nick were also looking at her as she sat, only half-listening to their conversation.

'You'll give it a go, won't you Florence? All those ballet lessons I paid for. Perhaps it was worth it after all.'

So she started to practise in her bedroom mirror, trying to mimic the swaying hips and circling hands that Eleanor Powell made look so smooth and effortless. A couple of weeks later, her costume arrived. Nick tossed the bundle to her as he walked through the door and told her to try it on. He waited downstairs with her father, while she went to her bedroom. Sita appeared, and together they laid everything out on the bed. Sita picked up the top half of the outfit.

'It's very small. You are wearing this on the stage?'

'It looks that way.' Florence pulled the cropped red halter-top over her head and tied it behind her neck.

Sita held up the skirt. 'And this is straw, from the stable?'

'Well, not quite from the stable. In Hawaii it would be made out of grass.' She slid the rustling, scratchy stalks up past her thighs and fastened the hooks on the waist band. 'There. What do you think?'

They both turned to look at her reflection in the mirror. All the work of the past few years, driving trucks and lifting supplies, had kept her strong and fit; still, her body didn't quite seem to match up to the sensuous curves the costume called for.

'This is not right. You should not be dancing and showing yourself like this in front of people.'

Florence saw how upset Sita was. She held her hand.

'Times have changed. People are used to seeing dancers in get-ups like this. It's really nothing shocking.'

'But why, *beti*, why? You are a respectable woman now. You are not a dancer.'

As always, Florence couldn't answer why. 'Oh, I think it might be amusing. Why not?'

'The *Sahib*, he is wrong. He was always wrong. And now, this Mr Nick. Him, too? And who is he? A singer from Goa. I tell you, he is not a good husband for you.'

'That's enough. There's nothing to be upset about, I promise. I really don't mind anymore.'

Sita refused to be consoled, however, and left the room. Florence tried to forget what she had seen in the mirror and went downstairs.

'Try to walk as if you're crossing the sand on a tropical beach somewhere. Not marching across the bloody Burma front.' Her father was handing Nick a drink as she entered the salon.

Nick gave her a long, cool look, and Florence felt aware of every inch of her flesh that was on display. 'Yes, yes. That'll do, I suppose.'

Florence had already noticed that the compliments he paid her under the banyan tree in the fields were much less forthcoming in front of her father. Nick went over to the gramophone and placed a record on it. The sound of a steel guitar slid into the room, accompanied by a chorus of voices crooning a lulling melody.

'Hawaiian Medley. We can use this. Let's have a go.'

Nick pushed back the sofas to create more space. Her father sat down on one, drink in hand, watching with a doubtful expression.

Nick began singing along and encouraged Florence to start moving. She tried to remember what she had seen in the film, the silky side-steps, the swinging hips, some hand gestures to fit the words, and after a while she began to think she was giving a passable performance. The music faded, Nick stopped singing, and she was left standing with just the bump of the needle in its groove breaking the silence.

Her father finished his drink. 'It was *Honolulu* I told you to see, not bloody Laurel and Hardy,' he said, laughing at his own joke.

Florence wondered if Nick might say something in her defence, but he appeared to be having some difficulty putting the record back in its sleeve. To her alarm, she felt her eyes start to fill with tears. 'That's a horrible thing to say. It's the first time we've tried it. You know, I'm not a dancer, I'm not an artist. All of that, it's your thing, not mine. You asked me to help out, so I did. I always say yes, I always try. I can't help it if I'm no good at it.'

'No, I suppose not. But, really, Florence, what are you going to do? It's not like you can spend the rest of your life driving a truck around. Can she, Nick? Sooner you get married, the better I say. Get you off my hands.' He was laughing again, and now Nick joined in.

'Papa! You don't mean that. Nick, say something!'

But at this moment, the three of them became aware that another person had stepped into the room.

'Hello. May I? Sorry to interrupt. They told me I'd find you here.'

Florence saw a woman, perhaps in her late twenties, with the same dark eyes, fine nose, and plump mouth as Nick. She was dressed in jodhpurs, and her hair was coming unpinned with dark strands falling around her face. Nick stepped out of the corner, looking astonished.

'Ester?'

'Little brother!'

She embraced him, then turned. 'Are you Harry? Nick's written about you in his letters.' She offered her hand, and Florence watched as her father stood and grasped it, appraising this bold young woman standing in the middle of his salon. Then the woman turned her gaze on Florence. 'Wonderful outfit. Hula dancing, is it? I loved that film. Eleanor Powell. She is so seductive.' She started to twirl her hands and sashay sideways across the room in a perfect imitation of the routine in *Honolulu*. The men laughed and clapped. Florence stepped forward and put out her hand.

'I'm Florence. Nick's fiancé. I take it you are his sister?'

Ester stopped dancing and shook hands. 'Yes, I'm Ester. Big sister, come to check up on him. I'd heard rumours he was engaged. Quite unbelievable. Someone willing to hitch themselves to this boy. Had to see it for myself.'

Through all this, Ester maintained a generous, wide smile. She didn't appear to be taking the situation very seriously, and Florence wasn't sure whether to laugh or feel offended.

'I'm afraid Nick hasn't told me anything about you.'

'Yes, well, Nick doesn't really approve of me. Do you, dearie?'

Nick, however, had placed the record on the player again and turned up the volume a notch. 'How about another practice, Florence?'

'Now? I don't think so. I might go and change, as we have a guest.'

The last thing Florence wanted was a second humiliation, and especially not in front of this woman.

For once, her father — whether intentionally or not — came to her rescue. 'Looks like Ester would make us the perfect Hawaiian dancer. Ever done any performing?'

'Yes, you could say I have.'

Ester looked at Nick and then around the room. 'Is that the

idea, Florence? Have they roped you into the band as a hula dancer? You know, it's simple once you have a few basic steps.'

Ester took Florence's hand and, still smiling that enticing smile, led her across the space and back again, winding and circling between the furniture, following the music. A sense of calm flowed from her.

As they moved together, and Florence fell in with Ester's rhythms, led all the while by that mesmerising smile, she finally forgot about her father's gaze and her fiancé's tepid appreciation. She started to inhabit her body again, in a way she had forgotten, that had only just begun to awaken in her teenage years and then had been subsumed in disappointment and work and loss. The music swelled, and their movements streamed together. Her body felt warm, began to glow, and at last she was in harmony with the music and with herself.

After, Ester fell into one of the sofas and fanned her face with her hands. Separated from Ester, Florence felt doubtful again. She smoothed the strands of straw around her hips and looked at her father, who was pouring more drinks.

'I think we've found our act.' He handed a glass to Ester. 'What are you doing next Saturday?'

Ester took a sip of her drink, waited for a moment, and looked at Florence before she answered. 'Ah, well, I think my husband has other plans. Give the girl a chance though. She was really starting to get it. If she wants to do it, that is.'

Florence, at that moment, felt the seed of an understanding planted. A bubble of courage – delicate, transitory, beautiful – rose up inside her and burst in her mouth. 'I'm not sure I do, Papa. I think you'll have to find someone else.' She braced herself for his reaction, but Nick, staring at his sister, interrupted instead.

'Oh, so you are here with Andreas then? And the show, I suppose? You hadn't mentioned that.'

'Of course I am.'

'I thought you might have finally changed your mind about all of that.'

'A snob as always, my little brother. And a hypocrite, I might add.'

'I'm sorry, Ester, but what I do in no way compares to—'

'Let's not do this now.' Ester turned her back on Nick. 'Florence, if you would like to become a hula dancer, I would be only too happy to help. If not, then good for you. But I think I had better be going. Before I get into any more trouble. Harry, thank you for the drink.'

She stood and faced Nick again. 'The show is coming into town next week. We're applying for the permits now. Bring Harry and Florence to see it. I'm sure they don't have your silly prejudices.'

After she had gone, Harry began to laugh. 'She's certainly spirited. Good dancer, too. What was all that about a show?'

Nick slammed his empty glass down on the table. 'It's not a show. It's a circus. She works in a bloody circus. Married The Great Gombar and embarrassed the entire family.'

Outside, a bell rang for lunch. Ravi appeared and handed a jacket to her father, who continued to seem amused. 'A circus you say? How very entertaining.'

Nick looked unsure. Florence could see his discomfort, could see that her father's opinion about the respectability of his family was crucial to his sense of identity. *Weak*, she thought, suddenly, and then as soon as the word had formed in her mind, she chased it away.

Nick turned his eyes on Florence. 'I think you'd better get changed, Florence. Cover yourself up. Not the sort of outfit a nice girl would wear to lunch really, is it?' The tone of his voice was unpleasant, calculated to make her feel awkward.

Florence left the room without replying. As she changed

back into her dress and shoes, she raged silently at the men. Nothing she did was ever good enough for her father. And Nick, for all his sweet words in the fields in the countryside, was so in thrall to him she might as well not exist whenever her father was around.

She threw the skirt, a pile of rustling straw, on the bed. *Well, damn them,* she thought. They could find someone else to humiliate. She threw the tiny top across the room, followed by the garlands of plastic flowers.

Then she remembered that moment, dancing with Ester. Not dancing for anyone else's approval, but simply her own pleasure. Ester shimmied across her memory — strong, sensuous, in control. A circus! Nick could protest all he liked. She was definitely going to see the circus.

Chapter Fourteen

AGRA, FEBRUARY 1946

Most mornings, Florence would rise early, and step out into the cool grey light of dawn. Oscar would be waiting for her, head over stable door, stamping the ground, as eager as she was to escape the confines of the house and roam the surrounding paths and fields — a moment of freedom and independence. Today, however, Florence headed towards the servants' quarters, where she could see Sita standing outside Cook's room. 'Not late, am I?'

'We are waiting for Shireen, don't worry.'

They stood together in a patch of sunlight, listening to Cook banging pots and pans in the kitchen, then the sizzle of eggs frying. Florence instead had only eaten a biscuit with her tea in the dark an hour earlier, thinking how important today was — the first time Sita would cast her vote. She hadn't realised that Shireen was coming, too. During Harry's years of absence, Cook had finally summoned up the courage to marry and brought his new wife to live with him after Ravi asked him to resume his duties. Florence had tried to welcome the new arrival, but Shireen had been reluctant to converse.

Florence felt there was some kind of hostility, perhaps. She wasn't sure. Sita, of course, had struck up a friendship immediately; nobody could ignore her warm greetings and gentle questions for long.

Shireen stepped out of the door. She glanced at Florence and bobbed her head, then turned to Sita. 'Come on. We want to arrive at the booths in good time. There will be a queue.'

The three women set out down the road that led to the bridge over the river and the centre. It would take them nearly an hour to walk, and later on it would be hot. For now, they enjoyed the cool air and the sun breaking through the mists to warm their heads. Bulbuls flew in and out of the bushes either side of the road, sometimes stopping to sit and chitter angrily at them as they passed.

Shireen walked quickly, a little way ahead. Florence and Sita kept a slower pace, quietly in step with each other, as had been their habit for years.

The image of Ester, dancing in their salon, sinuous as a serpent, came to Florence again. Then, too, Nick's anger. It wasn't the first time she'd seen him flare up. Well, artists expressed their feelings more volubly, she supposed. After all, her father wasn't the easiest of men to live with.

'Are you sure Mr Nick does not mind you coming with us today?' Sita asked.

Florence took her arm. 'I didn't tell him. Why should he mind?'

'You are too quiet these days. And always out on your horse. Never at home. A woman planning to be a bride should be happy. And he should be worshipping you. But all I ever see is cold. Like he is not here, even when he is. It gives me a strange feeling.'

'Really, *amah*, it's fine. I'm fine. You know, it's not some silly schoolgirl crush, all talk and kisses and …' The word stuck for a moment, glued in her mouth, as if it were a huge betrayal. She spat it out. '… letters. This is a proper relationship. An engagement. I'm sure Nick is taking it just as seriously as I am.'

Sita squeezed her arm. 'You are right. You know, after, we can go to buy the rose oil for your wedding bath, and ask the tailor if the dress will be delivered soon.'

At this, Shireen turned to Sita with a look of irritation. 'Are you not inspired by this day? By what we are doing?'

Sita stopped walking. 'Of course. I have never imagined times like these.'

Florence was surprised by Shireen's sharp tone. She knew that Cook and Shireen listened to the radio every evening in their small room. And that Cook was prone to small outbursts of political anger when her father wasn't around. It seemed Shireen had picked up the habit. 'But won't you be voting for different things?' she said, hesitantly, wanting to defend Sita from Shireen's unexpected and evident fervour, but still a little nervous of offending Shireen.

Shireen tutted. 'Congress or League, this is about freedom. There's never been a time like this'. She stepped up to Sita. 'We will have our country back. *Swaraj,* sister. Independence. That's what we will have.'

They walked on again. Florence thought about what Shireen had said, what she had heard on the radio, and her father's increasingly frequent outbursts when he read the paper. 'And what will this *Swaraj* look like?' she said.

'Freedom from famine. Freedom from rationing. Freedom from your rule.'

'Shireen!' Sita said. 'Please, control yourself.'

Shireen looked at the ground. 'I apologise.'

'No really,' said Florence. 'It's fine. You should be able to say what you believe in.' Florence increased her pace. Perhaps the queue at the polling booths might distract Shireen from the discussion.

Sita caught up. 'And anyway, Shireen. We live with the British. We work for them. What will happen to us? To them?'

'They will be just fine, I can tell you.' Shireen said, quietly.

Florence thought it was time the conversation moved on. This was a significant, historic day, and she had wanted to share Sita's moment with her, to support her in taking a new step forward. Shireen instead made her feel as if she shouldn't be there. 'Come on,' she said. 'There will be hundreds of people there. We want to get a good place in the line.'

They hurried down the road to the bridge. As they crossed, Florence looked out at the slow, silver waters, and the banks quilted with squares of colourful cloth drying in the sun, and children playing as they washed. She couldn't imagine it changing. She couldn't imagine what might come next.

They stood for hours in the crowd, slowly moving forward, one small step at a time, until they finally reached the booths. Florence waited in the shade of a tree and, after, they all slipped through the crush of bodies and into the bazaar.

'I think we should celebrate this special day, don't you?' Florence said, as they walked down the crowded street. 'Food and a visit to the tailor. New outfits for you both?'

'I want to visit the perfume seller first. Remember, rose oil for the bride's bath in the morning,' said Sita.

Florence was about to cross the busy road, watching out for wobbling bicycles piled high with boxes, other pedestrians, and a large cow that had stopped to help itself to a festoon of marigolds decorating the market stall next to her.

'Wait.' Shireen grabbed her arm and pulled her back. It was then they saw it happen.

There was a storehouse opposite, bags of produce from the fields stacked up on the road outside. A truck pulled up, scattering people and animals as it drove through the throng. The driver jumped down and began ordering the men who were waiting with the sacks to start loading the truck. One man, however, turned and shouted at the others, a sort of crazed desperation in his voice. The driver shouted louder and passers-by stopped and gathered round. Suddenly the man ripped one of the sacks open and started to throw handfuls of wheat at the crowd. The driver advanced on him, stick raised, threatening to hit him, but now the crowd pressed closer, and in a moment many hands were tearing open sacks and grabbing at the grain and barley, filling bags and pockets.

'We should leave,' said Sita, trying to step back, but Shireen held on to her, too.

'See. This is what they have brought us to. Squabbling in the street over handfuls of wheat.'

The scuffle opposite was becoming more heated, punches and missiles thrown. Florence saw blood and someone on the ground, curling away from kicks and blows. More men came out from the storehouse to join in, and from down the street the sound of whistles could be heard. Florence pulled at Shireen. 'Come on. The police are arriving, and this is turning nasty.'

Now another group of men, armed with sharpened *lathis*, forced their way into the mob, and that was when Florence stopped in her tracks. One man looked familiar: the lock of hair that curled down over his eyes, the angle of the jaw. It couldn't be … could it?

'*Beti*, please, this is very bad.' Sita tugged at her arm from one side.

'She's right, we have to go,' said Shireen, pulling from the other side. Florence had no choice but to follow them into the swell, and when she next turned, the crowd had closed around them, and she could no longer see him.

They pushed their way against the tide of people, holding on to each other's hands. The press of the bodies around them, elbows and hands and fists jabbing and jostling, was frightening. Sita pointed to a small alleyway, and they sidestepped into it, running now, leaving the noise and violence behind them. The alley led away from the main street, and soon it became quiet and empty. They slowed down, breathless.

'No harm, sister. No need to be upset.' Shireen gave Sita's hand a squeeze then let go.

Sita held on to Florence. 'Are you fine, *beti*? Don't worry. We are safe now. What's wrong?'

But Florence couldn't answer. She wasn't sure what she had seen, in the midst of that throng, with such a look of cold anger on his face. It couldn't have been him. Jay was never a man of violence.

'Nothing, nothing,' Florence said. 'I'm just upset by the fight.' She could still hear the sounds of it, echoing down the narrow corridor.

Sita looked behind, then ahead. 'This will bring us out by the river. We can walk along the bank to the bridge. Quickly, come on.' She took the lead, and Florence followed with Shireen.

She just wanted to get away, to be out of this place where there was so much rage, and where ghosts appeared with sticks as hate-filled versions of their former selves.

* * *

That evening, Florence sat in her room, trying to picture the scene again. The more she thought about it, the more she realised how unlikely it was that the man in the crowd was Jay. It was Jay himself who had once told her that the simplest solution to a problem was usually the correct one. And what was more likely? That Jay had died in the war? Or he had returned to Agra, joined the gangs of protestors, and had chosen not to contact her? No, that was not the Jay that she had known, and that meant that the Jay she had known was dead.

She felt a pressure in her chest, something she thought she had learned to suppress, but she refused to go there. She had already dealt with this. There would be no more tears. It had just been the strangeness of the situation, the emotion of the moment. She took a deep breath and pressed her palms to her eyes. Enough.

There was a knock at the door, and Sita came in holding a package.

'It's your wedding dress, *beti*. It's arrived.' She untied the string, unfolded the paper, and lifted it out for them to admire together. Layers of delicate, ivory lace, elegant and flattering.

'Just like a proper *mehmsahib*,' said Sita as she smoothed away the creases and hung it carefully in the wardrobe.

Florence watched but said nothing. Seeing the dress there, it suddenly all became very real. Whereas today's vision had been just that — a vision. And an aberration. She wouldn't let the past ruin her chance of a normal life now.

As if reading her mind, Sita said, 'This wedding is what you need. You will see. You will be contented once you become a wife. A child will arrive — and that will be enough future for us all.'

Florence smiled at her ayah and hid from the shadows in her heart.

Chapter Fifteen

AGRA, FEBRUARY 1946

In the days that followed, Florence tried to forget about what she had seen on voting day, and instead concentrate on her wedding, just as Sita had advised. She sent a card to Ester, wondering whether her future sister-in-law might like to come over for lunch, and had been delighted when she had received by return a letter asking if she would like to see around the circus instead.

The next day, she told Nick she wasn't feeling well and wouldn't be at rehearsals — there had been no more mention of hula dancing. Then, as soon as the house was empty, she asked Bikram to saddle up Oscar, trotted out of the back gate and down the road to the circus field, where Ester was in the middle of her daily practice.

'When's the wedding, then?' Ester's body was upside down, swinging forward and back, draped from the bar of the trapeze. As Florence started to shout her reply, Ester flicked herself upright, grabbed hold of the bar and then launched herself into a graceful backflip, landing with a bounce in the rippling grasp of the net. She rolled over to where Florence was applauding this unexpected descent and swung herself over the side. 'Sorry, when? I didn't catch that.'

'March, before the hot weather arrives. Ester, that was wonderful. How long have you been doing this?'

'Oh, so next month? Is everything ready?' Ester drank in large gulps from a leather flask of water that had been lying in the dusty brown grass near their feet. 'I've been with Andreas for seven years now. Performing for about six. But it only took me about six months to learn the basic routine. If you're fit and flexible, then the hardest thing to train is your mind. But, there's always the net, after all.'

It must feel wonderful, Florence thought, to swing like that, so high and unencumbered, and then release yourself into the air, rotating and twisting, floating and falling.

'You know, if you want any help with anything — the dress, the food, whatever — I'd be happy to assist.' Ester was walking away, across the field, towards the row of tents and the large rectangle that had been fenced off as an arena. 'Do you want to see the horses?'

Behind the tents, Florence counted seven horses tethered in the shade of the trees. A man — blonde, short, and stocky — was grooming one of them, with long, strong sweeps of the brush over its dappled-grey back and haunches. Ester walked over to him, indicating that Florence should follow. 'Come and meet Andreas.'

Andreas greeted Florence with a cool gaze over his high, Slavic cheekbones. She remembered he was Hungarian, and he certainly looked about as different from Ester as could have been possible. He nodded a few times while Ester caught him up on a problem with one of the horses. Then he turned back to his work.

'A man of few words.' Ester was walking away again. 'Which I always think is an advantage.'

Florence hurried after her, but before they had gone far, she heard Andreas call out after them.

'You can show her the cannon.'

Ester paused for a moment, seeming surprised. 'Well, you are honoured. He must have seen something he liked in you.'

'What do you mean?' Andreas had barely said two words to her. How could he know whether he liked her or not?

Ester had stopped outside another tent. The sound of mallets hammering pegs into the iron-dry earth rang across the field. A horse whinnied, and above them a pair of black kites screeched and circled, on the lookout for food.

'Andreas has a sense about people, a way of seeing beneath the surface, beneath the skin, if you like. He works in a different way to us, to other people. If he likes you, you should be flattered. He's not the easiest man to please.'

'Well, of course I am.' Florence was not sure at all what Ester was talking about, though the look Andreas had given her had been a little like a beacon lighting up the horizon to expose the enemy. She wondered what he thought he had seen in her. Perhaps she would rather not know. 'What did he say you should show me?'

'The cannon.'

Now Florence really did have no idea what Ester was talking about. Did Andreas keep military weapons as a hobby? 'I'm sorry. What cannon?'

Ester went to the tent opening and began to untie it. She turned that generous smile on Florence again. 'Oh, did I forget to tell you? I'm also a human cannonball.'

Inside the tent, Florence's eyes adjusted to the dim light while Ester pulled at a canvas sheet, folding it in towards her in long dusty tugs as she revealed the machine underneath. Florence estimated it to be about thirty-feet long. Huge. It squatted in the gloom, a solid dark presence with an even blacker heart. Instinctively, Florence placed a hand on the surface; the metal felt cold and pockmarked under her fingers. She wondered what it was made out of.

'I can't believe it, Ester. I've heard about this, but I've never seen it, let alone met anyone who did it. Do you really get fired out of this thing? How on earth does it work?'

'Dearie, I can't tell you how it works. Secrets of the trade, I'm afraid. This is why Andreas really is The Great Gombar. He had this thing built, and he does all the technical side of it — angle of elevation, trajectory, and so on. Of course, it's me that actually risks my life. But it is the most marvellous feeling. You have no idea.'

Florence walked around the cannon and, without thinking, stuck her head inside the opening. There was nothing to see, just a cramped space disappearing into the darkness. She pulled herself away, momentarily unable to breathe. 'It's not really gunpowder, is it, that launches you? I mean, that just wouldn't be possible. It would kill you.'

Ester was sitting side-saddle on the other end of the cannon. 'Why don't you come and watch, and then tell me your theory.'

Florence placed her hands on the dark metal again and then laid her cheek there, too. Her mind was churning through ideas, all she knew about propulsion and engines and explosives. What she would give to see inside the machine — a neat cross-section showing all its guts and workings. A brief shadow passed across her mind, a ghost of Jay's carefully drawn diagrams, his spiky annotations. She sighed.

Ester had begun to haul the cover back up the cannon towards her, so Florence grabbed a corner and pulled until it was hidden once more. Then she followed Ester out into the daylight.

'When are you going to perform? I have to come and watch. I don't care what Nick says.'

Ester had stopped and was looking out across the field. 'We're still waiting for the permits to arrive — the bureaucracy is always rather an ordeal — but within the next week or so, I hope.' Ester walked back to Florence, took her by the shoulders, and turned her to look across the field. 'And that's going to be our very special backdrop. The first human cannonball jump over the Taj Mahal.'

Beyond the expanse of grass in front of them, on the other side of the perimeter wall, rose those soft, voluptuous domes, tinted peach by the late afternoon sun.

'You stand in the correct place, get the perspective just so, and you'll see me fly right over it.'

As they walked back to the gate, where Florence had tied her horse, Ester again began to ask about the wedding, as if to reassure herself that it really would go ahead and that everything would be ready in time. Or perhaps she was just trying to be helpful, knowing Florence had little female support in her life. As it was, the tailor had copied a dress from the catalogue, with Sita's approval, and her father was happy to make arrangements for yet another party at the Club. Beyond this, she wasn't really sure what she should be doing. Or what she should be feeling. As usual, she let these thoughts pass, like clouds scudding across the sky. Nick could be sweet sometimes, and he was certainly talented, not to mention handsome, and Papa was obviously thrilled at the idea of him as a son-in-law.

'Well, there is one thing you could help me with, perhaps.' Florence untied her horse and pulled down the stirrups, preparing to mount. 'Are you any good at hair and make-up?'

Ester laughed a loud 'ha!' as she patted Florence's horse on its shoulder. 'Am I any good? Darling, I will make you look divine.'

Riding home, however, it wasn't the wedding, or hair and make-up, that Florence was thinking about. She was calculating angles of trajectory and whether someone of Ester's weight and size could be launched by some kind of spring-loaded propulsion system. Perhaps the cannon was actually just a giant rubber catapult inside. The problem would continue to gnaw away at her, over the coming weeks and months, providing her with endless material for distraction from what would become an increasingly unpleasant reality. It would be over a year until she would finally discover what really went on inside that machine.

Chapter Sixteen

AGRA, MARCH 1946

When Florence woke up on the morning of the wedding, she didn't stop too long in bed to consider the day ahead. She forced herself up and, after nibbling on a biscuit, decided that an early ride would be a good start and a way of clearing her head.

She found herself, perhaps through some subconscious sense of maternal lack on this day, riding past the cemetery and made a brief stop at her mother's grave. And what of her wedding all those years ago in England? The photo still took centre place on her father's dresser in his room. From the little she knew, her mother had done her duty, done what was expected of her, and then followed her husband to a foreign country on the other side of the world where she had made the best of what life had apportioned to her — until it killed her, anyway.

Looking down at the gravestone — *loving wife and tender mother* — Florence realised now that she couldn't, shouldn't, expect much more herself. Finding a husband and fulfilling her familial duties was what she should have been aiming for all along. After all, the last time Ruthie had written from London, she had just finished yet another disastrous engagement with a man and was back to square one. And at twenty-six, Ruthie wasn't exactly young. No, Florence was lucky to have found this path, and she should commit to it without any silly regrets, which after all were no help to anyone. And no more dwelling on the past.

She rode back to the house, happy to have convinced herself of something that she knew to be correct.

Later, at breakfast, where she sat on her own (her father was nowhere to be seen), she made sure she ate well. She did not want to come over all faint at an inappropriate moment during the ceremony, not in front of a church full of people – or Nick, for that matter. She spent some time in a bath, into which Sita dropped rose oil and rose petals, and then had a brief lie down.

By and by, Sita came bustling in, followed by Ester, long and slender as a bamboo leaf in a pale-green silk dress and heels. Florence sat up, a little groggy from the sleep she had fallen into, and suddenly worried about the time.

'Two hours yet, dearie. Plenty of time to make you look ravishing.' Ester dumped a bag on the dresser and began to take out a series of brushes and different pots of make-up. 'Now then, face first.'

While Sita sat and shook her head at Ester's distinctly modern and European take on the application of cosmetics – with frequent reference to a picture on the cover of that month's *Vogue* magazine – Ester began a conversation that Florence thought she had probably been intending to have for some time.

'Is it what you imagined then, your big day? I mean, every girl, no matter how independent, dreams occasionally, secretly, about their wedding, don't they?'

Florence was immediately alert. This was the sort of conversation that ran the risk of revealing those emotions that, she now realised, were much better left buried and never spoken of. The best plan in these situations, she found, was to distract the other person with questions about themselves. It worked with Nick every time.

'What was your dream wedding then, Ester?'

Ester loomed in close to Florence's face, blending colours over her eyelids then moving back to approve the result.

'I was dreadfully conventional when I was young. It was all clouds of white tulle, little bridesmaids like fairies, and a five-tier cake with sugar flowers and a figurine of the happy couple dancing. I never actually imagined my husband though — he was quite irrelevant in it all. Then, of course, Mummy and Daddy died, and I suppose all my ideas about security and permanence changed. I certainly never dreamed my wedding breakfast would take place in a circus tent. When I met Andreas, though, it just seemed completely natural that we would get married. I never really had any doubts.'

The word *doubts* signalled itself to Florence as a potential source of commotion. She needed to extinguish these dangerous sparks, and quickly. 'I know, isn't it wonderful when you are just absolutely sure you are doing the right thing. It's so calming. I mean, I haven't felt so at peace like this for such a long time.'

Ester was now stroking rouge on to Florence's cheek-bones. She hoped Ester wasn't going over the top with the make-up. It wasn't a circus show she was preparing for, after all. 'So, you are sure? Nick really is the man you want to marry? What you always dreamed of?'

'Yes, of course. I mean, he might not be exactly what I dreamed of when I was young, but then, like you said, circum-stances change.'

'I have to say, I've noticed you are awfully quiet when he's around.'

Florence thought it best not to respond to this, rather as evidence that she could be quiet in whosoever's company she chose to be. Sure enough, after a brief silence, Ester continued talking.

'Still, he can be quite chatty, which I suppose makes up for it. It must even out in the end. Perhaps it's quite relaxing, letting someone else make all the conversation. Andreas is the complete opposite, but I rather prefer that. And I know he's always listening.' Ester continued with her work, now on to the lipstick. She painted it on carefully then made a kind of 'mmm' with her mouth, pressing her lips together and releasing them, a little like a goldfish, and indicated that Florence should follow suit. 'Is Nick the first man you've been in love with?'

There it was, that word. The word she had being doing such a good job of avoiding. Because when she thought of it, another face came to mind. 'Oh, I had a schoolgirl crush once. But that was different, you know. I was so young. I think he just was just being kind.'

Ester picked up a hairbrush and stood behind Florence, gently easing the tangles and slowly transforming them into shining, corn-coloured curls. 'What happened to him?'

'The war. We wrote for a while, but then he was sent to Singapore. I never heard from him again.'

'I'm sorry, Florence. The war tore so many of us apart, didn't it?'

The wall. She had to keep the wall strong. Now was not the time to let things crumble. 'Well, we were hardly together. It was more of a 'disappointment'. Just think of all those families instead with no husbands, no fathers. That must be the real agony.'

Ester was pinning her hair now, doing clever things with grips and spray. Sita offered to bring some sweet lime water and, after she had left the room, Ester's tone changed into something more mischievous.

'Do I have to give you the talk about the wedding night? What to expect and all that?'

'Oh heavens, please don't! Anyway, he's your little brother. I'm sure you don't want to think about him like that. I'm quite *au fait* with the details, thank you.' Although, quite how *au fait*, she didn't really want to let on. Sita returned with drinks, and Ester swept the brushes and make-up back into her bag.

'Good, now let's get you into the dress.'

It was hanging inside the wardrobe, wrapped in whispering tissue paper. But as Florence took it in her hands, she became aware of a different sound, louder than the paper, though just as dry, like a fire about to catch. Then a shadow slid out across the floor towards her.

'Oh, Christ!' She jumped back, dropped the dress, and knocked into the table, sending her hand mirror crashing to the floor. The creature stopped at the noise, coiled itself, and then began to rise, swaying in front of her.

'Stay calm,' said Ester from behind her. 'Try to back away.'

Sita gave a small moan and rushed from the room. Florence took a step back, but this seemed to aggravate the snake more, and it grew to a greater height, hood inflated, hissing, tongue flickering in and out — seeing her, scenting her.

'I don't know what to do,' Florence whispered. 'Someone get Ravi, for God's sake.'

But there was no need to get Ravi, for at that moment, Sita returned and pushed in front of Florence holding one of Harry's antique scimitars high above her head.

'Get back. Get out of the room, both of you.'

'We're not bloody leaving you in here alone,' said Ester, as Sita stood there, warrior-like with her sword.

The snake froze at this new apparition, hissing louder now, and Sita lowered the weapon in front of her body as protection. 'I will cut you in two before I let you hurt her,' she said. 'Get out of here, snake, get out.' Sita stared, and the snake wavered for a moment, then began to lower itself to the ground.

All three women clustered together now, Sita at the helm, still ready with the sword. After a few more seconds, the snake began to move away, and Sita lunged to one side to prevent it returning to the wardrobe. 'It needs to go out of the window. Block its way.'

'Do we want it roaming around the garden?' said Florence, looking around the room to see if there was anything else she could protect herself with. 'It'll just come back in.'

The snake continued to wind its way towards the edge of the room, Sita advancing slowly behind it. It moved up the leg of the chair next to the window. 'Get out of here, snake,' shouted Sita again. 'Out of the window.'

As if it had heard and understood the choice it was faced with, the snake launched itself upwards and over the edge of the windowsill, then disappeared out of the room with a flick of its tail. Sita ran to check it had truly gone then shut the window, and the three women looked at each other in horrified relief.

Sita lowered the sword. 'We must send for one of the *Saperas* to take it away. I will tell Cook's boy to run to the village, and I will tell Ravi to keep watch in the garden.'

'Sita!' said Florence. 'You were magnificent.'

'Yes,' said Ester, laughing now. 'Like a destroyer of demons. I thought Kali had come to save us.'

'Oh no, Madam. You mustn't say that.' But Sita looked

more proud than embarrassed as she walked past them, still holding the sword. 'I must return this to the *Sahib*'s room. I hope he will not mind I took it.'

Florence and Ester watched her leave then looked around the room. Florence picked up her dress from the floor and shook it out. Ester brushed the shards of broken mirror into a pile. 'Watch out for your feet, dearie.'

'A broken mirror and a snake in the wardrobe. Not the most auspicious start to one's wedding day,' said Florence. 'Oh, God, what's the time?'

'Time to get you into that dress.'

* * *

Florence and Ester let Sita have her moment as she draped the layers of lace, wrapped and pinned and tucked, until she was happy with every single pleat and fold.

Tears pricked at Florence's eyes. 'Thank you, *amah.* I couldn't have done this without you. Promise you won't ever leave me. Even when I'm a married woman.'

Sita hugged Florence to her. 'My beautiful, golden one. I am always here for you. For you and your children. Be happy.'

Ester took the veil and secured it on Florence's head with a circlet of orange blossom. Florence wriggled her feet into a pair of white satin heels, and Ester and Sita stepped back to look at the final effect.

'Ravishing, just like I promised. Little brother ought to be devastated when he sees his bride walking down the aisle. Come on.'

She took Florence by the hand, and together they walked to the mirror. Florence saw a woman unknown: polished and refined, ready to start a life with her husband. She allowed herself one large, dry sob that heaved itself somewhere out of the depths of her chest, those depths where love and loss lived, joined in unhappy alliance. Ester squeezed her hand, and they all went to wait for the car.

* * *

Inside the church, Florence acknowledged the guests sitting in the pews as she walked next to her father down the aisle. The women admired her dress, and a few dabbed at their eyes with handkerchiefs. The men sat, impassive, thoughts elsewhere, pulling occasionally at their stiff collars in the heat of the small building.

As she neared the altar, Nick stepped forward, and there was a muttering of approval from the women at his film-star good looks. The music finished, and Ester came to take Florence's bouquet, soft cups of cream-coloured roses — their scent was the only element of the scene she allowed to drift through into her consciousness.

The vicar began to speak, and Florence, rather than listen to the actual words, heard it as more of a musical hum, the pitch rising and falling, the pace quickening and slowing as he intoned the beginning of the ceremony. The church was dark and getting warmer by the minute. She wondered how much longer until they could escape outside where at least there was a bit of a breeze. There would be photographs and then off to the Club for the wedding breakfast.

Behind her, she heard Ester sneeze. Probably all the flowers. Florence thought again about their earlier conversation. Imagine having your wedding celebration in a circus tent. They had finally been to the show two weeks ago. Even Nick had grudgingly come along, once Papa had said he thought it all sounded like good fun and an impressive spectacle, come to that. Inside the big top, they'd watched Ester perform her acrobatics on the trapeze, held at one point by a chain of five male trapezists, swinging in long, curling arcs before somersaulting into the net. There were men juggling flaming torches and breathing fire, then dancing horses and troupes of tumblers and contortionists creating a confusion of ever-changing patterns and formations. It had been exciting and colourful, but nothing compared to what happened after.

Florence became aware that the vicar had come to the part about lawful impediment. After a moment's silence, he began again. Florence wondered when it would be the bit where she had to speak. Nick passed the vicar the ring, a plain, thick band of gold.

Ester's outfit, when she finally entered the arena outside the big top, had also been hooped with glittering circles swirling around her figure and making her seem like a golden spring. The finale had been timed to coincide with sunset, and behind the field, the minarets and cupolas of the Taj blushed like soft, rouged cheeks in the orange light. The crowd gathered in excitement behind the ropes while Andreas walked back and forth across the field from the cannon to the net, and Ester waved and encouraged them all to cheer.

'Nick, how can you not be amazed by your sister? This is incredible.' Florence glanced at him and registered an expression she had never seen before. It wasn't, as she had been expecting, shame and embarrassment, but something that rendered him vulnerable. For the first time, she could imagine him as a little boy. Terror. That was it. Terror masked with anger. She took his hand. She hadn't truly considered the dangers until now. And Ester was the only family he had left.

Her father, bluff as ever, didn't notice anything amiss. 'She's certainly got some pluck, your sister. Bloody long way to that net. What is it, a hundred feet?'

Nick pulled his hand away from Florence and pushed his

way back through the crowd towards the gate. Her father watched him go, puzzled. 'Where's he off to? It's about to start.'

Florence now realised that the vicar was speaking the words she had to repeat. She began to echo those phrases about sickness and health and being parted by death, but even as she did so, her mind returned to that orange evening field and the sight of Ester disappearing inside the cannon, slipping away into the darkness. The crowd stilled, and Andreas began to speak.

'Ladies and gentleman. Please be stunned, be thrilled, be astonished, by the amazing, the explosive, the soaring flying lady. In a moment, I will light the charge of one pound of gunpowder, propelling her one hundred and thirty feet, at a height of fifty feet, across this field and into the net. For the first time, witness the illusion that she jumps over the domes of the Taj Mahal itself.'

Now Andreas walked to the back of the cannon, and Florence could see a spark as he lit the charge. He started to count down from ten, encouraging the crowd to join in. Florence's stomach was doing flips now, trying to imagine Ester inside and what was about to happen to her. The crowd was shouting, deafening around her as it reached a crescendo — *three, two, one.*

A flash of light and clouds of smoke surrounded the cannon, and then Florence could see a body, streamlined, straining, rigid, speeding above them, the domes beneath her gold like her glittering costume, gold like the ring Nick was putting on to Florence's hand as he finished his vows and bent to kiss her, while Ester landed safely and the crowd cheered as she took long bouncing strides across the net and jumped to the floor to take her bows, and Florence turned to the congregation and realised that she was married.

* * *

Their wedding night proper was delayed, as they took the sleeper train out of Agra that night. Nick seemed happy enough to get ready for bed as soon as the train pulled out of the station, after they had arranged their cases and the bearer had brought them a nightcap. She stood for a moment, unsure if she should try to lie down next to him, even though the bed was impossibly narrow, but he kissed her hand, told her she had looked beautiful in the church, then rolled over to face the wall. Back in the familiar surround of a night train again, Florence settled herself on the bed opposite and began the lengthy business of removing all the pins that Ester had spent so long placing in her hair only twelve hours earlier.

Twelve hours, and here she was, a married woman. She felt her insides seem to contract, a brief surge of adrenaline — or fear. No, she mustn't let her resolve leave her now. She was doing the right thing, making a life for herself. There would be children, and she would manage a household, look after her husband and her father, and be as respectable a member of society as it was possible for her to be. And times were changing — Nick was more or less accepted by that same society.

She pulled the brush through her hair a few times, but as usual it was impossible to do anything with. She would have to get up early and try to wash it out before Nick woke up. She wondered when it became permissible to let one's husband see you in your true morning state. Probably not until you'd actually slept with him, at least. She changed out of her going-away suit, hung it carefully on the hook by the window and lay down. From the bed opposite now came a repetitive sound, like a saw passing through wood. Heavens, she hadn't imagined he would snore. The sound grew louder and more staccato. Evidently it was a particularly knotty piece of wood to get through. It continued on, louder and louder, until it came to a sudden, choking stop. For a moment there was silence, then it began again.

They had breakfast in the buffet car together with another, older couple called the Pearsons, who were also going to Udaipur. Nick was uncommunicative, and Florence thought that perhaps he wasn't a morning person, so she attempted to cover the silences with inconsequential chatter — which is what she thought a considerate wife would do.

As a wedding gift, the Hansons had made the kind offer of their houseboat on the lake for the honeymooners, the same place Florence had stayed the year the war broke out. So she described what she recalled of Udaipur — the views, the palace that seemed to float on the water, the changing colours from sunrise to sunset. The couple seemed quite taken and asked for advice on the sights they should see, and if it were possible to hire a boat. Florence obliged with as much information as she could provide, considering it was seven years since she'd visited and she'd been little more than a child. Nick stared out of the window and only perked up when Mrs Pearson suggested a round of bridge to pass the time until lunch.

It was during lunch that the train juddered to a halt in the middle of a large, dusty plain, with distant hills purple on the horizon. Mr Pearson stood and went to the window to look out. When he returned, he seemed concerned.

'Not sure we shouldn't lock ourselves in our compartments, you know. There's a nasty looking mob surrounding the front of the train. I suppose they've blocked the line.'

'Oh, Edward, are you sure? They haven't brought the dessert yet.'

'My dear, I'm afraid you will have to forgo your sweet for

now. And I advise you two to do the same,' he said, looking at the newlyweds.

Nick went to see the situation for himself, leaning so far out of the window that Florence thought he might fall. When he came back, he stood next to Mr Pearson and took on the same look of concern.

'I think he's right, Florence. We might not be safe here. Come on.'

Now Mrs Pearson stood also, apparently resigned to missing her dessert. 'Perhaps we should all stick together for safety.'

The men agreed this was a good idea, and the four of them hurried down the corridor to the Pearson's compartment. Once inside, they pulled down the blinds and locked the door.

Mr Pearson, a rather large man who took up a lot of space even while sitting down, now began to pace around the tiny area. 'This is all that damn Gandhi's fault, giving people ideas above their station — strikes, mutinies. Great big mess they've created now. Self-government, separate Muslim state. It's a disaster, mark my words.'

Nick, who had been reclining on one of the seats, also stood up. Florence watched as he and Mr Pearson negotiated the space around them, each taking a couple of steps in opposite directions, then towards each other, then an awkward, dithering moment before they turned and inspected the furnishings.

Nick checked the lock on the door. 'I quite agree. It's one thing organising people to make a bit of salt. Quite another to run a country.' He jiggled the door handle and then turned, apparently happy with their security. 'Anyway, I wouldn't worry too much, ladies. It's probably just a bunch of peasants with their spinning wheels sitting on the line. We'll be off again soon enough.'

Florence frowned. She thought he ought to have been more sympathetic to what Congress was trying to achieve. At least her father had a more open-minded approach.

'Papa says Indian independence is inevitable, and we should be doing what we can to smooth the process.'

At this, Nick gave Florence a look, the kind she had never been on the receiving end of before. He suddenly did not seem handsome at all, but whatever he was about to say was interrupted by a loud crashing and banging that started up on the outside of the carriage. The thud of rocks hitting metal came intermittently. Mrs Pearson, evidently a stoical type, fanned herself with a drinks coaster and attempted to keep things light hearted. 'Sounds like they might be throwing their spinning wheels at us now.'

Then shouts came from inside the train, which made a sudden jolt forward, provoking louder cries and screams. The four of them locked inside their compartment stopped talking, and all at once Florence sensed how vulnerable they really were. No way out, no weapons – sitting ducks, really. The train jerked forward again, and this time continued moving. The shouts and pounding on the carriage grew more frenzied and then, thank God, began to diminish as the engine picked up speed. After a moment, the two men sat down. Florence peeked behind the blind and saw, disappearing into the distance, the ugly faces of angry men, still waving sticks and throwing rocks in their direction.

Mrs Pearson, ever keen to cheer the situation up, put the drinks coaster down and exhaled deeply. 'So, anyone for cards?'

* * *

The houseboat was of wood, painted in red and white, with pots of flowers around the deck. A small kitchen-boat was attached for the cook and his boy, and attached to that a small *shikara,* flat-bottomed and complete with cushions and a rower to convey the honeymooning couple around. It was this little watercraft that met them at the ghats where their bearer for the fortnight placed garlands of marigolds around their necks and steadied Florence as she stepped from the pier into the rocking boat. Nick was already sitting, squinting at the palace in the centre of the lake. Florence saw that he had taken the driest place, forcing her to wobble even more as she tried to avoid the puddle on her own seat. Finally, she was stable and the rower set off across the water.

It was sunset, and raspberry clouds stained the horizon. Florence realised she was hungry and hoped the cook had prepared them a decent meal for their first night. A kingfisher darted across the lake in front of them, and she turned to Nick, eager to point it out to him, but he had his eyes closed, and she thought perhaps she shouldn't disturb his moment of repose. He had had a very long day after all.

Dinner was light, but at least the cook knew how to deal with fish. For once, the fried pomfret hadn't been cooked into a tasteless mush, and the green beans had a satisfying crunch to them. After they'd eaten, Nick asked for a peg of whisky, and they sat on the deck at the front of the boat with the lights of the palace glittering out across the water towards them.

Florence thought she should encourage a little conversation. It was usually easy to prompt Nick into giving his opinion and much more besides. 'It's beautiful, isn't it, the Lake Palace. What do you think it's like inside?'

'Your father is supposed to be getting me an introduction to someone who knows someone who knows the Maharana.

What with the band getting so popular, I imagine he might ask me to sing.'

'Oh, Nick! How exciting. Jane will be so impressed when I write to tell her. We spent every evening inventing tales of what went on there when I was here in '39.'

'God, Florence. Don't go writing to the whole world about it. It might not happen, you know, and then I'll look like a bloody idiot.'

Florence thought about trying to explain to Nick that she had only meant to write *if* he actually sang for the Maharana, but she felt suddenly very tired and so lapsed into silence. After some time, Nick pushed his drink away (why he had asked for it in the first place, she didn't know — he never drank whisky) and stood up. The boat shifted, and Florence clutched at the side. The idea of sleeping in the middle of that dark expanse of water, just the two of them, gave her a vague sense of anxiety, but Nick and her father had been so enthusiastic about the idea of Udaipur that she hadn't wanted to complain. Now she understood why they'd been so enthusiastic, of course. It was all about the bloody band. But as soon as she'd thought this, Florence corrected herself — it was no way for a wife to think about her husband's profession. Instead she yawned, stretched, and looked up at him. 'Shall we go to bed?'

The bedroom below decks was small, low-ceilinged, and a little claustrophobic. While Nick was in the bathroom — not much more than a cupboard with a basin and a jug of water — Florence changed into her nightdress. She sat on the edge of the bed, also narrow, and tried not to think of anything in particular. It was inevitable, however, that her mind would wheel back through time to her only other night with a man, the one she'd met in Calcutta. He'd taken her to the cinema and then to a restaurant and then back to his leave apartment, where he'd been quite insistent, though if she had had the willpower or the wish to do so, she could have resisted him in the end. But, what with the war and the sense of futility and impermanence that surrounded her every day, she had decided to seize upon the moment as some way of escaping the sadness that she could never seem to shake. The experience hadn't been awful, and she'd heard enough from friends at school to know the basics of what would happen. Rather, she just remembered being curious — at one point, he'd told her not to stare so. What she hadn't confronted since then, and even now she was trying not to think about it, was what Nick would think of a bride who had been with another man.

Nick came out of the bathroom and stood for a moment, looking at her. 'What a charming nightdress.'

Florence felt that this wasn't quite a compliment. The sweet nothings and conversational chaff of their outings when they had first met had all but disappeared now. It hadn't taken long, she thought. She should probably give him the impression she was willing, at least.

'Would you like me to take it off?'

'Up to you. I can negotiate around it, if you prefer.'

Even the officer in Calcutta had wanted to see her naked and had been more than appreciative, as she recalled. She decided to let Nick take the lead. She lay back on the bed, and he approached her, hands smoothing paths along her legs and over her breasts, lifting the lace and cotton of her garments. She tried to encourage him. 'Tell me if there's anything you want me to do.'

He paused for a moment. 'I'd rather not have to talk about it, Florence.'

So she lay back again and let him do what he wanted, which didn't seem to have much to do with what she wanted. Afterwards he said nothing about what he had discovered, or if it had been pleasurable or not, or if he was happy or disgusted with his bride. Probably for the best, Florence thought, as she balanced on the available sliver of bed next to her husband.

The sawing of wood began. She listened to it for a while and attempted various positions for her arms — under the pillow, draped off the side of the mattress, placed over her chest. She crossed and uncrossed her legs, but no matter what she tried, the only way she could have been comfortable in that little bed was if she could have wrapped herself around her husband, and he around her. And that seemed highly unlikely.

After two hours of this torture, Florence had had enough. She slipped out from under the sheet, opened the door, and made her way to the second bedroom on the other side of the boat. Within five minutes, she was asleep. In the morning, Nick made no mention of her absence, and so their sleeping habits were arranged. They never slept the whole night in the same bed again.

The two weeks passed slowly for Florence. The boat had been a mistake — rather than encouraging romantic intimacy, it seemed Nick couldn't get far enough away from her, and she began to feel the same.

Still, she tried to make the best of things. Every morning, local merchants would paddle up to them to sell fruit and vegetables or souvenirs. This amused Florence, and she bought several carved wooden elephants of varying sizes over the first few days until Nick told her to stop encouraging them. He would sit and stare out over the water as if these people, holding up their wares, asking for attention with warm smiles and outstretched hands, did not exist.

After breakfast, their rower would encourage them into the *shikara*, and they would tour the lake. There were the ghats where women washed saris and laid them out in colourful tapestries on the bank to dry, then scrubbed down their small children who jumped with shouts and screams into the water to rinse off the suds. Further on, the walls of the City Palace loomed up, providing glimpses of exquisite balconies, cupolas, and turrets, and a hint of the lavish way of life it had hosted for hundreds of years. From waterside temples came the sound of bells and chants and the smell of incense on the air. At the edge of the lake grew water hyacinths, and Florence found herself mesmerised by the plash of the oars and the tugging of the plants as the boat nosed through the greenery studded with purple stars of flowers. Long-necked white ducks came swimming up to them, dabbling in the weed and squabbling over the morsels of food that Florence threw overboard.

On another day, they visited an island and walked in the lush and shady gardens of the Maharana's third pleasure palace. As they strolled along paths lined with hedges of sky-blue plumbago and jazzy sprays of red hibiscus, Florence took Nick's hand, and for a while it seemed some sentiment might exist between them after all.

Chapter Seventeen

AGRA, OCTOBER 1946

They returned to Agra in October after the heat and the rains, and a season in Simla where Nick and the band had a regular residency at the Saturday night club. They also played at the many tea dances that were becoming so popular for the British as a way of stoppering up that dead time between lunch and dinner. It seemed more and more that time needed filling with distraction from what was beginning to feel like a life in danger of extinction.

By now, Florence was becoming accustomed to some of the routines and rhythms of marriage and running a household. When she came back to her father's house, she was expected to take over the duties, keep an eye on the servants and hold dinner parties and entertain the neighbours, too.

All the domestic accounts were recorded in a ledger. Ravi held the daily purse strings until Florence was married. But Nick didn't approve of one of the servants having such an insight into the family finances, so Florence took it on out of a sense of wifely duty. Also recorded in the ledger was the day that Cook left, causing the sort of upheaval in the house that hadn't been seen since Harry and Florence had moved to Delhi in the war.

It happened a week after their return from Simla. Her father was away, working down the line at Jhansi, and the atmosphere in the house had been tense. In Simla, Nick had begun to claim that he could no longer stomach curry and spices every day and had a developed a taste instead for tinned vegetables and fruit, which he said was healthier and much more civilised.

Their first night at home, having arrived in the late afternoon, tired and full of dust and grime from the journey that had taken two days, they finally sat down to dinner, only to discover that Cook had served them his usual chicken curry – that same famous chicken curry he had been making for her father for over twenty years. Nick lifted the lid on the salver and pulled a face of disgust. It was a face that Florence had started to see more frequently, and one that again made her doubt how handsome he actually was.

Nick sent for Cook, who edged into the dining room looking at the floor.

'You'll need to learn to make some different food – more European. We won't be eating this anymore.' Nick pushed the dish away across the table. 'For now, I'll just have an omelette, and tomorrow Mrs Criado will go through the stores with you.'

Florence, who still was not accustomed to her married name, wondered what her father would think of this when he returned. 'But Nick, darling, perhaps we could compromise a little. After all, Papa will want …' She stopped, sensing something wrong. Cook picked up the dish of curry and hurried out of the room. They were alone.

Nick turned to her, and his words were like bullets as he

spoke. 'Do not contradict me in public, Florence. I'm warning you. You do as you are told, and especially in front of the servants.'

They ate the omelette when it arrived, without speaking, and then Nick went straight out on to the veranda with a drink. Florence went to the kitchen to look for Cook. He was sitting on the grass outside, smoking a beedi, while his assistant, a young boy from the village, finished washing up.

'Not to worry, Cook. I'm sure we'll sort this out. We'll go through the food orders and stores tomorrow and see what we can do. All right?'

Cook gave a nod that Florence knew was just out of deference to her but could hide a hundred different thoughts. She left him to finish his smoke.

So the next day, Florence forfeited her morning ride and went straight down to the stores. What was it that she had read in one of her magazines? A good wife should act as a buffer between her husband and any annoyance. Cook opened the door for her, and she entered the dark, cool room, trying to remember the last time she had been in there. Probably when she was a child, hiding in places she wasn't supposed to be.

Cook sat at a small table and opened up a large book. Florence recognised Ravi's handwriting, checking off the amounts of rice or flour or oil that Cook was allocated for the day, indicating what had been bought in the market and from which merchant and how much it cost. Florence thought for a minute, then looked around the shelves.

'Listen, I'll write you a list of all the things that Mr Criado likes and some ideas for dishes for the next couple of weeks. It's all very easy. Then, when Papa returns, I'll speak to him, and we'll come to some arrangement. Would that be all right?'

The nod came again, and Florence hoped that meant she

had managed to smooth things over with him. She took the pen and began to write a list.

In the early evening, she stopped by the kitchen. Cook was there surrounded by a collection of cans. The boy was peeling potatoes, and Florence could smell a chicken roasting. Satisfied instructions were being followed, she went back to the house to wash and change for dinner.

The next day, she took a recipe from a magazine to the kitchen, for fishcakes made from tinned salmon, and explained to Cook what it said. The day after, she suggested chicken rissoles accompanied by tinned peas, and the day after that a stew of lamb and tinned carrots. And like this, they managed to get through almost a week without further arguments in the dining room.

The following night, Florence had asked for roast chicken and potatoes again, confident this was something Cook could quite easily manage on his own. She sat down to dinner feeling refreshed after an especially pleasant bath and wearing a new dress of blue rayon, which accentuated her waist and made her feel a little like Bette Davis. Nick had been rehearsing a new set with the band, preparing for the Christmas season, and seemed in a cheery mood, even asking her opinion, in her father's absence, on which tunes would prove most popular this year.

When the dishes were placed on the table, Florence wasn't even thinking about the food, happy as she was to be enjoying what seemed to be a moment of marital togetherness. Nick lifted the lid, and then she saw that expression again. He slammed his fists on the table and roared for Cook. Florence placed a hand on his arm.

'Whatever is the matter? I asked for roast chicken and potatoes. I thought you liked roast chicken and potatoes.'

But Nick ignored her and sat, drumming his fingers on the table, until Cook shuffled into the room.

'What the hell is this?' Nick thrust the dish across the table towards Cook, who made apologetic noises and looked at the floor. Florence couldn't bear his discomfort. She wondered what on earth was in the dish.

'What is it that's such a problem? Let me see.' She pulled the dish back across the table, ignoring Nick's expression, lifted the lid and looked inside. There lay a roast chicken, with the skin browned and crispy just as he liked it, cut into neat portions. However, the source of the problem sat next to the meat: what seemed to be a large, whole, bright-green pear.

'Has the man absolutely no idea?' Nick banged the table again, and Cook gave Florence a brief glance of appeal. 'Who the hell serves a bloody great pear with a roast dinner? I honestly don't know where Harry found him, but he's a liability. How can we trust him not to serve custard with the roast beef next time we have a dinner party? He clearly knows nothing about proper cuisine.'

Florence, who had been looking at the object that had caused all the trouble, wondered which would be worse: to explain to her husband what it actually was and risk being accused of humiliating him, or to let him continue his rant until Cook finally exploded — a state he seemed to be getting closer to by the second.

'Nick, darling. I think you'll find it's not actually a pear.'

'Of course it's a bloody pear, Florence. I know what a pear looks like.' As he said this, he grabbed her wrist under the table, pinching hard at her skin. Florence froze, looked at him in pain and fear, and after a moment, he let her go.

Florence, shocked and still trying to calm the situation, pretended nothing had happened. She picked up a fork and prodded the offending piece of fruit. 'I know it looks like a pear, darling, but actually, Cook has been rather clever.' With this, she lifted a piece of the pear away — it had a soft and fluffy texture — and put it in her mouth. 'Mashed potato, coloured and moulded, and I think that's a clove for the stalk, that's all. It's very smooth. I'm sure you'll like it. I think Cook just thought it might be amusing.'

Nick sat for a moment, processing this information. A number of expressions crossed his face, like clouds streaming across a sky, and Florence waited to see which would settle.

'Don't stand up for him. It's bloody ridiculous.' Nick threw his napkin on to the table. 'I warn you, Florence. He'll make a laughing stock of us. Something will have to be done.'

He walked out of the room, and Florence could hear the veranda door open. A minute later he yelled for the car, and then a few minutes after that, there was silence. Cook disappeared from the room.

Florence reached for the dish once again and helped herself to a piece of chicken and half of the aberrant potato-pear. She wondered if the something to be done referred to Cook or herself, or them both. When she looked down, she could see the faint marks left by his fingers on the white flesh of her wrist.

The day after the potato incident, Florence rose early for her usual ride but was met by a worried Sita, who stepped into the bedroom after a cautious look around the door. The fact that Florence and Nick did not sleep the night in the same bed had not been discussed, and the pretence was maintained — a large matrimonial bed had replaced Florence's schoolgirl cot, and Nick's room was still referred to as the guest room.

Sita tugged at Florence's sleeve.

'You have to come. There's a problem.'

Florence, who hadn't had her tea, and as a consequence was still feeling sleepy, followed Sita downstairs and outside to the kitchen. The room was quiet, save for the small boy, who was attempting to stir a pot of something on the stove, even if he wasn't tall enough to see the contents inside.

Florence looked around. 'Where's Cook? He's usually here by now, isn't he?'

Sita took the ends of her dupatta and began to wind them round her hands, a sign Florence knew well.

'He has gone. He is not coming here anymore. Last night, he and Shireen took all their things and went. What are we going to do? Mr Nick will be so angry.'

Florence thought for a moment. Not only would Nick be angry, but there was her father, too. He was supposed to be returning home by the end of the month and would not be at all happy to discover that his cook of twenty years had left, insulted and upset, after just one week of Florence's household management. No, she would have to get Cook back, and that would entail going to his family's house on the other side of the city and thinking of some way of placating him.

Her head throbbed. She wasn't accustomed to dealing with these sorts of complications, let alone so early in the morning.

First things first, she would have to sort breakfast and then suggest to Nick that they have dinner at the Club that night. Perhaps by the next day everything could be back to normal. She went to the stove and looked in the pot. A glutinous porridge was starting to burn around the edges, despite the boy's efforts. He gazed up at her, and she took the spoon gently from his hand and asked him to fetch some milk and sugar and the bread for some toast. He ran off to the stores, and Florence got on with the task of preparing her husband's breakfast.

It turned out, she needn't have worried. When the bell rang, and she sat waiting for him at the table, nobody appeared. After ten minutes, having eaten a little toast and porridge herself — she was quite pleased with the result of her efforts — she went to his room to see what was delaying him.

She opened the door on to a still-darkened room. The curtains were closed, but when she opened them and looked around, she realised that the bed had not been slept in. It appeared he had not come home.

* * *

Florence kicked Oscar's sides and urged him into a gallop. Perhaps she could fool herself that this surge of emotion was down to speed and motion, but she had to slow down after a while, out of pity for the animal, and then she could no longer hide her upset. Without any conscious decision, she found herself heading past the Taj to the field where the circus had remained all summer, held up first by lack of permits in Poona, where Ester and Andreas had intended to perform next, and then by the reports of violence in the countryside that made them reluctant to move the troupe of staff and animals. It was the first time Florence had been there since her return.

She rode into the field and over to the big top, tethered Oscar to a post, and slipped through an entrance in the canvas. Inside was warm with the animal smell of sawdust and straw. Coloured lamps on a rig above cast circles of violet, yellow, and pink across the arena. When her eyes were accustomed to the light, she saw a familiar figure hanging from a pair of silk ropes, contorting into a series of unfamiliar shapes. Florence picked her way across the sawdust and waited until Ester unfolded herself and stood upright.

'Don't let me interrupt you, knotting yourself up like that. Reminds me — I must finish that jumper I was knitting.'

'Florence! What a lovely surprise.'

They had not seen each other for over three months, when Ester and Andreas had come up to the hills for a brief respite from the heat and humidity. At that point, Florence had still been trying to establish what the rules of a marriage might be and, anyway, there had been little opportunity to actually talk, with most of the time taken up by parties and dances and picnics by moonlight. She realised now how much she had missed Ester.

'No luck with the permits then?'

'It's not just the permits. Look at Noakhali. Look at Bihar. Ambushes, riots, attacks, massacres. Moslems versus Hindus, and everyone against the Brits. I think we'll be stopping here a while yet.'

Florence pushed the bloody events that Ester had mentioned to the back of her mind. She couldn't imagine that sort of thing happening in Agra. She knew it was selfish, but she was glad Ester was staying. It might just ameliorate whatever else was happening. She watched as Ester began to stretch and twist herself into a human tangle again.

'Is this the act, or just the warm up?'

'Bit of both, really. Feels fantastic and helps with the trapeze and the cannon. Strength and flexibility. But you were a dancer — you know how it is.'

Florence thought about her years of ballet training, all her father's hopes and money for nothing. 'I used to quite like the exercises, but Madame was ever so strict. She thought my arms were ugly — used to smack them into place when I got it wrong, which was every lesson.'

For a while there was quiet as Florence, sitting on the wall of the arena, thought about how she had disappointed her father and why he couldn't have appreciated her aptitude for numbers or been happy that she had shown so much interest in his work. And now it seemed she was all set to be a disappointment in her marriage, too.

Her troubles must have traced lines across her face, because Ester stopped what she was doing.

'Penny for them, dearie?'

Florence remained silent for a moment. What could she say? Ester was Nick's sister, after all, and it was Florence's job to be a good wife, to look after him, do what was expected. Nobody had forced her to marry him, and if it had been a mistake — well, it was too late now.

'Oh, no, nothing really. Problems with the household. Cook has abandoned us. I'm afraid my management skills aren't up to much.'

'How did that happen?'

'Differences of opinion, let's say.'

'I hope little brother is behaving himself.'

Florence didn't reply, even though she so much wanted to tell her everything. But that would be betrayal. And she wasn't there, yet.

Ester lounged for a moment against the edge of the net that floated above the floor of the arena and then grabbed Florence's hand. 'Try the trapeze.'

'What? No, I couldn't possibly.'

'Of course you can. Ballet dancing, horse riding — why not the trapeze? I think a good swing would do you the world of good. Make you forget all about Cook for a while. And anything else, come to that.'

Ester took Florence over to a fixed bar so she could test out how to support her weight then try hanging by the legs with the bar tucked into the backs of her knees. From here, she found it easy to pull herself back up to sit on the bar.

Finally, she practised locking her arms as she hung so it was easier to keep her grip and swing her legs. None of it was difficult, and Ester was very encouraging.

'I knew you'd be a natural. You got the sequence first time.'

They practised until the series of moves became automatic. Then Ester looked up at the platform overhead. 'Fancy trying it up there now? There's a harness, don't worry.'

Florence tilted her head back. A skeletal, metal ladder led up, up, up into the roof of the big tent. 'How high is it, out of interest?'

'Oh, about fifty feet. How are you with heights?'

Florence had no idea how she was with heights — she had rarely, if ever, had the chance to find out. 'I like being up in the hills, if that counts.'

Ester was attaching a rope to a harness and held it out for Florence to step in. She laughed. 'Not exactly the same thing, but there's only one way to find out.'

Florence followed Ester up the ladder. It shuddered and fidgeted beneath her hands and feet as she grasped the thin, cold rungs. *Probably best not to look down at this point,* she thought, as the roof of the tent drew closer. Better to wait until she had her feet on the platform before finding out if she did have a head for heights or not. Speed, she was fine with. There was nothing better than putting her foot down on the pedal when she was driving the car and charging along. She'd been reprimanded more than once during her service for doing exactly that — there'd also been the time when she'd not seen that boulder in the road and put a hole in the chassis. She'd been put on canteen duty for a month.

The ladder stopped twitching as Ester stepped on to the platform, holding out a hand a few moments later to steady Florence as she did the same. The platform seemed small for the two of them — an intimate place over a plunging absence.

Florence looked steadily into Ester's eyes and then, counting silently to three, forced her gaze down. The arena, with its coloured rings of light blossoming across the sawdust, shimmered into vision.

'Nothing can happen. You're very well strapped in. And there's the net. It's all in the mind, you know.' Ester gave the harness one final check. Outside somewhere, an elephant trumpeted, brief and discordant.

Despite the harness, and despite the net, and despite the fact she knew she was as safe as she had been on the ground, Florence still felt the fear that started in her stomach and then flooded into her legs and arms. She felt weak and shaky as she prepared to grip the bar.

'Just turn off your brain, Florence, and let your body do the rest.'

Turn off her brain. Now that was something she knew how to do very well these days. Don't think, don't feel, just take yourself somewhere else inside. Or outside. Outside yourself, your body, your situation. Let it happen.

She heard Ester give the command *ready,* and she bent her legs and pushed her hips forward, *steady,* and she pushed her weight back and extended her arms and legs, *hup* – and she kicked herself out into the air.

Momentum and timing. Breathe in and breathe out. Legs forward, legs back.

The walls of the tent and the lights above moved in a blur while she let unseen forces push and pull her, push and pull, like a lullaby, like rocking in a mother's arms, *rock-a-bye baby, in the tree top... and down will come baby.* But the bough did not break, and she did not fall. Just gave herself over to the release, and the freedom of aiming high.

After, she stood on the ground, and her body felt electrified, sparks flickering in muscles, tendons, ligaments, jolting through her cells and jumping across synapses. She had the sensation that if she looked closely, perhaps she would see tiny flames of pleasure and vitality dancing on her skin.

* * *

The ledger squatted on the table between them, the edges of its pages browned and consumed with use. Opposite, sat Ravi, these days a quiet and impassive presence around the house. Florence remembered him differently. Of course, he had been younger then — but once he had loved to canter her round the garden on his shoulders, or impersonate an elephant plodding along while she rode on his back.

Now he had grown silent, though devoted as ever to her father. Over the years, he had seen other staff come and go and, she had discovered, had slowly taken over the running of the house, managing the kitchen, the stores, the purchasing of goods, and keeping an eye on the amounts of oil and sugar and rice that Cook siphoned off as an extra little commission for his troubles.

Cook had returned, thank goodness. The visit to his small home, the gifts for his family, and above all the frank conversation with Shireen about their situation if he didn't find another job, had been a success. The next day Cook had reappeared, and nothing more was said.

Still, from this moment, Florence had decided, if she were to fulfil the duty she had signed up for — the formation of a home — then she needed to keep a closer eye on things, or at least create some semblance that this was happening. Nick, who had also reappeared, and about whose absence nothing was said either, delivered a lecture comparing Florence to a monarch who needed to rule her subjects and keep control of her kingdom. Florence had nodded and given the impression she was in agreement with this vision of monocracy, but it was not at all the way she really intended to take care of things on the domestic front. It would require a delicate subterfuge – enough to give Nick the impression she was taking these regal duties seriously, while in reality letting the people who had looked after her and her father for so many years get on with their jobs as they knew best.

So now she made a daily show of picking up the large bunch of house keys, perhaps when she left Nick's bed (for she had not given up on the physical side of her marriage and found, if she crept under his sheets in the hour before dawn and lay next to him in his blurred dream-state, he responded willingly and to their common satisfaction). As the light of the morning sun slanted through the cracks in the shutters, she descended the stairs with a percussive clinking of these symbols of authority in her hand to greet the other members of the household.

This morning, Florence sat and turned the pages of the ledger, scanning down the columns filled with Ravi's neat handwriting, a meticulous recording of every bag of flour, sack of rice, and tin of sardines that had made its way from the bazaar to the storeroom shelves. There was chicken and mutton from the butcher; potatoes and squash from the market; candles, matches and soap from the general store – all the precise quantities noted down together with price and date. She continued to examine these chronicles of their daily lives, the numbers adding and balancing in rapid succession in her mind's eye until, coming to the entries for the past week, she noticed an amount of tinned truffles and caviar – even foie gras – present on the list, alongside a crate of champagne. She tapped a finger on the page and sent an enquiring glance across the table to Ravi.

'This all looks a bit luxurious, Ravi. It's not Christmas yet.'

Florence had the distinct impression that Ravi disapproved of her sitting there, doing this job, asking him these questions. He remained silent for a while longer, as if struggling with the ethics of what he was going to say. Then he appeared to make his decision.

'Mr Criado, Madam. He insisted we have these in the storeroom, in case of guests.'

'Oh, yes of course. That's fine then.'

Florence kept looking at the page. What bloody guests? Papa had always put on a good party for a special occasion, but lavish dinners had never been their thing at all. And there had to be some limit to their finances. She was sure the band's weekly engagements at the Club didn't pay enough for the regular consumption of foie gras and Moët & Chandon.

She closed the ledger and passed it to Ravi. 'Thank you. Keep up the good work.' Then she picked up the keys and allowed him to leave before locking the storeroom door behind her.

Back in her room, Florence picked up her hairbrush and began to stroke the tangles of her curls, trying to soothe herself and chase away the questions and doubts that buzzed around her mind. It was no good.

She threw the brush down and turned to look out of the window, defeated in her chair. A sunbird hovered in the tree below, searching the blooms for nectar, swinging from branch to slender branch. Watching it move, Florence thought again of the circus, the sense of ease she felt there. The trapeze not only made her feel strong and in control, but it fascinated her, too. The forces in play, the pure physics of it. It was maths and science and engineering all in one, and she felt herself part of a beautiful equation.

She imagined herself again, a mass accelerating, increasing in velocity from the moment she launched from the board –

gravity exerting its rule on her — through a perfect arc to the peak of the swing, and thought of that purest of moments, where gravity seemed to disappear, before the descent into freefall. And as she pictured herself as this pendulum, full of potential energy, kinetic and dynamic, she began to find a way back to herself again, despite the problems with Nick, and despite all the loss and pain she had buried in her heart.

She needed the circus, and she wouldn't give it up, not for anyone. It was the one place she felt understood. Where she felt supported by forces greater, more important, than she could really comprehend.

Thinking of all this, Florence sat up straighter, pulled her shoulders back, and took several slow breaths. Her husband, her father, their domestic situation — she wasn't going to let them turn her into someone she had never wanted to be. Jay would have understood, she felt sure.

* * *

On Saturdays, her father would take his paper into the garden after breakfast and sit in the shade with a pot of chai, which Cook's boy would replenish at frequent intervals. It was the end of November, and overhead, bee-eaters whirled and swooped like gold and green paper kites, drawn to the little lake nearby that had not yet dried up after the rains. Not that Papa would have noticed anything, Florence thought as she walked down the path, so taken was he with the news these days.

As she approached him, he gave a sharp laugh and shook his head, and she heard him mutter the words *Pakistan!* and *Resolution!* as if someone had told him a bad joke.

Florence sat down and waited, knowing it was best not to interrupt him when he was reading. After some minutes he registered her presence and lowered the paper, looking at her over the top of his spectacles. 'This is not going to end well, mark my words.'

Florence was so preoccupied with the problems she needed to resolve, that she thought for a moment he was referring to the conversation she had been determined to have with him, ever since both the tailor and the owner of the general store had arrived at the house last week brandishing bills for enormous amounts of money and demanding that somebody pay them.

'I mean, I'm all for self-rule, can't argue with that. But after Calcutta, Noakhali, Bihar ... I can't see this two-nation folly ending in anything other than mass slaughter. We might as well still be at bloody war.'

He snapped the paper taut and wide with a sharp crack, then folded it into four and lay it down. Florence waited until the frown cleared from his brow, and he finally seemed to notice she was there.

'What do you want anyway? Aren't you usually out and about on that nag of yours at this time?'

Florence marshalled her thoughts, sat forward in the chair, and fixed her father with a serious eye. 'Papa, you know I'm managing the house now, the stores, the kitchen, the accounts.'

'Oh yes. Right up your street, I imagine, all those numbers.'

'Well, yes. I mean, the numbers side of things is fine.'

'Jolly good. Never interested me much, have to say. Ravi's been looking after it for years. You should talk to him.'

'I know, I have. I'm sure Ravi has done a wonderful job of things. But it's a little more complicated now, with the three of us here.'

'I don't see why. One extra person, that's all.'

Perhaps she was being too vague. If she wanted to penetrate her father's lassitude regarding the household expenditure, she probably needed to be more direct.

'Papa, I need to know our financial state. I need to know how much money is coming in. Who earns what, who pays what. How much are you supporting us? Are you giving Nick money as well as what he makes from the band? If I'm going to do this properly, you need to tell me.'

Her father looked bored. 'Trust you to make such a meal of things, Florence. Ravi just got on with it. Ask him.'

'Ravi is too discreet, for one thing, and for another, he doesn't have any control over Nick.'

'Of course he doesn't. That's your job. You're the wife.'

Florence let this comment fall to the ground without examining it too closely. She mustn't lose sight of her intent. Perhaps if her father had a less rosy view of his new son-in-law, he might be more forthcoming. 'I'm a bit worried about Nick, actually. It's as if he thinks we have the Viceroy over for dinner every week and that the stores need to be stocked accordingly. You should see the jars of caviar, truffles, foie gras.'

'So he's developed a taste for a few fine foods. Let him enjoy it. Anyway, we're coming up to Christmas. We'll use it then.'

Clearly, the money and extravagance was of no interest to her father. Really, she should have known this was not the approach to take. Florence felt a renewed respect for Ravi and the years he had managed to keep the household running so smoothly. Her father was, on the other hand, completely irresponsible on the domestic front. Still, he always claimed to be an artist, so perhaps she could appeal to his other sensibilities.

'It's not just the food and the money.' She waited, hoping her hesitation might build the drama, emphasise the distressing nature of what she was about to say. 'He goes off, at night, and I've no idea where. Sometimes he doesn't come home. Can't you talk to him?'

Her father remained quiet for a moment. No doubt this last, this insult to his daughter's honour, had given him pause for thought. She knew how much Nick wanted her father's approval — and, so it seemed, the handouts of money that came with it. If Papa even hinted that he knew about these nocturnal activities and would censure any potential discourtesy to his daughter, she was sure it would bring Nick into line. And then Nick would have to listen to her about the house, the accounts, and everything else that he seemed to be intent on ruining.

'Talk to him? Let me tell you, Florence, that your marriage is none of my concern now. If you can't keep your husband at home at night and in your bed, then that's your problem. Perhaps if you were a bit more supportive, showed some interest in his music, and made a bit more of an effort to look attractive, he might not feel he has to go elsewhere.'

Florence began to feel as if she were moving away backwards down a long tunnel, with her father at one end continuing to lament her many inadequacies as a wife and daughter. As the tirade continued, she tried to take herself elsewhere, but his words echoed and bounced around her skull, and there was nowhere to hide from what she now realised was the truth of her situation.

'Honestly. I gave you every opportunity to be something special, but what did you want to do? Work in my bloody office and talk about trains every day. And what did you end up doing in the war? Driving a bloody truck. Well perhaps, just perhaps, you could manage to make a success of your marriage instead. You have a handsome, talented husband. An artist — you should be so lucky — so hold on to him. And if there's a problem in your marriage, you need to bloody well sort it out. You are no longer my responsibility, thank God.'

Having finished what he had to say, her father picked up his paper and stomped off into the house.

Florence remained, determined not to let the tears spill out as the truth finally penetrated — she was truly on her own.

Chapter Eighteen

AGRA, NOVEMBER 1946

Well, not entirely on her own. Sita was still there, trying to keep an eye on her, even though Nick let it be known that her presence irritated him. Florence was well aware that Sita waited until he left the house before she would knock on Florence's door or enter the salon to ask how the day was going. Sita never asked why the couple did not share a bed at night, and Florence did not want to discuss it. She hoped Sita would assume it was something to do with a British sense of propriety, and well, why not, when they had so many rooms in the house.

This afternoon, not wanting to be around either her father or Nick when they came back in the evening, Florence had agreed to go with Sita to visit Shireen, who had recently moved with her new baby to live with Cook's family in the town. As they set off, later than they had intended, she could see how happy Sita was at the prospect of being able to hold the baby again — it wasn't the first time she had gone to see the infant. Florence, still slightly put out by Shireen's open distaste for British rule, had avoided visiting until now. Still, she knew she should be a good *memsahib* and take a gift and enquire after everyone's well-being.

When they arrived, Shireen had seemed pleased to be able to hand her child over to somebody else for a while. They drank tea, and Sita rocked him and hummed a song. Out of the window, Florence could see across the street into the bazaar. Shadows were creeping up the walls opposite and people were bringing out lamps in preparation for the night.

Sita smiled across the room at Florence. 'I hope soon you will have a child. I think this is what will make you happy. And perhaps make your husband fall in love with you.'

'Is that all you can think about?' Being a mother had not dulled Shireen's edge. If anything, she seemed even angrier at the reports of fighting, destruction of villages, and mass violence that seemed to pour from the radio these days. 'Think instead what we are bringing these children into.' Shireen paused, as if remembering who was there, and her tone softened. 'I am sorry. Thank you, both, for coming to see me and little Hasib. And for the gifts. It's just ... it's driving me crazy sometimes here, with my mother-in-law, and now there is talk of a curfew, and you never know what is going to happen when you step into the street, how people will speak to you. You know, some of the Hindu shops won't serve us anymore. Here ...' Shireen reached out her arms as Hasib began to cry, and Sita passed him back.

Florence looked out of the window again. 'Perhaps we should go. It will be dark in an hour. Less. I don't think it's wise to walk the road too late.'

'Yes, you must. But thank you again. And forgive me.' Shireen turned to Sita. 'Please know that I value your friendship.'

In the street, Florence watched as Sita pulled her shawl

over her head so that it covered her face. 'What are you doing? You don't need to hide.'

Sita pulled another scarf out of her bag and gave it to Florence. 'You should cover your head, too. There is an atmosphere these days. The men, they can be strange. They say things when I pass.'

Florence took the scarf. 'If you say so.' She glanced up at the darkening sky; it was later than she had thought. They walked quickly past the stalls selling bolts of glittering cloth, down the street with pots and pans made of gleaming copper and metal, and turned left into the park where the local evening market was in full effect. Stalls selling stolen junk; stalls selling medicines and promises of cures for any and every ailment; a man sitting under a tree playing a sitar in the criss-cross shadows thrown by the flaming torches and lamps that served to light the path. Smells of hot oil and fried food and spices filled the air.

Sita hurried on in front, taking a shortcut. Florence was thinking about dinner when a man almost walked into her, bumping her shoulder and causing her to stumble. She turned to say something, but he had already moved on. Startled, she realised it was Nick.

What was he doing here, in this market, at this time?

'*Amah*,' she called. 'Wait.'

Sita stopped, and Florence, without considering what she was doing, turned back and followed Nick.

He walked to the end of the market, where the light ran out and the trees and bushes thickened. Florence, aware this was not a good place for her to be, stood by the last stall, pretending to decide which of the sticky sweets she wanted to buy, though the stallholder was not at all interested in her business.

Sita stood beside her now, and Florence indicated where

Nick was smoking by the fence. She could see his face lit faintly by the orange glow of the cigarette. He finished it and threw the end away, then looked up. A young man, his white tunic and pale, baggy trousers luminous in the murk, jumped over the fence and went towards him. They spoke, heads close, words Florence could not hear, and then together they disappeared into the darkness of the park behind them.

'Well, what was all that about?' said Florence. She looked around and suddenly felt uncomfortable, uneasy at where she was at this time, and all she wanted now was to be home.

'We should go. This is no place to be at night,' said Sita. Together they retraced their steps back along the path, following the flickering lights to the exit and stepped into the street.

Florence felt disorientated. 'Which way is the river?'

'Down here.' Sita began to walk down the street to their left, but it seemed to lead away from the crowds.

'This doesn't feel right,' Florence said. She stopped and looked around. It had become a narrow path, low blocks of houses with corrugated iron roofs on either side of her, doors closed, windows darkened. They walked a few more paces then stopped again. From ahead she heard the sound of drums growing louder, pans being struck, a gong being hit. It was moving in their direction, and now she could hear voices, men's voices, chanting and shouting. She grabbed Sita's hand, turned and ran.

They found themselves on the main road near the bazaar, back among the people. Safety in numbers, for now at least. But the sound of that unseen procession in that narrow, dark place, and the sense of threat that she now saw everywhere, left her disturbed, panicked. She stepped into the road and hailed a rickshaw. Sita gave him directions to the house, then they sat back and left the noise and assault of the centre behind, jolting over the stones of the bridge.

'What was that, Sita?'

'Bad people, looking for trouble. We shouldn't go there anymore.'

Then Florence thought again about what she had seen in the market. It wasn't good, whatever it was. 'And Nick?'

Sita remained quiet for a minute. 'Nothing, *beti*. You shouldn't worry about this. You don't need trouble at home.'

The rickshaw rumbled and jerked along. Florence rubbed at a bruise on her arm. Sita was right. No point saying anything to anyone. Her father wasn't interested, and Nick would only get defensive, which was the last thing she wanted. She briefly considered talking to Ester, but a mild sense of shame rose up at the thought of it.

No, whatever it was — gambling, debts, or something else entirely — she had to forget about it. She lay her head on Sita's shoulder and closed her eyes. Out of the dark, another face appeared, looking down at her under the shade of a peepal tree. For once, she let herself be transported back to a time when love had felt like a very different proposition altogether.

Chapter Nineteen

AGRA, MARCH 1947

Florence had developed the habit of shortening her morning ride — the one moment in the day when she was free to roam — so that she could trot over to the circus field to see Ester. And not just to see Ester, but to train with Ester on the trapeze, improving her technique, strengthening her body, and perfecting the timing needed to make a successful catch. This was something for her and her alone, the feeling of bliss as she launched herself into the void, the childish delight squirming in the pit of her stomach as she arched and flipped through the air.

It was also a time and place where the anxiety and boredom she felt at home, the petty frustrations — and the significant — could be put to one side as she enjoyed a drink after their workout, with Ester pouring the tea and offering biscuits, or sometimes they helped Andreas groom the horses. Andreas, despite his dour countenance, seemed to approve of Florence and had commented more than once that she was one of the fastest learners he had seen. He joked one day that she could join the troupe any time she wished, and that's how she came to her first small rebellion, her first act of defiance in the face of the life she now lived at home.

Nick would certainly not approve, would have been incensed to see it, but he was so involved with the band — and whatever he did on his covert trips into town — that it was easy to keep it a secret from him. Her father, on the other hand, so easily impressed by any kind of performance, might finally have given his approbation to something she had done. And so — bloody-minded — she made sure he knew nothing about it.

In the event, it was easy. The costume and make-up were so elaborate that no one would recognise her, and when she tumbled out of the roof of the tent on silken streamers alongside nine other acrobats to the whistles and applause of the audience, there was anonymity in numbers.

More and more, she began to feel that this was the only place she could be herself, or forget herself — she still wasn't sure which it was. Being with Ester gave her some sense of belonging and alleviated the loneliness, and the fear, that otherwise filled her days.

Still, she had to be careful, and Ester had sharp eyes and a sharp understanding. Ester also had an allegiance to Nick, a sibling bond that couldn't be broken, and Florence was afraid if the truth came out it might ruin everything.

But Florence should have given Ester more credit. After all, she had colluded in Florence's secret performance, had encouraged her first insurrection, and dismissed Nick's contempt of the circus and everything associated with it.

* * *

A few days after her first public appearance in the big top, Florence finished her usual morning practice and gathered up her clothes to change for the ride home. Ester had gone to fetch water and, as there was nobody else in the small changing area behind the arena, Florence stripped to her underwear and quickly stepped into her jodhpurs. She was just buttoning her shirt when she realised Ester was standing in the entrance. She knew by the look on her face that she had seen.

'What's that, Florence, over your back and shoulders?'

Florence felt a flush of shame, but she continued to fasten her buttons as if there was nothing unusual.

'Did it the other day, fell off the horse. Just a couple of bruises is all.'

'Really? You never mentioned it. That's a lot of bruises. Did he run over you? Horses don't normally do that.'

Florence sat on a chair and pulled her boots on. The space around them was small, and the air was clammy.

Ester began again. 'Are you sure it was a fall? I've never seen anything like that from a riding accident.'

'Of course I'm sure. What else would it be?'

This last hung in the air, and Ester gazed at her with a troubled expression.

'Please, Florence. Tell me it's not Nick.' Ester walked up close and waited. 'Tell me it's not him. Because, God knows, I've had nightmares about this. I know what he's like. I'm the one person who understands. You can talk to me.'

There was a long silence now. Eventually, Ester sat down by Florence's feet, by her riding boots with their coating of dust and crust of manure on the heel. Florence stared into her lap, noting a green streak of horse slobber on one of her thighs, dirtying the cream cotton of her jodhpurs. She couldn't get her thoughts in focus. All she knew was that if she said it out loud, whatever needed to be said, then everything changed.

If she continued to keep the words hidden, then it could still be ignored. Speaking them would mean setting things in motion, and while she understood, really, that something needed to happen, she wasn't sure she could face the process. Still, the words began, each one a step towards a looking glass in which she could see only her humiliation and abasement.

'A couple of days ago, a man showed up at the house. I'd never seen him before, but he was screaming that Nick owed him money, and he wouldn't leave until someone paid him. He had a handful of chits for some very large sums with Nick's signature on. I have no idea what it was for, but he wasn't the most salubrious type I've ever met. And this is on top of the tailor, and the general store, and the catalogue. Ester, you would not believe the debts he's run up since we've been married.'

Florence faltered, and dead air hung around them. Ester remained anchored at her feet, as if she knew that any disturbance might send Florence into flight, while Florence again considered a retreat from the mirror. Did she really want to see herself like this? She could choose not to tell, choose to have a story without this dreary, sordid disgrace. Hers could be a tale of happiness and contentment, love and success. *Truth is a secret, keep it close,* her pride whispered. But Ester continued to sit and wait, and the silence pressed down so heavily upon them that Florence felt compelled to speak again.

'Papa is hopeless. I don't know why I thought talking to him would help. After all, he let Ravi run the household for years. I think Papa believes all that sort of detail – accounts, money stuff – is beneath him. Anyway, he made it very clear that he has washed his hands of me, as far as any kind of advice or help about my marriage goes, so the only thing I could do was try to talk to Nick myself. As Papa said, I'm the wife. That's my job.'

Ester frowned, and Florence felt the words dry up. Whatever way you looked at it, it was shameful. Either she wasn't adult enough, or strong enough, or intelligent enough to be able to have a rational conversation with her own husband about money, or she had chosen to live the rest of her life with a man who could not be reasoned with and whose response to any difference of opinion ranged on a scale from childish temper tantrums to outright fury.

'Let me tell you about Nick when he was a little boy.' It seemed Ester had a sense of Florence's shame and wanted to alleviate it, and Florence was grateful. 'I remember times when Mother would hold him in her arms for hours while he screamed and screamed, because he didn't want to go to bed, or he had to tidy up his toys, or eat a certain vegetable. Four years old, and he would hit her and kick her and yell until he vomited. Father couldn't bear it — he usually left the room, if not the house. Of course, he himself had a vile temper, too, on occasion. Mother would just continue to carry Nick around, telling him she understood, telling him she loved him, while the rest of us had entire afternoons, evenings, and nights disrupted. A few years later, when we were left to play together, he would fly into such rages if I didn't do as he wanted, punching me, taking running kicks at my shins, or tearing at my hair. But I was older, and he was the baby of the house, and so it was more or less indulged as childhood caprice. As we entered adolescence, the incidents were fewer, but now there was a nastiness to his character that would stay hidden for months and then, for no reason that I could understand, would begin to seep out: threatening conversations, pushing me up against my bedroom wall, telling me what I could and couldn't do as his sister and as a member of the family. A few times he slapped me. Once, he nearly pushed me through a window. I had bruises on my lower arms where he would pinch me under the dinner table if he thought I was behaving in a way he didn't approve of, usually in front of other men. And he had a paranoia about being laughed at — he hated people making any kind of joke at his expense.'

Florence absorbed this information in a fog. Why hadn't Ester ever told her this before? Perhaps she could have mentioned it before she married the man. Then again, was it anything that Florence hadn't really been aware of during her brief courtship with Nick? His aptitude for stinging barbs aimed directly at her weaknesses yet all disguised under the cloak of his easy, public compliments.

And if Ester had divulged this previously, would it have made any difference? Florence had chosen to float unthinkingly into her marriage. She had sought out a path along which she could stumble, eyes shut and unaware. She would have reasoned away any hint of difficulty in order to prove she could be as normal as anyone else. But now Ester was taking all that away from her, forcing her to admit that there was horror in the looking glass, and she had to stare it directly in the eye.

'Why didn't you tell me this? Before?'

'You know, the last time I saw him like it, it was years ago. After Mummy and Daddy died, and he was wild with grief. I'd just met Andreas and when I told Nick, he attacked me, verbally and physically. So I left and went to live with Andreas. Nick wouldn't dare to do anything to me then. I thought Nick had changed. When I arrived here, I thought that someone like you would never agree to marry a man like that. There were no signs that I could see, and who was I to ruin my brother's shot at a happy marriage? For all I knew, it was something about our sibling relationship that triggered it inside him. But I'm sorry now that I kept quiet.'

There was silence again until Ester finally prompted her. 'What did he do to you, Florence?'

Oh, the shame. If she said the words out loud, the illusion of herself she had created through her marriage would vanish. And yet she wanted Ester to know – she wanted everyone to know what kind of a man he really was. Far from the movie-idol his good looks led you to believe. Far from the crooning romantic that his audience cheered on stage. She wanted everyone to see the bruises that spread like mould across her back and ribs and know that he had done it, but please, let her tell them she had fallen from her horse. She wanted her dignity, but she wanted to be saved.

'It seems so banal. I asked him about the bills, and he immediately got that look in his eyes. It's like he's playing some sort of villain in a cheap melodrama. I tried to be rational and reasonable, tried to tell him Papa wouldn't stand for it. He began to laugh, and then … then he called me an interfering whore trying to pass herself off as a respectable wife. He said I'd married him under false pretences, and my father knew damn well no one else would have me.' The words were rushing out, and Florence paused for a moment, wondering if she should go on, but somehow it was as if someone else was speaking – as if she was listening to another woman's story. 'By now he has me up against the wall, both arms pinned there, and I shout something savage at him – call him an uneducated thug. And then he throws me to the ground and kicks me, again and again.' A moment's silence, then the voice – her voice – continued. 'After he finished and left, I lay there a while, curled like an infant, wondering if he had broken me. Some time later I stood up, locked the door and had a bath, and then I had dinner with Papa.' There. It was done.

On the ground, Ester leaned against Florence's legs. Now it was Florence's turn to stroke Ester's head.

Ester leaned in, hard. 'I'm so sorry, Florence. I had no idea.'

Florence, having finally spoken out loud the events, given a name to the horror, suddenly felt annoyed by her friend. She pushed Ester away and stood. 'There's nothing to be done. I'll remember not to confront him when we are on our own in future. And Papa will have to pay the bills. It'll be fine.'

Ester, too, stood up. She looked shocked. 'You can't pretend nothing happened. You can't stay with him, always wondering when the next time will be, never able to speak your thoughts or be yourself. Stay with us. Come away with us!'

But Florence still wasn't ready to accept that things wouldn't work out as they were supposed to. Some part of her still thought that it would be all right. She walked to the entrance of the tent, dismissing Ester's concern as she went. 'I can't do that. I don't want that. You shouldn't worry. It's not going to happen again. I can fix this.'

She rode Oscar fast back to the house, hooves kicking up dust in the surprised faces of the people she passed on the road. When she arrived home, she sent Cook's boy out to deliver dinner invitations to the Hansons and a number of other well-to-do friends of Papa, then prepared a menu full of all the luxury foods that were still gathered on the store-room shelves. She informed a surprised Cook that it all needed to be ready for eight o'clock that evening. In the afternoon, she spent a pleasant hour cutting flowers in the garden and arranging them in vases around the dining room and salon.

Later on, she washed and changed, poured herself a large gin, and waited on the veranda for Nick to return from golf and Papa from the office, so she could tell them to expect company for dinner. She'd decided the best thing to do with the vision she'd seen in the looking glass was cover it up with a large, heavy drape.

* * *

With the troubles that had intensified across the country, the local council had denied more permits for the cannon show. When Florence asked, Andreas replied in angry Hungarian, and Ester explained later that numbers for the circus were down; either they needed to move on, or another cannon jump was required to pull in the crowds again. But moving was too risky at that moment.

From Bombay to Bihar, across the Punjab and Bengal, mob violence invaded town and countryside alike. Shouts of 'blood for blood' could still be heard in villages and cities and on the roads at night. There was no safe way to travel with their company of European, Anglo-Indian, Hindu, Sikh, and Muslim staff, and so they stayed on in Agra and paid lower wages and hoped there would be enough left over to buy food for the animals.

Florence had not forgotten the cannon. Ester's flight still soared through her mind from time to time, but more than this was her curiosity at how the damn thing worked. She had her theories, but she wasn't going to be satisfied until she saw what really went on inside. To this end, she assured Andreas that the civil servants would give in eventually — it just needed some special event or celebration that they could offer to perform at, and that was sure to happen soon.

PART III

Chapter Twenty

PORTSMOUTH, 1955

After the events of the day — Robert, the train tracks, the police — Florence thought for a moment that she had finally lost her grip on reality. She stared and stared at the visitor on her doorstep.

'Ester?' she said at last and wondered when the hallucination would dissolve.

The silence was only broken when a small girl also standing on her doorstep spoke up. 'Aren't you going to let us in? We've come all the way from India to see you. We're your lovely surprise.'

They followed her inside. Ester was talking, to cover the silence. 'Your rather sombre Aunt Sarah gave us your address. I can't quite believe you live here — all these little houses and quiet streets. Is everyone always so tucked away behind their front doors? And married to another man, too. Is he home?'

Florence was suddenly horribly aware how small and flimsy the house must seem — the walls and ceilings so thin that every noise could be heard from everywhere. Ester stood in the middle of the living room while Florence pulled up another chair and then pulled up Robert from the sofa to stand beside her.

'This is Robert. He must be about the same age as…'

'Tara,' said Ester.

The two children looked at each other. Ester gave Tara a gentle nudge, and she stepped forward, a little wary of this strange boy with his bandaged leg and dirty, tear-stained face.

Florence turned to Ester again, and now the two women saw each other properly.

'I can't believe you're here.' Florence stepped close and then, finally, embraced her long-lost friend.

Ester held Florence tight. And in Ester's arms, Florence understood many things. The smell of her own unwashed hair, and the sweet taint of stale alcohol on her breath. Her body, gone soft, weak and tired. She knew all she had to give was the clutch of someone who was desperate for love, and a friend.

They sat, and Ester recounted her trip on the boat, how they had looked after the horses and the elephants, and how Andreas was following, once he had sold the other acts, the tents, and the caravans. Florence listened, stunned by this other world so vivid and unexpected inside her sad front room.

Outside it was getting dark. Florence rose from the chair and pulled the curtains, then turned on the lights. She saw now the wallpaper above the window, stained with damp and curling away from the wall, and the dust on the table and shelves. She felt the chill in the room that made it seem unlived in. And unloved.

Tara and Robert, after ten minutes of quiet, mutual observation, were now playing with toy cars in front of the unlit electric fire, with that unguarded ease of the young. Florence watched them, noting their similarities: dark hair falling over dark eyes, the fine, straight nose and full lips.

Degree by degree, Florence felt herself waking up. Now she leant forward in her chair and held Ester's hand. 'Who will you work for?' she asked. 'When Andreas arrives. I don't understand. Will you still be the amazing Flying Lady?'

'I've asked him to sell it. I want to work with the horses now. Nothing else. That cannon — it's become my nightmare.'

'Nightmare? Why?' Although Florence had an idea, for she had suffered the nightmares, too.

'Since Tara's birth, the idea of the cannon has haunted me. I dream of being broken, snapped in half, flipped from the net. The last time I jumped, I saw visions of a body, dragging itself across the floor, reaching out with a twisted hand that melted before my eyes into gleaming bones.' Ester paused and seemed embarrassed by her admission. 'After Independence, we couldn't travel. It was far too dangerous. And by the time it all calmed down, we'd lost our best people. We've tried to keep it going, but this year we realised we'd have to sell it all. And that wasn't easy, either.' Ester paused and glanced around the room. Florence followed her gaze to the set of wooden elephants, marching from left to right across a shelf above the fireplace.

'Aren't those from your father's house?'

Florence nodded. 'One of the few mementoes I allowed myself.' She looked down at her feet, then up again with a wistful smile. 'How I miss it. How I miss it all.' She stopped and frowned. 'I should have kept in touch with him. It's been more than two years, I think.'

Ester took a breath. 'Florence, I have to tell you something. Even after Nick left, we continued to see your father. He stayed on at the station for a year or so, but the change — the new way of everything — it was all too much after a while. He stopped working. And then he became ill. I'm so sorry, Florence …' Ester gripped Florence's hand. 'He died last month. I came here to tell you. And to bring you this.'

Florence took the envelope and unfolded the letter inside. It was from her father's lawyer, giving details of the will. As she read, her eyes filled with tears. Finally she stopped and looked up. 'What happened?'

'Heart failure. I think it was quick, at least.'

Florence placed the letter on the table beside her. 'Well, he did right by me, in the end. And not just me. Ravi and Sita, too.' At this, Florence began to sob.

'Florence, dearie. How an earth has it come to this? This isn't who I expected to find at all. What's happened to the woman who used to ride across the fields under a Rajasthan dawn to practise the trapeze and more?'

Florence shook her head and covered her eyes with her hands. 'I'm a mess, Ester. It's all an absolute mess.'

On the floor, the two children stopped playing. Robert shuffled over to Florence and leaned his head on her legs. After a moment, Tara went to Ester and climbed on to her lap. Ester stroked her daughter's hair. 'Well, dearie, we're here now. And we're here to help. You need to get out. You need something to make you smile. And we have just the thing.'

Florence took her hands from her face, retrieved a handkerchief from her skirt pocket and blew her nose. 'What are you talking about?'

But before Ester could answer, she heard a key in the front door, the sound of boots on the doormat, and then Billy walked into the room. Florence jumped up from her chair and went to him, taking his coat and kissing him on the cheek. 'Billy, this is Ester,' she said, looking anxiously at them all. 'She's come from India. Ester, this is Billy, my husband.'

* * *

Billy was snoring in his chair. Ester and Tara had left an hour before, after a stilted and awkward conversation over a hastily bought fish supper. Billy had not been impressed to find Florence's past had arrived on his doorstep.

She looked down at him, wondering — not for the first time — what she had been thinking when she had decided to marry him. Florence turned out the lights and left him there. Normally she would pour herself a drink, something to send her to sleep, ensuring she wouldn't wake up when he came blundering into bed. But tonight she didn't feel like numbing herself. She wanted to be alone with her thoughts, and the dreadful and marvellous events of the day. Passing Robert's room however, the panic and terror came back to her again. And the guilt.

She pushed the door open wide enough to let the light of the hall lamp fall across his face. His eyes opened. 'Sorry,' she said. 'Did I wake you?' He shook his head, and she sat beside him on the bed. She stroked his forehead, pushing back his soft curls. 'I love you, Robert. I am so sorry for today. Not just today. I'm going to try harder. You do understand how much I love you, don't you?'

Robert nodded and curled up closer to her. 'Tell me about Auntie Ester. Tell me the story about the cannon again.'

Florence lay down next to him and tugged the cover over them both. He was such a forgiving little boy, and such a sweet thing, asking about Ester and wanting to know about their past. How lucky she was to have him. A ferocious love rose inside her. She would never let anything like today ever happen to him again. 'Okay, darling. This is your Auntie Ester's story.' She pulled him closer to her.

'The circus had been in town all season, and Ester, a beautiful young woman, had often seen the horses exercised along the soft, palm-lined sands of the beach, and the elephants, slick as wet tyres, bathing in the river. Andreas — he of The Great Gombar fame — was a stocky, blond Hungarian with eyes that scanned you like a searchlight across prison grounds.'

Robert looked serious as he considered what this meant. She continued touching his forehead until his eyelids drooped.

'He galloped past her on his dappled steed, kicking up spray from the waves as they hissed and foamed and expired on the shoreline around her feet, and she — angered the first time and amused thereafter — would laugh and wave until one day he slowed his horse, jumped down beside her and asked her name.'

Robert smiled at her. 'You like horses, don't you, Mummy?'

Florence nodded and, carried away in her imagination to the beach next to Ester and Andreas, continued.

'Unfortunately, her brother was a violent, jealous man and when their parents' car crashed over the edge of the road, down the hillside, tearing a swathe through the green velvet of the tea bushes, Ester knew she could not stay with him.'

Florence stopped, aware that Robert was gripping her hand, eyes open again, anxious. 'Oh, don't worry, darling.' She slipped back into telling the story. 'The next time she went home, it was to pack a few belongings into her bag while Andreas guarded the door. Her brother arrived just as they were leaving, and, for a moment, the two men faced up to each other on the path, and she knew then that she was safe.'

Robert yawned and closed his eyes again. Oh, how he looked like Nick. But there was something of her own father, too, in the dimple on his chin and the line of his brow. His breathing slowed, but Florence kept talking, quieter and quieter, telling the story now for herself, a fairy tale for a girl who had never wanted to be a princess.

'The two of them made an unusual couple. Ester was tall and slender, with her father's sleek black hair, full lips, and dark eyes; her mother's fine nose; and the height that came from her Scottish ancestors. Andreas was a muscular little gnome in comparison. However, he gazed upon her adoringly, followed her as she walked from tent to tent and caravan to caravan to discover her new world. Everyone from everywhere – here there was no division, no partition, and no one was untouchable.' She looked down. Robert's mouth had fallen open slightly, and his breath was steady and even. But Florence continued, lost in the world she was rebuilding for herself with her words.

'The next day he asked her into his office. He pulled a roll of paper from a large cardboard tube, unfurled it across his desk, lit a cigarette, and sat back in his chair, giving her that searching look once more. Ester studied the plans in front of her, what looked like the designs for a large weapon. What this had to do with the circus, she couldn't fathom.

'"It looks like a cannon," she said. "Why are you designing a cannon?"

'Andreas stood up and came round to her side of the desk. "It is a cannon. But it is not a weapon. This," he said, dropping cigarette ash all over the paper, "this is why I am truly the Great Gombar."

'"A human cannonball!" Ester could hardly believe it. She had thought he was just a Master of Ceremonies, an overseer of elephants and acrobats – and that would have been enough for her. But this was something else indeed. The next day, he asked her to marry him.'

Florence's own eyes were closing now, and the story wove

itself into her exhaustion, as the details of her own life, and Ester's melded into one.

'First, she mastered the trapeze. There was a practice bar where she learned to support her weight, hanging by her knees and with her back perfectly arched. It was easy to pull herself back up, and locking her arms as she hung seemed natural to her. Then again, she'd always been an athlete, running rings round the other girls on the lacrosse field at the expensive boarding school her mother had insisted she attend. Not that she had ever really belonged. Not like the circus, where her mixed blood was no more unusual than a piebald pony. After a week of training, Andreas nodded in approval and then pointed up into the roof of the tent. "You have the sequence. Now try up there."

'Up on the tiny platform that shuddered and swayed with the least movement, she willed herself to look down. The net seemed far away and far too flimsy to provide much in the way of safety. A member of the troupe stepped on to the platform beside her, placed the bar into her hands, and steadied her with his hands on her shoulders. From below, she heard Andreas shout. "It's all in the mind. Turn off your mind."

'After, Andreas took her in his arms and kissed her until she didn't know what was happening ...'

Florence's head sank back on the pillow next to Robert, but it wasn't Andreas kissing Ester that she saw as her dreams crept up on her — it was Jay under the branches of a peepal tree, holding her, telling her he loved her. And finally she felt her resolve, her vigour, her appetite for life return.

* * *

Sundays were for cooking the huge lunch that Billy expected, and then he might stomp about in the garden for a while before settling into his chair with a rum and the paper. Florence distracted herself by helping Robert with his homework, the two of them in the kitchen repeating times tables over and over, inventing songs for each one, then seeing if they could say them backwards without mistake. As Sunday afternoons went, it hadn't been a bad one.

She had to wait until Monday, when Billy had gone to work, whistling down the street on his bicycle, before she could see Ester again. She left the house with Robert and told him she would see him to school and back for the next week or so — just until she was sure those boys weren't coming to get him again. When she had walked him up to the school gate and waved him inside, she returned to the roadside and waited for the number twelve to take her all the way to the sea front.

The bus stopped at Clarence Pier and she began walking along the esplanade. The gates to the funfair were closed, shutters drawn down on the windows beneath garish signs in yellow, blue, and red for sweets and shellfish and ice cream. Behind the roofs of the buildings, she could see the twisting top of the helter-skelter, and the rollercoaster, still and silent. Next to them, the giant spokes of the big wheel remained motionless. Florence picked up her pace. There was a cold breeze that lifted her hair from her neck and insinuated itself inside the collar of her jacket. She didn't mind; the chill made her feel awake in a way she hadn't felt in a long time. To her right, the sea threw itself on to the pebbles of the beach with a constant suck and clash, and she took deep breaths of the stinging, salty air.

* * *

The sign for the Royal Southsea Hotel was new: fresh black paint on a bright white background. It only served to highlight the shabby stucco exterior, patched like a map of the world in mouldy tones of grey and green. Gulls sat on the windowsills and cawed and chuckled. Southsea common spread out in front, and beyond that a steel-grey sea. The big top — a gaudy, ruby and gold crown — sat on the muddy grass, surrounded by its attendant trucks and caravans and tents. As she entered the hotel, she almost thought she could hear the cough of a tiger, the trumpet of an elephant.

Florence waited in the tiny lobby, smiling at the elderly couples who were making their way back from breakfast. A fishy smell hung around the gloomy room. Kedgeree, was it? Kippers? After another few minutes, the doors to the lift opened, and Ester and Tara stepped out.

'Sorry to keep you waiting. I was just trying to find you something to wear. That,' and here she indicated Florence's clothes, 'is not going to work.'

Florence looked down at her jacket and skirt. She'd thought she looked presentable. 'What's going on?'

But Ester was already heading out the door. 'Come on. We can't keep them waiting. They'll be getting agitated.'

'Who? Why?' said Florence, but Ester and Tara were already outside and crossing the road over to the common.

In the early morning sun, the big top looked a little tired and saggy. Loose canvas flapped around the entrance. Ester swerved left and led them around the side of the tent. Here there were trucks parked and cages on wheels. As they hurried past, a large striped head raised itself and looked around. It yawned and then lay down again. Florence stopped. *A tiger.* Immediately a memory she hadn't dared to revisit for years came back to her with great clarity — a Christmas camp, and another tiger, surrounded by the bloody parts of a dismembered deer, and Jay gazing in wonder. At that moment she heard the shriek of an elephant and for a second wondered if she really had been transported back in time. She stood, transfixed, allowing the past to wash over her.

Then Ester was grabbing her arm. 'I thought we'd lost you,' she said, and Florence returned to the present.

'What's going on? Do you work here? What about Andreas?' Florence could not piece any of this together.

Ester pulled her by the arm, and Tara took her other hand, and together they walked past the cages towards a row of smaller canvas tents just ahead. 'This is Copperfield's Circus. One of the oldest circus families in the world. And now it's run by Dickie Copperfield. We just happened to meet him when he came out to Bombay. He was looking for elephants, and we had them to sell, so …'

'So you're here with the elephants?'

'I helped look after them on the boat, yes. But that's not my act.' Ester stopped outside the row of tents. Tara had already gone on inside. 'Nowadays I travel with these beauties. Come and meet my new dancing horses.'

Florence followed Ester through the canvas flap into the twinkling, twilight world of her dreams. Five palomino Arabians stood with their heads over the partition, eager for attention. Even in the shadows, Florence could see how their coats gleamed like gold. Under the lights they would look spectacular.

Florence walked up to the nearest and offered her hand. The horse blew air down its nose and stamped, then grew still. Florence moved her hand up to its forehead, rubbing the stiff hairs under the snowy forelock. She felt the velvet wobble of its lips and nose, then ran her fingers through its mane, inhaling the sweet and oh-so-familiar smell of hay and sweat. The acid that usually flooded her body, eating away at her guts — and her mind — suddenly seemed sweetened, became mild and something kind. Overwhelmed by sensations, by memories of herself in another world, as if it were an old story she had read a hundred times as a child but then forgotten, she leaned against the animal, wrapped her arms around its neck and cried.

Ester waited, tactful, for a few minutes, then said, 'They need mucking out. And exercising. Don't suppose you'd want to help?' She threw her bag at Florence, who caught it and looked inside. A pair of jodhpurs, boots, and an old checked shirt. 'You can get changed in here,' said Ester picking up a shovel that lay on the ground. 'No one cares. Well, you remember how it is, don't you?'

* * *

They shovelled dung and refilled the buckets and nets, and Ester and Tara fetched the halters. Florence looked at the blisters on her hands, then rolled her shoulders and twisted her head from side to side. She wasn't used to this sort of physical work, and yet, despite the pain, she felt good.

Tara led the way with her favourite, and Florence followed Ester with a horse on each side. Inside the arena there was an atmosphere of focused activity. To one side, jugglers were practising, clubs flying in a blur, while next to them a young boy was learning how to breathe fire. The horses waited patiently by Florence's side while Ester demanded that the ring be cleared. The trapeze artists above pretended not to hear and continued to swing themselves back and forth until Ester threatened to remove the net from under them. In five minutes, the arena was ready. Florence gazed at the acrobats as they descended, twisting and somersaulting down the ropes and ladders, and somewhere inside her own body, her muscle-memory awakened, and she remembered how it felt to move like that.

Florence joined Ester in the centre of the ring, while Tara settled in the front row. Once released, the horses bunched together then, at the first command, curved as one to canter round. As Ester called out, they spun and whirled in perfect synchronicity, like the mechanism of a precious timepiece — shining and precise.

Next, Ester vaulted up on the lead horse and sprang neatly to her feet, swaying in rhythm to his pace. She made it seem effortless. Balanced there, her body looked lithe and strong. Again, Florence felt a desire for movement, for physical expression, stir inside her. As the horses continued, round and round, Ester pirouetted, leapt from the back of one animal to another, and finished with a somersault to the ground. The only sign of exertion was the rising and falling of her chest under her shirt. The horses stopped, turned to her and again, in complete accord, melted to their knees, bowing their heads, before drifting on to their sides. Ester herself lay backwards across them, in a languorous arch, and the whole group stayed in this silent tableau until Florence could contain herself no longer.

'Bravo! Bravo!' She clapped and cheered, and Tara ran across the sawdust to join her.

At the sound of the applause, Ester flipped herself upright on the back of her horse as it stood, then the group did one final lap of the ring before coming to a halt in the centre. Under the lights, a sheen of sweat glistened on her face as she laughed and blew Florence a kiss.

The animals were breathing hard, and Florence held one by the halter, whispering her approval into its ear. Ester slid down to the ground and looked at her. Florence saw how alive her friend was, at one with everything around her, and she wanted that for herself again.

Back in the stables, grooming the horses, Ester unfolded a plan.

'We haven't had the official opening yet. Animals needed to get acclimatised; the poor elephants haven't quite recovered after their time at sea. But Saturday we have the parade. All the way along the prom, down — what's it called? Kings Road and back around to the common. Then it's the opening show. Why don't you ride one of the horses with us?'

Tara, who was hard at work brushing the tail of the horse Florence had walked, stopped what she was doing. 'Ride with me and Ma. It's going to be fun. Everyone will be watching.'

Florence thought about it. She tried to imagine herself in some sequinned outfit, feathers in her hair to match the plumes on the horses, trotting down the promenade, surrounded by elephants and clowns and jugglers and acrobats. And who would be watching? Billy? Aunt Sarah? Robert? She knew at least two of those people would be unimpressed, to say the least.

She put her brush down and leaned against her horse. He bent his neck around towards her and nibbled at her hair. 'I don't know. It's years since I've ridden. I'm not the same person as I was ... then. People change.'

Ester made a sound of exasperation. 'Nonsense. A few years older, but that's it. And riding — it's second nature to you, I know it. Come on, Florrie. Where's the woman who jumped over a rainbow? You can do anything you want.'

Perhaps it was the name: Florrie. Memories of Jay, explaining the workings of an engine, taking her to inspect the boiler of a train then teaching her to drive. Or perhaps it was the mention of her greatest act of daring. The one she'd never been allowed to talk of since. 'Christ, Ester. Do you remember that day? I mean … I can't believe I did it. Did I really do it? It seems like a dream.'

'Dearie, you certainly did do it. And flew like a dream, too.' Ester came closer and waited.

Florence turned to the horse and ran her hands along his back. He shivered and stamped in response. 'I suppose I could give it a go. Get myself back in the saddle, literally. What about this one? I think he likes me.'

Ester laughed. 'Good choice. He's a darling. Does anything you ask.'

Florence put her hands on her hips. 'Okay. Right. I will. I damn well will. What's his name?'

'We call him Mor.'

'Isn't that Hindi for peacock?'

'Yes. He's completely vain. Likes nothing more than being tarted up with jewels and feathers and prancing around in front of a crowd. You'll have a lot of fun with him. Try him out.' Ester disappeared for a moment then returned with his tack and gave him an approving pat on the neck.

Florence led him outside, checked his girth and then, almost without thinking, hopped herself into the saddle. She adjusted the stirrups, gathered the reins, and squeezed him into a walk. Behind her, Ester and Tara clapped and cheered. Florence gave a wave and pushed the horse on into a trot. Within a minute she had left the tents and bustle of the circus behind and was setting out across the common. After another minute, feeling the rhythm, she pushed him on again into a canter. He responded to her touch, and together they sped across the grass, and Florence shouted her joy into the wind.

* * *

Perhaps it was the horses — igniting something long dormant inside her. Rebellion, a new refusal to accept the mediocre, the knowledge that there was so much to do and see, and she wouldn't be confined by the lives and conventions of those around her. Something had changed, and when Billy came home that evening, she greeted him with her coat already on, tying a scarf around her hair in the hallway mirror. 'You'll have to take care of your own dinner,' she said, running a stick of rouge over her lips. 'Robert and I have to go out. There's someone we need to visit.'

'Take care of my own dinner?' Billy squeezed past her into the kitchen. 'What do you mean by that?'

'We'll be back in an hour or so, but if you can't wait, you can go to the pub, or the chippy. Up to you.' She didn't wait to hear his reply. 'Come on, Robbie.'

She couldn't walk too fast — Robert's ankle was still sore. It was the last week of term before the summer holidays, and though she was glad he wouldn't have to see those boys every day at school for a while, she worried what on earth he would do with himself for nearly seven weeks. Then again, if Ester stayed, at least there would be Tara. She knew, however, that it all needed to change, if they were going to do more than just survive the future. And she had started to remember just how to go about making a change. How to throw herself into a challenge and ignore anyone who told her she couldn't do it. Seeing Ester again had brought it all back to her.

At the signal box she hesitated for a moment, wondering if he would be there. Evenings and weekends, he'd said. She thought about calling up but wasn't sure if her voice would reach. Instead she inserted two fingers into her mouth and whistled long and loud.

Robert jumped away from her in shock, hands on his ears. 'Mummy! Stop it.'

But Florence ignored her son and called up instead. 'Haresh?'

A second later a head appeared out of the window. It was him. He looked puzzled for a moment then seemed to realise who she was.

'Can we come up? Or can you come down for a moment?' She hoped she hadn't misjudged the situation.

He frowned. 'I'm not sure it's a good idea, visitors in the box. And I can't leave my post.'

'We have to speak to you, Haresh. You have no idea. You saved Robert's life.'

'What are you talking about?'

'Let me come up, and I can explain. It won't take long.'

She watched him look around. The road was quiet. No cars, no people. She didn't want to get him into trouble, but no one would ever know.

'When's the next train due?'

He checked his watch. 'Oh, not for another half an hour.'

'On Saturday. You saved his life.'

His expression cleared, as if he suddenly understood. 'You can come up, but quickly. And don't touch anything.'

She pushed Robert up the steep metal steps in front of her, thinking momentarily of the ladder that had swayed under her grip high over the sawdust of a circus arena. At the top, Haresh opened the door and ushered them inside. They looked at each other, silent for a moment, then Haresh crouched down to Robert's level. 'So that was you on the line on Saturday. Nobody gave me a name. A man in a car just pulled up and started shouting at me to stop the train. You were lucky it was still two blocks away.' He touched the bandage on Robert's ankle. 'You were very lucky indeed.'

He stood again and Florence, who had felt so determined and confident on the way here, now stammered over her words. 'I just … I just had to thank you. To let you know the … the miracle you performed. To tell you that you are our hero. Right, Robbie?' Robert nodded, serious and quiet, then suddenly threw himself at Haresh, hugging him.

Haresh laughed. 'I was just doing my job, you know. But still,' he patted Robert's head, 'I'm thankful you weren't hurt. What were you doing on the line, though? You know you shouldn't play there, don't you?'

'It wasn't his fault,' Florence began, and then she found herself telling Haresh the whole story — the ripped shirts, the names, the gang of boys in the alleyway. At the end of it, she found herself asking, 'What will you do? Will you have children here? How could you bear it, knowing what they will go through?'

Haresh shook his head. 'I live in a small house with seven other men, all of us Indian and all of us trying to make our way here, to find some kind of life. I'm afraid having a family is a long way off for me. Even if my parents did find me someone back home, I don't know if I could bring her here, and expect her to fit in. This, I think you can understand.'

They stood in silence again. Florence looked around her. Robert was sitting on the floor, making sure he didn't touch anything, as he'd been told. She looked at the bank of levers, at the telegraph machine next to the desk. She picked up *The Signalman's Journal*, which was on the desk, and started flicking through the pages until something caught her eye. 'Oh, look!' She held it out to Haresh, who took it from her and then nodded.

'Yes, this has caused a lot of controversy, as you can imagine.' He handed it back to her, and Florence began to read the article. 'Barbara Wooding, former porter at Willington station, has become the Midland region's first female signalman.' She looked at Haresh. 'I didn't think this was possible. They wouldn't even let me study at the technical college. I went to ask, after I talked to you.'

'Perhaps times are changing,' he said. 'But it's a slow process. Still,' he took back the journal from her and looked at the photograph of Barbara Wooding, smiling on a station platform between two men in railway uniform, 'you shouldn't give up. Anything is possible, really, with a bit of luck and knowing the right people. Well, look at me. And if there's ever anything I can do ...'

Florence felt embarrassed, as if her difficulties could ever be compared to what he had been through and would continue to go through for the rest of his life if he stayed here. 'I have to ask,' she said, apprehensive but curious, 'and don't take this the wrong way, but how did you get this job?'

'I know, I am the exception to the rule. You don't expect to see me here. I was lucky ... the war. The Superintendent at the new apprentice training school in Eastleigh — my brigade fought with his.'

'Where?'

'Kohima.'

Florence gasped. 'Some of the things I heard about Kohima ...'

'Yes, and all true, probably. And I'd only joined up a year before. I was very young.' He stopped, and Florence wondered if she should change the subject. Heaven only knew what sort of trauma the man had been through. 'I was at Jotsoma,' he continued, 'but we were sent to reinforce the Kohima defenders, and that's where I met Hugh — Hugh Woolf.' Again he stopped and Florence imagined the scenes, the flashes of blood and body parts and explosions, that he would be trying to suppress in his mind. 'It was a terrible two weeks. The bitterest close-quarter fighting — things I never expected to see.'

'I'm sorry, Haresh. You don't have to talk about it.'

He smiled at her. 'No, it's fine. It happened, but it's in the past. Anyway, let's just say, I saved Hugh's life, and he hasn't forgotten. He was the one who helped me when I arrived, got me in at the college. And he gave me a place at the training school. I've been lucky.'

'How difficult has it been since?' Florence again looked at Robert, thinking of the shouts and taunts of the local boys.

'Honestly? Every single day is a challenge I must overcome. The other men ... First it was isolation. Most wouldn't sit near me, talk to me, work with me. Then there were complaints about me — they said they couldn't understand a word I was saying, that I would be a liability as a signalman.'

'But that's ridiculous,' said Florence, blushing with indignation on his behalf.

'As I said, I was lucky. Hugh put them all in their place, and gradually it's settled down into a sort of grudging working relationship. Donald, the other signalman here, he doesn't really talk to me, but on the other hand, he doesn't make comments about curry and sacred cows either.'

How sad, Florence thought. How unfair. He would have sacrificed his life in that war and all for the people who now mocked him and insulted him in return. 'Why do you stay?'

'I promised my family. And for the money. And I believe there will be opportunities here in the future that I wouldn't have back home.'

Florence wasn't so sure. From her perspective, the future here did not seem to be a place paved with gold and full of opportunities. And if it was, only for certain kinds of people. Haresh checked his watch.

'I suppose we had better leave you to do your job,' she said. 'Although,' and she looked around again longingly at the bank of levers, the ledger with its rows of neat handwriting, the telegraph machine, silent for now, 'I'd much rather be here than at home.'

'I'm a bit hungry, Mummy,' Robert piped up from the floor, evidently alarmed by the prospect of no dinner and an evening spent in this tiny box with no toys to play with.

Haresh laughed. 'Duty calls. Thank you, though, for coming to visit, and for letting me know what happened. I cannot tell you how happy you have made me, knowing I saved a life — it's an incredible feeling.'

'Thank you, Haresh. We are always in your debt.' She held out her hand and he took it in his, warm and strong. She looked away, feeling awkward, and instead pulled Robert up from the floor. 'We'll visit again, if that would be acceptable.'

'It would be a delight.'

She made her way easily down the steps, Robert clutching on to her hand, and at the bottom looked up once more. Haresh was there, leaning out of the window, giving them a wave. Then she heard the bell start to ring, and he disappeared from view.

She began to walk away from the track, up the hill. She didn't want Robert to be there when the train went past this time.

* * *

Florence took easily to the horses again, and to the circus itself. That week, they trained every day, Florence regaining her balance and her strength, as well as her confidence. In the mirror at home, she noted the colour coming back to her complexion, the frown between her eyes a little less pronounced.

It was Friday afternoon, and Florence was just thinking about leaving to pick up Robert from school. She sat with

Ester and Tara on a wall outside the hotel in the sunshine, finishing ice creams – slabs of the stuff that looked like butter, pressed between two wafers by a sullen man in his van. Tara had smeared ice cream all round her mouth and was dripping it on to the ground by their feet. Ester took two bites and crossed the road to throw hers in the bin. Florence, enjoying the rich, sweet taste after months with no appetite, looked the other way towards the big top, then looked again. Walking towards her, head down and unseeing, was Ester's husband.

'Ester,' she shouted.

Ester turned. 'Andreas!' She waved and ran to meet him.

Florence watched as Ester kissed him and held him close, and he smiled. Slowly, she approached them, unsure whether she should leave them to their reunion. Tara was still concentrating on her ice cream.

'They told me you'd finished for the day,' Andreas said. 'The horses look in good condition.' Then he saw Florence. 'And here you are, too. All is well, I hope.'

Florence nodded. 'All is well since Ester turned up on my doorstep.'

Ester took his hand. 'Why didn't you tell me you'd arrived? I've been worried. Never mind, you'll be in time for the parade. You can ride with us.' She stopped and smiled at Florence. 'You'll never guess who else is joining.'

Andreas did not look interested in the parade. 'We have to talk,' he said. 'Copperfield wants to pay us good money, a lot of money.'

Ester laughed. 'I know, don't worry. The elephants are fine. I can't wait to see them walking along the seafront on Saturday. The crowd is going to love it.'

'No, Ester. He wants to pay us more money. For the cannon.'

Florence watched as Ester took this information in. She saw the expression of fear on her face, and she understood.

'No. No, Andreas. I told you, before we left. I told you. Never again. I can't. I won't. It's enough.'

Andreas stared at Ester. 'I promised him a flying lady. He wants the machine, and he wants you to do it.'

Ester pulled away from him. 'How could you? After everything we talked about. Just the horses, you said. Just one more season. And no more cannon. For Tara. Remember?' Florence could almost feel the panic that rose up from the pit of Ester's stomach, could hear it in her voice. With Tara, everything had changed.

Andreas's voice was calm. 'With this money, it will be just one more season. And then we can buy the land. We can do everything we've dreamed of.'

Ester turned to look at the circus behind them. 'Is it here already?'

Florence understood she knew it was there, somewhere in a tent, squatting under its tarpaulin cover. Waiting for her.

'You can't ask this of me. You just can't.' Ester walked away, back to Tara.

'Then you can forget a house here,' called Andreas. 'And a home for Tara, for us. We'll be on the road for years to come.'

Now Tara looked up with a cream-smeared face. 'Mummy?' Ester grinned at her, but Florence could see tears in her eyes.

Ester wiped Tara's face with a handkerchief. 'Look who's here.'

Tara jumped off the wall and ran to Andreas who bent down and picked her up, holding her high in his strong arms. Tara giggled and shrieked, then covered his face in kisses as he lowered her. Florence took Ester's arm in solidarity.

'Can we show Daddy our room?' Tara was skipping around

them now, clearly delighted to have her parents united again, at last.

'Yes,' said Andreas, raising an eyebrow at Ester. 'Lead the way, my sweetheart. Then your mummy and I need to talk.'

Florence was already late to collect Robert from school. As she sat on the bus, she thought again about the cannon, about the sensation of an oblivion entered and confronted, about the dreams she knew Ester had suffered since Tara had been born. There was no way she should have to endure the terror of it any longer.

* * *

Florence drank her tea down, finished her toast, and dumped the dirty dishes in the sink. Billy was still slowly eating his eggs and bacon and turning the pages of the paper.

'So you'll bring Robert down to the parade at twelve? Get a good spot, won't you? By the funfair, perhaps. Then we'll meet at the Royal afterwards.'

Billy nodded and carried on reading. Florence hoped he'd actually heard. The whole topic of Ester and the circus was apparently off limits; he'd made his indifference to her past quite obvious this week. And so Florence had simply not told him that she would be starring in the parade. She'd just let him think she was helping Ester get the horses ready — that much he was prepared to accept. Still, she would whisper to Robert before she left, and make sure he knew to look out for her on her golden mount. Billy, on the other hand, probably wouldn't even recognise her.

Walking down the promenade that morning, Florence felt like a different person. It was incredible how Ester's presence and the work with the horses had revived her. She felt as if she had woken from a long slumber, as if someone had finally broken the spell that had held her ensnared all these years. She crossed over to the common and made her way to the stables.

Inside was warm and filled with the scent of hay and the odour of the animals. Florence breathed it in, a nostalgic jumble of fragments and feelings whirling around her body. She called out, but there was no answer, except for Mor, who stuck his head over the partition and whinnied. Florence rubbed his neck and was about to call out again when, from the furthest stall, she heard voices raised in argument.

'I don't care what you promised. I'm not doing it.'

'We can't let him down now. He'll kick us out completely.'

'You should have thought of that before you agreed to it.'

'And our house, our dream, our new life?'

'If I die in that thing, there won't be a life, will there?'

'I don't understand why you've changed. You know I would never harm you. I love you.'

'Then show it by listening to me and understanding that I never want to get inside that contraption ever again.'

The voices stopped for a moment. Just then, Florence heard a sob from the back of Mor's stable. In the gloom, she saw Tara huddled in a pile of straw.

'Tara? Sweetie, what's wrong?'

Tara raised her head and sniffed. 'They've been arguing all morning. And last night.'

'Why? What's happened?'

Tara dropped her chin on her knees. 'Daddy brought the cannon with him. He was supposed to sell it, but now he wants Mummy to fly out of it again. And she said no. And it's all because of me. Because they want me to have a proper home and not live in the circus anymore.' Tara started to cry again. Florence was about to go to her, when she saw Ester come out of the last stall along the row.

* * *

Florence eased her arms into the spangled sleeves of her costume and turned to let Ester zip her up. She couldn't see much of herself in the small mirror propped up on the table. She hoped she didn't look ridiculous. Then again, Ester looked fabulous, and their outfits were the same — sparkling and shimmering in shades of green and blue and gold. Even Tara's costume was dazzling, though hers had gauzy wings attached. She looked like a little butterfly.

'Anyway, dearie. Even if you were fit enough, I wouldn't let you do it.' Ester was applying lipstick now, speaking between each stroke. 'You must have heard about Zazal and Zacchini? There have been so many accidents. I just don't have the stomach for it anymore. And you have Robert to think about.'

Florence watched her friend as she finished her make-up and gave herself a nod in the mirror and thought, not for the first time, how bold she was, so self-assured. Where did that come from?

'But Andreas is so insistent.'

'Don't worry about that. I can handle him.' Ester laughed. 'You've seen what I can do with horses and elephants. Husbands are no different, really.'

'Mummy!' Tara frowned at them, but only for a moment. Outside, someone started ringing a bell, and Tara clapped her hands.

'Is that us?'

Tara answered by running out of the tent. Florence attempted one more look in the smeared glass of the mirror, adjusted her head dress and followed Ester outside into a confusion of noise and colour. The band was warming up, and everyone in all sorts of costumes gathered with the animals in preparation for the parade.

* * *

The streets were lined with people cheering and waving. Ahead of them, at the front of the parade, were the clowns, the jugglers, and the acrobats. Then a marching band, drums rolling, xylophones, trumpets, and flutes playing melodies of popular tunes. After this came the horses.

Ester rode in front, stopping now and then to whirl her horse around on the spot or rear up, to the applause of the spectators. Florence and Tara followed, throwing handfuls of confetti up in the air so that it fluttered away over the heads of the children in the front row of the crowd. Mor did indeed love an audience, pawing at the ground and shaking the bells on his bridle every time they came to a halt.

Florence looked about her, at the people, the colours, and the animals. Behind them came the elephants, decorated with garlands of flowers. Occasionally one would trumpet, and Florence laughed out loud at the idea of these giant, exotic creatures walking in the road where she was more used to buying a pint of cockles for Billy after he'd been for a swim.

They continued on, the funfair on Clarence Pier now visible. Florence scanned the crowd, looking for the dark curls of her son, hoping Billy had made it in time. And she hoped that Aunt Sarah was there too, and her cousins, and the people she'd worked with at the factory, and anyone else who had known her since she'd come to this country but who had never wanted to know about her past, about who she really was. About India.

Finally, she saw Robert, concentrating more on the candyfloss he was eating than the spectacle in front of him. Billy was there too, pointing down the road at the elephants. Florence nudged Mor to the edge of the parade and, as she'd seen Ester do, gave the command. He reared up underneath her and stood for a moment, strong and steady as a statue, and she saw Robert's face light up as he looked at her. She blew him a kiss and Mor returned to the ground, and she waved to them all, then joined the pageant once more.

* * *

It was when they returned to the big top, that the trouble happened. Florence was in the stables, grooming Mor, preparing him for the show, when she heard Andreas shouting, calling for Ester. Florence stuck her head out of the tent.

'She's taken Tara to your caravan. The girl was tired after all the excitement of the parade.'

Andreas didn't answer. He just turned on his heels and walked off. He was accompanied by a large man in a suit. Florence, curious and anxious, followed them.

At the caravan, Andreas knocked on the door and, in a low voice that did nothing to conceal his temper, ordered Ester outside. After a few minutes, she opened the door and came down the steps, clutching her dressing gown around her.

'What is it? I need to get ready, and Tara is asleep.' Florence had never heard Ester speak with such irritation to Andreas. 'Can't this wait?' Then she stopped and saw the man in the suit. 'Oh, Dickie. You're here. I'm sorry.' Ester pulled her robe closer around her and frowned again at Andreas. Florence took a step nearer, behind the circus owner.

'Dickie just wants to be sure you'll do the jump tonight, as we discussed,' said Andreas.

Florence couldn't believe it. After everything Ester had said.

'Then he might as well leave. I'm not doing it. As we discussed.' Ester turned and walked back up the steps into the caravan.

Dickie Copperfield shook his head and started walking away in the opposite direction. 'I told you,' he said. 'I don't need the horses. Anyone can do horses. It's the cannon or nothing. If not, you're out.'

Andreas looked desperate. He ran up the steps and tried to open the door, but Ester had locked it. He banged his fists on the thin metal, threatening dents around the door frame.

'Andreas,' Florence called. 'Andreas! You have to let it go. How can you do it? How can you want to send her into that machine? You know the risks. And let's face it, unless you've done it yourself, you can never really understand what it is.'

Andreas stopped and sat slowly on the steps. 'I just want us to have our dream. To escape this,' he gestured around him at the tents and caravans, the muddy grass, 'and have a normal home, a normal life.'

Florence shook her head. 'No such thing, I'm afraid. Least of all here, in this country. Not for people like us, anyway.'

Andreas looked up at her. Behind him, the door of the caravan opened. Ester stood there looking down at him. 'Then what do we do?' he said. 'Go back to India? Live out the rest of our lives there, travelling around? Doing what, I don't know.'

For a moment, Florence considered it. Returning to the house in Agra. Her house now. They could live there, perhaps, all together. And then there would be Sita ... But Florence knew that this wasn't her answer. She knew that whatever was there now was not what she had left behind, and that what she had left behind, she could never have again.

'I don't know, Andreas. But what I am sure of is that you cannot send your wife into that cannon again. There's a promise of something when you jump, even among the delirium and the glory, that is so threatening — evil, even. It's there waiting, biding its time. And if you carry on, one day it will have what it wants. It will come for you. And you will be broken.' Florence looked up at Ester and felt the understanding between them. 'You have to find some other way.'

Ester sat down on the step behind Andreas and put her arms around him. He closed his eyes, and Florence turned and left them to their peace-making.

* * *

Florence sat with Robert and Billy in the front row of the audience, applauding with everyone as the trapeze artists swung and somersaulted above them, as Ester stood on Mor's back while he galloped around the ring, as she lay in the sawdust with the other showgirls and the elephants stepped carefully over them, an absolute silence inside the tent until the last pace had been taken. There was no sign of the cannon, however, and as the final procession circled the arena, coloured spotlights spinning and the band at a frenzy, Florence held Robert's hand and knew this would always be a part of her, and she would hide it no longer.

She had told Robert her stories, and perhaps he would one day tell his children about his mother and his aunt, the two women who had dared to do, and lost and won, and flown across the domes of the Taj Mahal.

In the meantime, they needed a plan, and watching the horses cantering round and around, an idea for the future began to form. She kissed Robert's hand and, with the rest of the audience, stood and cheered as the performers paraded out of the ring one last time.

Chapter Twenty-One

AGRA, JULY 1947

Lord Mountbatten finished his speech and, before the presenter had a chance to start his summary, her father turned the radio off and walked over to the piano. He sat down and flicked through some sheets of music then threw them on the floor and slammed the lid shut. He sat tapping his fingers on the ebony surface, while from the divan, Florence waited for the inevitable. In a few moments, it came.

'It's a disaster. It's all very well saying there will be no toleration of further violence, but how will that work exactly? And I don't agree that partition is the only alternative to coercion. What the hell is going to happen in the provinces? Avert civil war? I can't see how, just by rushing things through. Just wants to wash his hands of the whole affair, I think. Fifteenth of August — what's that? Six weeks? It's absolutely incredible.'

Her father sank lower in his seat and covered his face with his hands.

'Papa, please. You can't get so upset every time you hear the latest news. It's not good for you. Look, even Gandhi has given up and left them to it. Of course they have accepted the plan.

What else can they do? They aren't going to risk losing independence, are they? And everyone says there will be civil war otherwise.'

'And you don't think hundreds of thousands of people are going to die anyway? Haven't already died? Gandhi wanted freedom for a united India, not two hostile countries. We are abandoning them to a bloodbath. It's terrifying.'

Her father continued to sit, staring at nothing, still tapping. He'd been increasingly irascible over the past few months, with each new announcement from Attlee, Mountbatten, and Congress pushing him a step further up the mountain of his anger. He'd also been complaining of stomach pains and nausea, and the doctor had diagnosed an ulcer — this latest news wouldn't help with that.

Florence went to the gramophone and selected one of his favourite records, but by the time she had lowered the needle, listened to those first few bars of *Moonlight Serenade* smoothing their way into the room and turned around again, she discovered he had left.

The next day, Florence rose earlier than usual, eager to get to the circus field. She had a polite breakfast with Nick and her father, both men scanning the headlines as they buttered their toast. Nick seemed mostly concerned about the future of the band — already there was talk at the Club of people booking tickets on ships. Auctions of furniture and house sales were being arranged, and in quiet corners, conversations could be heard discussing potential positions in good companies or government departments back home.

Florence somehow did not see any of this as affecting her in any particular way, as if she would be immune to the huge upheaval to come. When she thought about it, she seemed to have been in a perpetual state of turmoil since the day she'd been called in to see her headmistress and sent away to

Udaipur for the holidays, and after all these years she'd come to believe there wasn't much that could be done. As she rode out on the path away from the house that morning, her main concern was Ester and Andreas and helping the circus survive.

She found Ester sitting down at the table in the kitchen tent, finishing her breakfast. Florence, agitated by her thoughts, refused a chair and continued to stand and fidget until Ester finally asked her what on earth was the matter.

'Of course, you've heard the news. Independence Day on the fifteenth of August. That's only six weeks away. *That's* your opportunity!'

Ester appeared rather subdued considering the whirlwind of events that would soon arrive. She stirred her tea and when she spoke, it was with muted tone. 'It's hard to take in, don't you think? In six weeks, India will finally govern herself, and the British will leave. And not only this, but a new nation will be created, and that dream of unification will be forgotten, and God knows what will happen to all those people who no longer have a place to live.'

Ester was being rather gloomy, in Florence's opinion. She clearly hadn't understood the opportunity that this news presented. They could sell a thousand tickets, cover all their recent losses, and still have enough to make the journey to Bombay or Cochin or wherever they wanted to set up their business next.

'Ester, stop being so cheerless, will you? It's not all bad. Apart from the fact that India finally gets what she's wanted for a hundred years, Independence Day means parties and celebrations, and what do people love at big celebrations to mark something hugely significant? A big spectacle. Like a cannon jump! I'll get Papa to pull a few strings at the Club — you can be the main event. Sort of symbolic too, don't you think? Raise the flag and fire the Brits out into space.'

Ester at least smiled at this last comment. 'I'll have you know, I do not consider myself entirely a British subject. Daddy was as Indian as any member of Congress.' She slumped again at the table. 'I'm sorry, Florence. I'm afraid I can't stop thinking about what it's all going to be like, in two months' time, in a year, in five years. All this violence is so frightening. How are they going to make them stop? It's civil war, just under a different name. In this little circus we have everybody all under one canvas roof: Moslems, Hindus, Sikhs, and whatever Andreas and I are. We all come from everywhere, but when they partition the provinces, communities will be split whichever way they cut it. We will no longer have anywhere to call home. And what future is there for people with no roots?'

Florence watched her friend as she sat, solemn and pensive at the table. There was something strange about her today. Florence hadn't thought the news, which after all had been on the cards for a long time now, would have affected her so.

'Come on. It's a time of change, but honestly, don't you feel that's all we've ever lived in anyway? Change and upheaval?'

'It is a time of change. You're right. Perhaps this is *your* opportunity, Florence. Perhaps you should think about leaving. This can be your chance to start again. A new home and a new life for yourself.'

Florence was taken aback. Leaving was what other people were going to do. Papa would no more consider going to live in England than he would going to live on the moon. And Nick – well, she assumed he wouldn't want to leave behind the sort of life he enjoyed here, with servants and polo matches and parties every weekend, for a poky flat in town or a cottage with roses around the door in the countryside.

'I really don't think so. Can't imagine Papa or Nick living

in year-round drizzle and toddling off to play shove ha'penny in the village pub every Saturday night.'

At this, Ester laughed out loud, and Florence, relieved, saw her chance to change the subject and return to her earlier proposal. 'So what do you think? I'll tell Papa today, and Andreas can go back to the paper-pushers and tell them he's doing them a favour, giving them a spectacle that will equal that of Delhi. Just think, you'll be a part of history.'

Ester shifted in her seat and looked uncomfortable. Florence beat the table top in frustration.

'What's wrong, Ester?'

'There's nothing wrong. Quite the contrary, in fact. It's just ... I can't do the jump now, or any time soon. Because I'm pregnant.'

Well. This was news indeed. Florence pulled out a chair and sat down.

'Oh, Ester!'

It was something they had never really talked about. Florence had thought perhaps, what with the circus and Ester's act, that they had been delaying things. Or they hadn't been able to. Or simply hadn't wanted to. It was certainly a subject Florence avoided bringing up anyway, in order to dodge those conversational bullets being aimed in her direction. Her own ambivalence about having children with Nick was yet another thing she glossed over in her mind, preferring to believe that at some point the situation would magically resolve itself. But she could be happy for her friend.

'Well, that's wonderful news. Congratulations.'

'Thank you, dearie. You'll be Auntie Florence. And Godmother, of course.'

'Of course. But, I have to ask. What are you going to do about money? What about the show?'

Ester didn't answer. Clearly, she didn't have one. But they

needed to do something, or the circus would not survive. Florence grabbed Ester's hand. 'Let me do it.'

'What?'

'Let me do it. Let me do the jump.'

Ester sat back in her chair. 'Oh, Florence. You can't be serious.'

'Why not? Look, I'm fit, I'm trained on the trapeze. It can't be that different. You can teach me. We have six weeks.'

'What about Nick?'

'What about Nick? He won't know. He never watches you anyway, and even if he did, I'd be wearing your costume, the mask, the helmet. Nobody will be able to tell. Anyway, this is more important than Nick's stupid prejudices.'

Oh, revenge is delicious when it presents itself as such an enticing dish, heady with the aroma of intrigue and steaming with the unknown. Florence, having let this thought take shape, would not be shaken, despite Ester's doubts. 'I can do it,' she said.

'I don't know, Florence. Six weeks? It's dangerous. I'd be responsible …'

Then, from behind, at the entrance to the tent, came Andreas's voice. 'Let her. Let her try. She has the aptitude. We need this.'

His words were flattering. He believed she could do it. And she wanted to. She wanted to so much. Ever since she had first pressed her cheek against the cold metal, she had known she would one day climb inside, would see first-hand how it worked.

Andreas moved to the table. 'Of course, I wouldn't want to create any problems between you and your husband. We wouldn't want to upset him, would we? But if you think there's a way we can do this without troubling Nick, then really, what's the harm?'

Ester looked Florence directly in the eyes, searching for something, it seemed — doubt, fear, the wrong motivation. Florence held a steady gaze in return. This was to be more than the sum of her experience so far; this was predestined, the culmination of her fascination with the machinations of various mechanisms. Pistons and pressure and compression and combustion, spring-loads and cylinders, crankshafts and valves, and the whole concept of propulsion in one shocking, explosive, life-defining moment.

Andreas stood in silence, and Ester, in the end, gave in.

'All right, dearie. Let's do it. I'll be the trainer, and you do the jump on the fifteenth of August, with all the flags and pomp and ceremony to cheer you on. After that, God only knows what happens.'

Florence jumped up and embraced her friend then turned to Andreas, promising not to let them down. This was it. This was to be her moment. It started now.

* * *

Resolute, Florence trained. Every morning, Ester had her lifting weights and stretching and bending until her body was as hard and as explicit as the cannonball she would ultimately purport to become. She continued with the trapeze, making ever-higher and more daring launches and catches, with somersaults mid-air and a firm, assured grip on the bar when it smacked back into her palm for the hundredth time of the day. The feeling of autonomy, the increasing sense of control — of power, even — as she grew more confident, was intoxicating. Each week, Andreas would take the callipers, the tape measure, and the scales and record all her physical details — height, weight, circumference — in order to perfect the dummy he would use to establish the angles and distances of her jump, the position of the cannon and the net.

With thirty days left to go, Florence wanted to know when she would actually start to practise with the cannon. Ester remained cautious, but Andreas was optimistic, and soon enough she approached the yawning interior for the first time. That dark, suffocating space, willingly entered into.

The helmet fitted on her head, tight and firm, and the shiny, figure-hugging jumpsuit let her slip and slide without difficulty down into the depths of the cylinder. Ester had explained the mechanism, but most important was the position to take, with total rigidity required in the flight phase. Aiming for the net was crucial, and even though this was the first test, over a much smaller distance, there was no room for mistakes. Above all, a complete commitment to the act and an abandonment to the forces of nature harnessed to evoke the illusion.

As Florence reversed inside the tube, pushing herself backwards with her hands until she felt the flat surface of the sprung platform against her feet, she told herself over and over: be determined, be strong. Be metal. She couldn't afford even the smallest hint of doubt.

* * *

With fourteen days left before the show, Andreas finally received the permits, and the order of celebrations was confirmed at the Club. Florence opened the stack of posters that had been delivered and read one out loud to Ester.

'Have you seen this?'

> 'Look who's here: The Great Gombar and his cannon. Ready to thrill. See the amazing flying lady and commemorate this special day.
>
> 'After, Harry Hunt and his leading band of Agra. Noted for their hot and sweet dance music. Introducing you to Nick Criado — the guy you'll never forget. Boy??? He's good. This is something you have been waiting for. The night of nights! Book your tickets to avoid disappointment.'

'Well, that does sound impressive.'

'The amazing flying lady,' said Ester. 'You know who that is, don't you?'

Florence shook her head. 'Don't say it. It's better if I don't think about it. Anyway, I'm more concerned about this hot and sweet dance music. And three question marks? Who wrote this?'

'I think the printer must have been a little carried away with excitement.' Ester laughed and took the poster from her. 'Come on, like you said. Best not to think about it.'

Everything was organised: marching bands and a parade of the cavalry, and speeches by the Governor of Agra and Major General Banks. After this, a champagne reception, followed by the spectacle of The Great Gombar's human cannonball, and all finished with a flag-raising ceremony and a twenty-one-gun salute. Dinner, music, and dancing. Carriages at midnight. It would be an unforgettable occasion.

* * *

Monday the tenth of August, and with five days to go, the Club was closed for preparations. Despite the heat, the humidity, and the ever-present threat of the rains that still had not quite arrived with their usual fury, Army and Navy delivered its finest foodstuffs and champagne, and servants strung bunting and coloured lights around doors and window frames, from rafter to rafter, and among the branches of trees. Soldiers on horseback rehearsed their formations — all curved, prancing steeds and polished boots and medals. And then the cannon arrived, Andreas in attentive custody, ensuring its safety and posting guards so that nobody could interfere with the precisely tuned apparatus.

Agra that season had remained full, though people were making arrangements to leave the country. Houses had not been rented in the hills, and anyway the journey those days was perilous. Attacks on trains seemed to happen daily, and already there were reports of long caravans of citizens and beasts making their way from one side of the country to the other. Desperate people in desperate times. In part, these events permeated Florence's conscience, and in part she simply let the last-gasp hedonism of those around her in those final weeks — more dances, more parties — act as some kind of cushion, muffling reality. She thought about Sita and Ravi, but never found quite the right moment to talk to them about it. And afterwards, everything happened too quickly for her to do anything anyway.

With three days to go, Andreas conducted test after test with the sandbagged manikin that was Florence's counterpart, her stand-in until they had perfected the set-up. The dummy hurtled through the air, falling short, over-shooting, rebounding too vigorously from the spring of the net to crack its skull on a rock or twist its body into the trunk of a tree.

Ester watched each trial with a grim expression, and Florence — without any sense of anxiety — watched Ester. But perhaps it was harder to send someone else into the dark confines of the cannon than it was to decide for yourself. Watching the dummy crash once more to the ground,

Florence wondered how Andreas had done it all these years, and why.

But there was no time for such shadowy thoughts now. If the day was to go as planned, then they all had a part to play to ensure everyone was in the right place at the right time with a jubilant bearing appropriate for the occasion, without any inkling of what Florence was about to do.

At 11 pm on the fourteenth of August, they gathered around the radio to listen to Nehru being sworn in. As the clock struck midnight, he delivered his historic speech. His words of destiny hovered in the air over them even after the transmission ended. Harry raised his glass, solemn and severe. Nick, rather more relaxed, reached for the bottle again, while at the side of the room Ravi and Sita smiled and stared at each other as if they could not believe what had just occurred. Harry turned to them and raised his glass once more.

'To life, and freedom.'

Florence, silent, thought then of the day to come.

* * *

The rest of the household woke late, and an air of festivity was palpable as Florence had her breakfast. Singing drifted in snippets from the kitchen, and through the window she could see the kitchen boy throw a paper kite up into the air to catch the breeze, its saffron, white, and green stripes dodging the trees and bushes to whirl and ripple with a buzz of its tail, up and away into the sky.

She had ordered a new dress, made with a pattern from the catalogue, and it hung in the wardrobe wrapped in tissue paper. She didn't quite have the appetite for the New Look that filled the fashion magazines that season. To wear a corset again after the comfort of the war years, and all that padding on the hips and shoulders, like armour. No, this dress was from a pattern that promised movie-star glamour — it was pure Judy Garland with black and white ankle-length stripes that sheathed her body. This was off-set by a feminine bustle, a sweetheart neckline, and cap sleeves that only just managed to hide the muscular definition of her shoulders and arms. She slipped it over her head and turned approvingly in front of the mirror. Whether it was the dress or the knowledge of what was to come, Florence had never felt so assured in all her life.

The marching bands were due to start at four. Canopies and gazebos had been erected down the sides of the polo field, but everywhere the butterfly wings of women's fans fluttered in ceaseless motion against the overwhelming humidity. People muttered recollections of Simla and fresh mountain air as they waited for the ceremony to begin. Florence was sitting with Nick, Papa, and the Hansons. She sipped sweet lime water and nodded at the conversation, but she was grateful when the drums and pipes struck up as the troops entered the field. They all applauded politely as the men rode by in slow-moving rectangles of clinking metal and the thud of hooves in a high-stepping trot. Two rounds of the perimeter were deemed sufficient, then they all lined up in formation to wait for the Governor to approach. Overhead, heavy clouds had gathered, and people started to comment that he ought to hurry up before the whole thing got washed out. Sure enough, as the speeches came to a close, the first heavy spots of rain began to fall.

There was a surge of people hurrying from the gazebos to the marquees that had been erected around the main building of the Club itself. Florence followed Nick and Papa with her fan held ineffectually over her head against the rain. They reached the tent just as it began to gather strength. She dashed inside the entrance and smoothed herself down. Her dress had not suffered, and her hair still felt in place. She accepted a glass of champagne from a passing waiter and stood on the edges of a conversation, listening instead to the tattoo of the rain on the canvas overhead. She had to slip away soon, when Nick went to set up with the band perhaps, as she assumed he would, instead of watching the show. Of course, they wouldn't do the jump while there was such a downpour, but even as this thought crossed her mind, the roar of the drops, which had been constant since they entered the tent, switched itself off, and then there was only the hubbub of chit-chat and the honeyed notes of the string quartet playing in one corner.

Time ticked by. People grew rowdy and the atmosphere more celebratory as glasses were emptied and refilled and emptied once more. Florence sipped at her drink and wondered when Nick would make a move. The Hansons had returned, and Mrs Hanson was obviously keen to make an impression on Nick.

'I hear it's your sister who does the actual jump. How awfully brave of her. I don't suppose you know how it works, do you?'

Florence watched her husband try to mask his irritation at this reminder of Ester's role in the proceedings. Oh, if only he knew. But Mr Hanson, a man who was always right, interrupted before Nick could answer.

'Apparently, it's all a trick of the eye. No-one actually flies out of the cannon. They distract you with all the smoke and explosions, and then someone just pops up in the net at the last moment.'

Mrs Hanson frowned. 'No, darling. That can't be true. You can see her flying through the air.'

'Just a manikin. Stuffed with straw and what-not and put in the same costume. Nothing to it.'

Mr Hanson took a satisfied swig of his drink while his wife

continued to shake her head in disagreement. 'No, I refuse to believe—'

'I'm so sorry, but if you will all excuse me, I have some business with the band to attend to.' Nick slid away from them, distracting Mrs Hanson from her argument. Papa signalled for more drinks, and Florence, seeing her opportunity, excused herself from the group. They would just think she was with her husband, and he would think she was with her father.

Instead, she edged through the crowd to the back of the marquee. There was an entrance and exit for the waiters. She slipped through and, picking up the hem of her dress so that it would not get splashed with mud, ran to the tent behind, where Ester and Andreas were waiting for her.

She stripped to her underwear, not caring that Andreas could see her — all the performers walked around half-naked in the dressing room — and flung her Judy Garland over the back of a chair. Ester picked up the dress and hung it on a rail, commenting that Florence would need it afterwards if she were to maintain a successful subterfuge. She wriggled inside the jumpsuit with its shiny stripes of scarlet and gold, easing it up past her thighs and waist and over her shoulders before Ester zipped her in, tight and contained. A red satin half-mask, rather baroque in design, disguised her goggles and completed the outfit before she picked up the helmet and fixed it securely on her head. There. She was ready. Ester and Andreas looked at her, then at each other, then back at Florence once more.

'Well, dearie. You certainly look the part. You could be me.' Ester came close, held her shoulders for a moment, then embraced her hard. 'Shall we do this?'

Andreas left, and the two women stood in the flap of the tent watching as he made his way over to where the cannon stood, covered in tarpaulin. Florence recognised a pair of fellow acrobats helping him prepare the space, hauling the material clear, standing by as he checked and re-checked the angles and co-ordinates of the contraption. Now she saw people starting to fill the area behind the ropes, cordoned off fifty feet or so from the flight area. Voices filled the afternoon air, laughter and shouts, the occasional pop of a champagne cork — the party was ready for a show.

Florence realised she was holding Ester's hand, that they were gripping each other as they looked over the scene. She eased herself free and took three deep breaths. It was time. One final smile at Ester, and then she stepped out into the field. Seeing her, a glittering splash of scarlet and gold in front of the tent, Andreas picked up his megaphone and began to incite the crowd.

'Lad-ieeees and gen-tle-meeeeen!'

Florence walked slowly and evenly towards him. The grass, sun-browned and flattened, was slippery with the rain under her thin ballet pumps. She felt the damp seeping in around her toes.

'Welcome, welcome, welcome to the grrrea-test show on earth!'

She kept on walking, drawing closer to the cannon now. As she appeared in view of the crowd, a cheer went up. She stopped next to Andreas and raised her arms, facing each different section of the audience with a gymnast's salute.

'The sensation of the century!'

Florence gave one more wave, her body arched and tense. A bow stretched by an arrow.

'For your entertainment and pleasure, for your delight, delectation, and diversion ...'

Now she approached it. It loomed over her, a giant machine of war — summoning ghosts of soldiers struggling to light the touch paper, ramming gunpowder and driving the ball to the breech to bombard the enemy and advance the artillery across muddy battlefields, the fleet across flaming waters.

'The astonishing, the amazing, the astounding flying lady!'

More cheers as she climbed the ladder and stepped backwards into the jutting column. Down, down and reversing until the light faded and she was sucked into the dark.

Muffled now.

'Shooting from the mouth of a monster ...'

The platform solid against her feet. Arms firm against her sides. Pressure building.

The dreamy, underwater echo of the crowd chanting. 'Ten, nine, eight, seven ...'

Breathe and prepare to brace. Fists, thighs, buttocks, stomach clenched, and chin tucked in.

'Six, five, four ...'

Lungs too — filled with air and held ready for ...

'Three, two, one!'

* * *

Violence. Punched forward and up and out. A flash of light and up through the smoke, and she must, must aim straight, with body exact and unyielding. Her vision starts to speckle and darken, but she cannot black out. Time has become meaningless — these four seconds as long as the life she has lived. And the life she has yet to live. She is immortal, infinite, boundless. A kaleidoscope of pictures turning and encircling her, in and out of focus, all the colours of the rainbow. Departed love and present hate; future grief and former joy; a mother, a father, a home — all gone; and love and lust and loss, alone; another man in sickness and health; then a woman, obscured, turns her head, mouths a warning that cannot be heard. But now, all at once, there is the net zooming into sight — a somersault required as she plummets towards it. A flip, a turn, and then she lands in its bouncing, elastic cradle. She must grab and hold and cling on as it bounds and rebounds around her, determined to hurl her to the ground.

* * *

She swung herself over the edge of the net and, with another somersault, landed with both feet on the ground, soft knees and then a straightening of her body back into that proud arch, arms flung high to the spectators. Andreas arrived by her side and grabbed her hand, and together they spun and bowed while cheers and shouts rang out from the entire field. One last salutation and then she turned and ran with slow, sure strides back to the tent where Ester was waiting for her.

'Oh, my! You did it!' Ester held her tight and close, and Florence pressed her face into Ester's dark, soft hair. They stood, holding each other, until Florence suddenly felt her legs go weak and had to reach for a chair.

'I did it!' She began to laugh. It was incredible. Had that really just happened?

'Did you see it?' Ester sat opposite her. 'I bet you didn't see it, did you?'

'Did I see what?' Florence removed the helmet and mask and rubbed the place where the goggles had sat too tightly on her nose.

'It was wonderful. Just the perfect timing. The rainbow. As you flew out, a rainbow appeared in the sky behind you. It was just perfect.'

Florence shook her head. 'I wasn't looking at anything other than the net.' Then she thought for a moment. Perhaps she had seen it. Perhaps, somehow, it had filtered into her subconscious as she hurtled through the sky. 'I don't know what I saw. My life — all of it. The past and the future. I don't know. I don't know what I'm saying.' She covered her face with her hands and thought she might cry.

'Dearie, you don't need to explain anything to me. Just know, you were incredible. That's enough.'

Then there was silence. Florence felt the strength returning to her limbs, the agitation starting to seep away. She thought, now, about her father. Had he seen? What would he say? Would she ever tell him? Nick, on the other hand — well, he would have been hidden inside the Club somewhere, sulking at the huge affront to his dignity he thought his sister had committed by daring to perform in a circus. Ha! Well, hi-di-ho, Nick. Now your wife is a human cannonball, too. Florence looked at her dress hanging on the rail. She should get changed.

'Help me get out of this costume?'

* * *

She slipped back into the marquee and picked up a glass from a passing waiter as she moved over to the corner where she could see her father and the rest of them. Piles of food were being loaded on to the buffet tables — platter after platter — and she joined the group as they moved towards the line.

'There you are, Florence. What happened to you? Did you see the show? Extraordinary woman that Ester, absolutely extraordinary. Don't know what you've got to be so sour about, Nick.'

Her father was in a festive mood, and several glasses down the line to being drunk, as he slapped Nick on the back and turned to the business of filling his plate, having seemingly forgotten his question to Florence. Nick however, stared at her.

'Where were you? I looked for you. You know I can't stand it when Ester does that thing.' He stopped and leaned forward, then pulled something out of her hair and looked at it. 'Straw? What were you doing? Feeding the elephants?'

Florence patted at her curls, which Ester had pinned back into place after the crushing tightness of the helmet. There was straw everywhere in and around the circus tent. Probably when she was getting changed.

'I couldn't find you. Ended up watching with some of the girls.' She hoped this was at once vague yet normal enough not to raise any suspicion. She took the piece of straw from his hand. 'Must have been blown by the wind — or the explosion. Wasn't she wonderful?'

Nick continued looking at her. 'Oh, yes. Wonderful.'

Soon after they'd eaten, Nick left to take up his place on stage with the band. The first song raised everyone on their feet to dance, and the evening continued with the same sense of abandonment and adventure. Older couples tried out daring new swing steps, and more than one tray of drinks was knocked to the floor from the hands of a waiter as a result.

Ester and Andreas appeared and caused another small storm on the dance floor, cheered by the encircling crowd as much for the daring of The Great Gombar's earlier spectacle as for their bold and modern moves. Florence danced with her father at first, then he turned to the other women in his coterie, so she sat and watched Nick up there in his element, twinkling with charisma and grace.

Around her a thousand points of light glittered in crystal candleholders and reflected in the jewels at the throats of the women and refracted in the cut-glass bowls holding masses of ruby roses on every table. The dancers turned, and the music whirled around her until the room started to fragment and spin away, and her head filled once more with those brief, forever moments of before.

Later, she found herself next to Mrs Hanson in the powder room. Mrs Hanson, dabbing at her nose, looked at Florence in the mirror.

'That is a lovely dress you're wearing. Really eye-catching, those stripes. Catalogue, was it?'

Florence, who was once again trying to put her hair in place, smiled with gratitude. 'A pattern. Judy Garland's *Vogue* dress. I took it to the tailor in the bazaar. He's a wonder. Probably could have done it from the photograph alone.'

Mrs Hanson snapped shut the little lacquered case she'd been using and came closer. 'Not such a wonder, it seems. Look, the sleeve's coming away at the seam. Still, I'm sure it looked lovely at the start of the day.'

Mrs Hanson gave herself one final glance in the mirror and walked away. Florence remained for a while, trying to hide the rip, but there was nothing to be done. She gave up and went back to join the throng.

When the band finished, and all that was left in the air was the babble of voices and clattering of crockery as the waiters began to clear the tables, Nick arrived at her side. Her father sat down and called for brandy and was soon embarked on a long and complicated joke, one that Florence had heard a hundred times before. No doubt the tittering women around him knew it, too.

Nick refused a seat. 'I want to leave. Come on. Your father can get a lift home with one of his cronies. Or one of his women.'

He pulled at her arm, and she stood. True, it was late, and if she thought about it she was feeling tired herself. But she ought to say goodbye to Ester. 'Fine, darling, but can we just find your sister to say good night.'

Nick had her by the hand now. 'Forget Ester, and that bloody husband of hers, will you? Come on. I said I want to go.'

He began to walk off, still grasping her hand, and Florence had no choice but to go with him, following with small hurried steps out into the dark of the night.

When they arrived home the house was dark – either everyone had gone to bed, or they were still out celebrating in the bazaar. Florence sat at her dressing table and began the tedious process of removing make-up from her face and the pins from her hair.

Her door opened, and Nick entered. He sat on the bed and looked at her. She could see him in the mirror as she continued to wipe at her face. Was this an advance? Perhaps, excited by the historic events of the day, he had come to be with her.

She waited for him to speak, wondering if she should leave her hair pinned or take it down before they moved to the bed. He stood and moved towards her, placed his hands on her shoulders, and she began to lean her head against him. It was a gesture she never finished, as his hands moved quick as spiders over her skin and tore at the hole in her sleeve.

'Tell me where you were.' He grabbed her now and forced her round to face him. 'Your dress hanging off you, straw in your hair, mud up the back, like a common tart. Tell me. I want to hear it from your lips.'

Florence took a moment to process what was happening. 'I … I was with the girls. Watching the show. Like I said. It's not my fault the rain made the place into a mud bath, or that the tailor can't finish off a dress properly.'

'Liar!' Nick's grip was tight now, beginning to hurt. 'I saw you. I saw you!'

What had he seen? Florence floundered, not knowing what, if anything, she should confess to. Had he seen her jump? Did he know?

She feigned outrage. 'What? What do you think you saw? I don't know what you are talking about.'

'Don't play the innocent. I watched you leave the marquee. And I saw you enter their tent. And then Andreas came out, and then Ester in that ridiculous costume and did that … that *thing*. And you. You were nowhere to be seen. Still inside, with your latest toy no doubt. Whoring it around once again. Who is it this time? Elephant keeper? Acrobat? Clown? Don't think I don't know you've been there these past weeks, visiting, hanging around. People see things, and people talk.' Now he pulled her up to her feet and shook her, like a child might shake a snow-globe, a jealous little god creating a storm in its tiny dominion.

Disorientated, shocked, Florence began to realise what he was saying. He thought she was having an affair? At the circus? Oh, how his suspicious, nasty little mind worked.

'What? You really think that I would … Well that's rich, coming from you. I've seen you. Sita's seen you, skulking round the market in the dark, meeting God knows who about God knows what. You're the one with secrets and sins, not me. Are you out of your mind?'

The hand came from one side, struck her a blow so hard it rang in her ears. She dropped to her knees in pain. There was a moment's silence, then he had her by the throat. She could feel his thumbs on her windpipe.

'Tell me. Tell me. I want to hear you say it. What were you doing? Tell me the truth.'

But Florence knew she would never give him that. She

would never spoil it, dirty it with his contempt. Better his fury at something she hadn't done. Let him think what he wished. She was keeping it for herself.

'Nick, please. You're wrong. It's not what you think, I promise. Please, trust me.'

'Trust you? Trust you! When could I ever trust you?'

He had her pressed down on the floor now and banged her head on the wooden floor with a hollow thud to emphasise his words. His hands tightened, and for the second time that day her vision began to blur and dull. She struggled to breathe, tried to kick herself free of his weight and then, at once, the pressure had gone, the heaviness had gone, and she was able to turn herself, gasping, pushing herself away from the floor as she tried to understand what had happened.

She heard Ravi's voice, raised and terrible, and saw Nick dragged out of the door. Then gentle hands crept around her shoulders and drew her close, and she breathed in Sita's comforting scent and finally allowed herself to weep.

* * *

She took breakfast alone the next morning. As she finished, her father walked in. He paused at his chair, looking down at her, at the darkening skin on her cheek bone. She brought her fingers protectively to her throat to cover the chain of red circles that sat there like some ghastly necklace.

He sat down next to her, and for once he was quiet. After a moment, he took her hand. 'Oh, my dear girl,' he said. It was more than he had given her in years. They stayed there, a silent couple, until Ravi brought fresh tea and toast. Her father picked up the newspaper, then put it down again. 'I don't think you should be here alone today. Not until I've had a chance to talk to him. I've no idea where he's gone. I assume he'll be back at some point. Come to the station with me. The whole place is upside down with everything that's going on. I could use your help. What do you say?'

She knew it was his way of trying to protect her, that he knew it was too little too late, but she grabbed at it, as she would at anything that might make her feel in some way less vulnerable, less defeated.

In her room, she sat at her mirror and looked at the bruises. She wondered where Nick was. He had not been seen since Ravi had carried him down the veranda steps and dropped him on the lawn outside. Gone to his friends, or whoever, in the town, no doubt. How little she knew him, her own husband, that she had no idea where he could be.

She had never known him though. Had never wanted to know him, really, if she was truthful with herself. Their so-called relationship had just been a convenient curtain to draw against the dark night of a lost love that she saw reflected in the window of her heart every time she allowed herself a moment to stand and stare into the past.

She rubbed at the creases between her brow. Nick wouldn't dare return for some time. And going with her father to the station would be a distraction. She couldn't sit here with her thoughts all day.

There was a tap at the door, and Sita came in. She looked at Florence and raised her hands to her own throat and moaned. 'I knew there was something wrong with him. I should have protected you.' She went over to the dresser and took a silk scarf from the drawer. 'Put this on. It does you no good to keep looking at what he did to you.'

Florence turned to her. With great gentleness, Sita wrapped the delicate material around her neck until the dark stains on her pale flesh could no longer be seen. The two women sat in silence for a while until Florence moved to the bed and lay down.

'What shall I do?'

'Ah. How can I answer this? Only you know what will make you happy.'

'I thought it was my fault, the first time. That I provoked him. So I tried to forgive him, and I tried to make him love me. I went to him. Nights. I wanted him to stay. It would have been easier that way.'

Sita stroked Florence's head. 'You should have told me. Instead, pretending you fell from your horse. Why, *beti*, why?'

Florence curled on to her side. 'I don't understand what is happening. I don't understand anything anymore.'

Sita sat there by her side until they heard Ravi sounding the car horn outside. Florence stood up. 'I'm going with Papa to the station. He needs some help.'

Sita squeezed her hand and let her go.

* * *

In the back of the car, still sleepy, eyes closed, Florence let thoughts of Jay dance around the edges of her consciousness and through the ruins of her marriage. She thought back again to the day of the vote and the street brawl. Could it have been him? What if he'd returned but heard of her engagement and decided to leave her be? What if her father — so taken with Nick at the time — had found out and warned him off? How different could her life have been if she'd refused Nick and done more to find out what had really happened to Jay?

As she sat there, jolting on the hot seat while Ravi navigated the disintegrating road, another name came to her, out of a long-distant conversation. Someone who might be in Agra again, and who she was sure would know the truth. It was just a matter of getting hold of him. She opened her eyes, adjusted the scarf on her neck, and sat up.

She spent an hour in the office, filing papers, waiting for the right moment. When the next train to Delhi had passed, and her father was in the middle of a telephone call, she gestured to him that she was going out to get some air.

The station was busier than ever, people milling around, arguments flaring in the heat and confusion. The humidity was oppressive, but Florence hurried to the end of the platform and waved up at the signal box. As she'd hoped, Prakash waved back from the window, then beckoned her up.

It had been years since she'd seen him — her eighteenth birthday, wasn't it? She wondered how she had changed in his eyes. He, on the other hand, looked the same. He delved into his drawer and offered her a bag of sticky sweets. 'Gulab jamun. Always your favourite when you came as a child.'

Florence took one and savoured the sugar syrup that coated her teeth as she bit into it.

'It must be nearly ten years since I saw you,' he said, as she licked the remains of the sweet from her fingers. 'And today of all days. A new start. A new world. Will you be leaving? Have you come to say goodbye?'

Again, the question of staying or leaving. She pushed it to one side for the moment. 'Papa will never leave. You know that. I'm not sure ... Are you well?'

Prakash offered her another sweet. 'I am well, personally. But I am worried about what will happen. Soon this place will be very different.'

Florence swallowed the sticky mass and ran her tongue around her teeth. The clock above her head ticked on. 'When's the next train due?'

'In five minutes.' Prakash stuck his head out of the window. 'Look at the rabble down there. This is what I mean. Things will get worse before they get better. Perhaps your father should retire, and perhaps you should go, too.'

Florence wasn't sure if he was referring to the present moment or her future again. 'Perhaps you're right. But I need to ask you a favour. I hope you can help.'

While the crowds seethed below, and the platform bell began to ring, Florence gave Prakash the name she'd been thinking of since the car ride, and the note she'd written when her father had been distracted in the office.

'I will try. He was again working here but then became sick. He did not do so well in the war. I will ask if anyone visits him. I will do this for you.'

The bell in the box began to ring, and his demeanour changed. Florence took this as her cue to leave, to let him concentrate on the job. She thanked him again and descended the steps.

She passed the rest of the afternoon in the office, organising her father's desk and all the piles of documents scattered around, grateful for the distraction. She knew there was still only a small possibility, but she had a feeling this might bring her the resolution she needed. Perhaps finally she would find the answers she had been seeking for so long.

* * *

When they returned to the house, her father, complaining of a headache, went straight inside. Florence, in need of company, went around the side of the house to the servants' quarters to look for Sita. Instead she saw Cook loading his possessions into a handcart.

'What are you doing? Where are you going?'

Cook heaved another box on to the cart and then looked at her. 'Leaving. We've had enough.'

'What? What's happened?'

'Last night, after I returned here, men broke down the door to my family's home in the town. They looted it. They beat my father and threatened my mother and my wife. We have no place here any longer. We will leave, just like the rest.'

Sita came running up beside them, then sank to the ground, the wet grass soaking her sari. 'This cannot be happening. You cannot leave. Have you told the *Sahib*?'

Cook put the last box into the cart and turned to Sita. 'I am sorry. Sorry for all of this. I hope they will look after you. Shireen thanks you for your friendship. As do I. *Ma'a as-salaama*, my friend. Until we meet again.'

Florence watched in shock as he picked up the handles of the cart and began to push it down the garden path. 'No, Cook, wait. We can help you. Won't you let us help you?'

But it was too late. He splashed through the puddles by the gate then turned on to the road and away out of sight.

Florence knelt down next to Sita, who continued to sit, face in hands, clothes wet through. And even as they sat there together, the sky overhead darkened, and drops of rain, like the spots of a leopard, began to fall again.

In the space of a week, everything changed. What she had done that day — the cannon, the flight, deceiving them all — began to seem a dream, as the violence closed in around them. Mobs gathered in the streets and in the bazaar. Bloody, fatal fights between former friends and neighbours. Then refugees from other towns and cities started to arrive wearing the blank, uncomprehending faces of people who had lost everything and had never once thought to find themselves thrown upon the mercy of strangers. Makeshift homes of sheets and card provided no respite from the rains that now fell with vengeance, filling the roads with stagnant water that festered in the heat and humidity. Sickness spread through the camps and, on more than one occasion, Florence saw carts piled high with corpses being pushed along the road to the edge of the city to be burnt.

Attacks on trains increased, and her father spent long days and sometimes nights at the station. The Club was quiet, with a few remaining members gathering in the evenings for a quiet drink, if the roads were deemed safe enough to pass.

Sitting in her room for hours at a time, Florence walked the paths of her memories. She took Jay's letters from the sandalwood box on her dresser and read through them, again and again. Thoughts of Jay bled into images of the cannon, and she felt again the physical sensation of flying into the unknown. At night she dreamt of the act, but now it had transformed into something that terrorised her – waiting in the suffocating darkness to be hurled into oblivion.

Her bruises faded, but she continued to wear the scarf around her neck, telling herself as she knotted it in the morning that she would never make the same mistake again. Time passed slowly, oil leaking from the engine of her life. And then, one afternoon, Ravi announced she had a visitor.

'Mrs Florence. There is a Mr Gopal Sharma to see you in the salon.'

Her heart beat faster as she walked downstairs, preparing herself for the worst. Gopal – the boy who had gone away with Jay, trained with him, had disappeared with him into the jungles of Malaya. At least now she would know for certain.

She walked in, and he stood stiff and upright as he shook her hand. Florence indicated he should sit. 'Drink?' she offered. He shook his head, and she remembered Jay had always called him a good Hindu boy. 'I think I might have one.' She needed something to numb her from what was coming. She poured herself a peg of whisky and sat down opposite him.

'You received my letter then,' she said when he didn't speak. He nodded and looked away. 'Thank you for coming to see me.' She waited for him to begin, but he said nothing.

She could see his youth, despite his thinning hair and pinched face. He must have suffered – he looked like he'd been starved, and there was a criss-cross of scars on his cheek. Then she noticed the two missing fingers on his left hand.

'You were in one of the camps?'

'Yes, we were taken there, Jay and I, after Singapore.' He seemed to come to life at the thought, as if remembering what he had come to her for. 'We'd been stuck in a drainage ditch for three days, defending a field across from a rubber plantation, when we heard the British had capitulated. Apparently, the Japanese had access to the water supply for the island and were threatening to turn it off. Anyway, we all lined up on a road and later on were marched off to the camp. I couldn't believe how many of us there were.'

Florence sipped her whisky, trying to let the burning liquid distract her from the inevitable. 'I hear the camps were brutal places.' She finished her drink. 'How did he die?'

Gopal looked surprised. 'Oh, no, Madam. I am so sorry. I should have told you from the start. Jay did not die in the camp.'

She clutched the arms of her chair. 'Then he's alive?'

'Please, madam, let me continue. First, you have to understand that his life was very much in danger in the camp. They were sending men to work on the Burma railway. We knew we would be transferred there sooner or later. At this moment, he had several bouts of malaria, then dysentery, and he was starting to suffer very seriously from malnutrition.

There was no way he could have survived hard, physical labour.'

'He didn't much like getting dirty, it's true. But he was strong and healthy.'

'I think, somehow, his mind let him down, and his body followed. He was questioning everything. He talked about your father, the other bosses, and his job and how he had been mistreated, disrespected. He said he couldn't remember why he had joined the army, and he didn't know who the enemy was anymore.'

Florence looked out of the window. Rain was falling, drawing a grey curtain across the garden.

'I can't imagine what it must have been like.'

'I don't think you can. And he became very depressed. But then, they sent in recruiters for the Indian National Army. They gave great, rallying speeches in the camp. *Give me your blood, I will give you your freedom. You are fighting for the people who enslaved you.* This kind of thing. They talked about the famine and how the British did nothing to help. Many of the men were swept up in this feeling of renewed patriotism for India.'

'And Jay?' Florence couldn't quite believe it of him.

'Yes.'

'And so he left, with the INA?'

'Yes.'

'And now? Where is he now?'

Gopal shifted on the seat. 'Madam, he is back in Agra, but …' He hesitated.

'He's back?'

'Madam, he does not want to see you. After I received your communication, I went to see him.'

'Here? In Agra?' Florence could still not truly believe it.

'He told me to come to you and to tell you ...' Gopal stopped.

Florence went to the cabinet and poured herself another drink. 'Tell me what?'

'To tell you he was sorry. That you and he never had a chance, and he should not have been so naïve. That you are a good woman, and you should find yourself a good English man to be with. That, when he walked out of the camp, he forgot you and everything that had gone before. And that you should do the same.'

Despite the humidity, the heat, and the whisky, a shiver ran across her skin. She could have forgiven him, his change in loyalty, but not for betraying what she knew they'd had together.

'And you?' She stared at Gopal.

'Yes, madam?'

'You didn't join the INA. Did they send you to work on the railway?'

'Yes.'

'And you survived.'

'Apparently.'

'Are you glad you stayed on our side?'

Gopal gave an ambiguous, circular shake of his head. 'It cost me a great deal.' He looked at his hands, then touched the scarring on his face, pushed what remained of his hair away from his face. 'I will never be the same young man I was before the war. But I hope the British will recognise this, somehow, one day.' He stood. 'I must leave you. Please, do as Jay wishes. Go forward with your life.'

'Forward, onward, always onward.' Stunned, Florence shook his hand, then remembered her manners. 'Thank you, Gopal, for coming today. It's a kind thing that you have done.'

After he left, she finished her drink and went back to her

room. She placed the letters back in the box, covering up the dried brown leaf of a peepal tree that once had meant so much to her. She sat for a while, as the light began to fade.

Jay was in Agra. She had seen him after all, the day of the street brawl. If he'd been in the INA, then no doubt he was also involved in the protests about the trials, the general unrest. The anti-British violence. She remembered the look of anger, the coldness in his eyes, and felt sick. He'd been back all this time, and he hadn't even bothered to come and see her. To tell her to her face. He'd just left her, not knowing, imagining the worst, hoping for the best. Always in a state of limbo. And now she was married to a man who beat her, and she'd done the craziest, most dangerous, unimaginable thing, being fired out of cannon. She could have died. She was no circus performer. She was just a fool.

The days dragged on. Florence, confined to the house, was conscious that something had changed. Not just Jay. The cannon, too. What she'd done had drawn a line, created a before and after. And as of the moment when Ravi had dragged Nick out of her room, she had no more feelings of guilt, remorse, or penitence regarding her marriage. Just contempt for her husband.

One morning she went to her father and said she wanted Nick out of the house. Harry said nothing, but later she saw Nick being driven away by Ravi. Where, she didn't know, and didn't much care. It was as if he no longer existed in her sphere. Somewhere, somehow, she had been released. Then, another afternoon as she walked in the garden after the day's downpour, her father approached her.

They stood under the frangipani trees, fat droplets falling now and then around them. 'Listen, Florence,' he said. 'The situation is very unstable here. We can't know what will happen next. And then there's this business with Nick.'

So that was it. He thought she'd brought shame on them. 'But you've sorted it. We'll be fine now.'

'I can't sort the political situation, I'm afraid. What will you do, here? Your friends all went home years ago. There will be no one for you to see. Nothing for you to do.'

Florence began to feel uncomfortable at the direction this conversation was taking. 'I'll be here with you. I can take care of you, of the house.'

'That's no life for a young woman. It's not even safe for you to ride your horse anymore. You'll go stir crazy.'

'What about Ester and the circus? I can help them.' Florence felt herself blush at her own duplicity. If only her father knew what she had already done.

'You know as well as I do that they won't be staying around for much longer. I wouldn't be at all surprised if they went to Europe, too. No, I've given this quite some thought, and it's about time you left. Go to England. Find yourself a life there.'

Hearing the words out loud, Florence's stomach churned with fear. 'A life? What would I do there? I don't know anyone. I can't do anything.'

'Nonsense.' Her father put his arm around her shoulder in an unusual gesture of closeness. For a moment, Florence felt herself calmed. He did want the best for her, after all. 'I've heard from your mother's sister. Your Aunt Sarah. She'd be happy to have you. She's a bit dour, but decent enough. And I'm sure I can put in a good word with a few people. Get you a job in admin somewhere. I have some connections with the rail companies there. Isn't that what you want?'

Florence had no idea what she wanted. This conversation had come from nowhere, but it seemed as if her father had it all arranged already. Perhaps packing her off to England was just the easiest thing all round.

'But what about you, Papa? What will you do on your own?'

'Don't worry about me. I'll never leave this place. I thought you realised that. Doesn't mean you have to stay on, too. No, I really think this is the best thing for it, Florence. The Hansons are leaving in ten days. You can go with them. They'll look after you on the journey. You might even be able to see Jane again when you get there. I'll get the ticket. You better think about packing.'

With that, he let go of her shoulder and left her standing in the garden alone. Silver beads of water laced the drooping stems of flowers next to her, and she thought about Jay, and Nick, and the cannon. And Ester's words came to her once again. *Perhaps this is your opportunity, Florence. Perhaps you should think about leaving. This can be your chance to start again. A new home and a new life for yourself.* And this time, for the first time, she thought she could imagine what that might mean.

And anyway, what choice did she have?

She hadn't expected to be quite so ill, for quite so long on the ship. The doctor's prescription was for seasickness, advising a tonic of lime and ginger, with plenty of fresh air and rest. Over the course of the voyage, however, she realised something more than seasickness was the cause.

At night she lay alone, in the smallest of beds, held fast by the sheets tucked around her. Her feet hung over the end of the thin, lumpy mattress. On the deck above, the Hansons had a cabin that was three times the size of hers, not that she visited them very often. Mrs Hanson took a vague interest in Florence's health, calling in on her for half an hour in the morning, but apart from this, the days and nights passed in a blur of nausea and a delirious whirl of memories and thoughts.

She began with her goodbyes: to her father who, shockingly, had wept as she left the house that Sunday morning, as she hauled her cases down to the car where Ravi waited to take her to the station. 'Take this,' he'd said, passing her an envelope. 'Read it on the ship.' She tucked it in her bag. As they drove away, she gave him one last wave and watched as he picked up Jackie, who had woken from sleep on the veranda, and sank his face into her old, grizzled fur.

She had informed Nick of her departure via a letter, in which she also requested a divorce. She wasn't sure how she would proceed with this, given that they would be living on two separate continents, but she hoped time would make the case easier. He had not replied and had not come to see her. She was relieved at his absence.

Florence turned in her ship's cot, the sheets tangled around her now as the floor rocked and the walls swayed and another bout of sickness flooded her body.

To say farewell to Ester was an ache that spread through her whole body, though Ester praised her for her courage and believed in her decision. The two women clung to each other, with tears and whispers. It was not likely they would see each other again.

But worst of all there was Sita. Florence waited until she was sure, until she had the ticket in her hands. Then there was no hiding it. She had a week to pack and set everything right. When she arrived back from town with her father after their visit to the agency that would arrange her travels, she went straight to Sita's room.

Florence knocked on the door then pushed it open. Sita was there, brushing her hair. Florence loved to see her do this, the way it shone and hung like black satin all the way down her back. Nothing like her own straw curls. Sita patted the chair beside her. Florence sat and took the brush, then began running it through Sita's hair, wondering as always at the absence of any knots or tangles.

'Thank you, *beti.* It is always such a treat to have someone else do this.'

Florence continued brushing smooth, slow strokes. 'I have something to tell you,' she said. 'But I don't know how to say it.'

'Just spit it out. What is it?'

Florence put the brush down, took the ticket from her bag and passed it to Sita. Florence watched as Sita's eyes filled with tears. 'Please, *amah.* I don't know what to say.'

Sita took her hand and gripped it tightly. 'I know, I know.' Sita rocked gently and held Florence's hand to her face. 'You have to go. I want only your happiness.'

Happiness? Why did everyone else seem to know what would make her happy, when she herself no longer had any idea what that could look like? For a moment Florence felt a rush of doubt, a premonition of a life over which she would have no control. Then grief took over as her own tears rose. 'Papa is staying on. He says you can live here as long as you wish.' Sita remained silent, holding Florence's hand. 'I'm so sorry. Please forgive me.'

A week later, she had closed her last suitcase, the clothes inside folded and wrapped in paper. Everything was ready. Sita stood by her side, an arm around her waist. Florence turned to her. 'I'm afraid. I wish you were coming with me.'

Sita took Florence by the shoulders and looked into her eyes. 'You were always so brave, my golden one. Don't stop now, or ever. I will be with you, and you will always be in my thoughts and in my heart.'

But Florence didn't feel brave. Foolhardy, perhaps. Frightened, absolutely. What was this place, this England, that she was running away to? How could it possibly justify leaving behind everything and everyone she cared about to take their chances in an uncertain world? No. She didn't think she was being very brave at all. She wiped away the tears that seemed to flow constantly these days. 'I love you, *amah*.'

At Agra Station, Ravi piled her cases on to a trolley and accompanied her to the platform. The Hansons were already on board, and Mrs Hanson leaned out of a window and beckoned. Florence ignored her and turned to Ravi. 'Look after Papa, won't you?'

Ravi nodded. 'For as long as I can.' They held hands for a moment, then Ravi stepped back. A bell started ringing somewhere overhead. 'You must go now.' He signalled to a porter and turned and left. She watched him disappear into the crowds and knew she would never see him again.

The ship heaved once more, and Florence hung her head over the edge of the bed above a bucket, miserable and lonely. The night passed, like all the others, in a confusion of sickness and shards of her past, which appeared to her now, as vivid and as detailed as when they had occurred.

As a child chasing butterflies and stalking peacocks. Running the length of the garden with a piece of silk, gossamer and radiant, held high like a sail in the morning sun. There was Oscar, his chestnut coat gleaming, shoulder muscles rippling as he trotted out underneath her across the dew-heavy fields. Land, still fogged, dreaming of its trees and silvered rivers, and workers that appeared like ghosts out of the cloud.

School came and went — the chill of mountain air on her legs as she chased the hockey ball, the snuggled conversations made by lamplight in the dorm. Sita leaned over her, singing a song. Jay smiled up at her out of the dark of the locomotive, then pressed her against the peepal tree and kissed her. Her father, seated at the piano, turned to her, expectant, when it was her moment to sing.

And then there was Ester unveiling the cannon and helping her on to the platform above the arena as the trapeze swung towards her. The cannon, its mouth gaping, luring her in, back down into its liquid dark where she would dissipate in its chrysalis and emerge a different kind of being.

And as the ship continued its way, across the rolling seas, and these memories rolled around with her, a knowledge, a certainty, grew in her, that she was carrying more than just diaries and photos as a reminder of the life she had left behind.

Chapter Twenty-Two

PORTSMOUTH, 1956

The April sunshine made a watery kind of light as Florence and Robert walked down the hill to the bus stop. Their cases were heavy and bulky, and every now and then they would pause and rest. Birds called from the trees along the road, a bright and hopeful sound. Florence picked up the cases again and strode on ahead, and every few steps Robert had to run to keep up with her.

At the station, Florence held his hand, wondering if he, like her, was recalling that dreadful day last year on the railway tracks. He seemed happy enough as he waited on the platform for the train to arrive.

There it came, with a thunder of wheels and a screech of brakes, followed by a great hissing of steam. Florence's heart beat faster as the ground trembled and the giant locomotive slowed to a halt a few feet from the buffers. Doors opened and people stepped down, porters unloaded luggage, trolleys trundled towards the exit, and finally they could board. They settled themselves in a compartment, Robert swinging his legs with excitement. Florence was excited for him. His first time on a train. It was something to be celebrated.

At last the whistle. Robert grinned up at her and pressed his nose to the window. They pulled out of the station and began to pick up speed.

After a while, Robert sat back. 'Where do we get off?' he asked.

'Southampton. Where the big ships come in. That's where I first set foot in England when I arrived from India.'

'How long are we going to stay there?' He eyed their cases again.

'I don't know at the moment. We'll have to see how things work out.'

'What about Billy?'

Florence didn't answer for a while. The train was going at speed now, countryside flashing by outside the windows. 'Billy knows where to find us, if he wants to.' But she really didn't think he would, not after all the arguments of the past few months. How he'd wanted to get his hands on her money, telling her it was his by law, because she was his wife. Her inheritance! Half of the sale of the house in Agra (the other half divided between Ravi and Sita) and the money that her father had managed to put away, despite all appearances. No, she would never let Billy take it from her and squander it on gambling and binges down the pub. If she gave it to him, she knew she would never see it again, and she would live forever in that cold and lonely house on the hill.

'But what will we *do* there?' Robert was looking out of the window again, his fingers leaving little prints on the glass.

'Well, you will go to school with Tara. And you'll have her to play with whenever you want. No more Andrew Leach and David Poole. Won't that be nice?' Robert nodded, still gazing through the glass as if mesmerised. 'There are fields to run around in. We can get a dog, if you'd like.' At this, Robert turned and gave her the biggest smile she'd seen for a long time. 'And if you want, you can help your Aunt and Uncle. It's going to be hard work, so only if you want to.'

Robert thought about this for a moment, a serious frown creasing his brow. 'Actually,' he said, 'I think I prefer maths to horses.' Then he added, 'But I'd still like a dog.'

Florence laughed. 'Of course. I'd like a dog, too. I used to have a dog. My Papa gave her to me on my tenth birthday. Jackie, she was called.'

Robert turned back to the window and so did Florence. She thought about the place she'd bought with Ester and Andreas. A farm for sale, going cheap after the death of the father — the grown children not interested in carrying on the family tradition. They'd walked the fields and talked about the horses, about stables and livery and the different events they could train clients for. Eventually there would be a dressage arena and a cross-country course. She silently thanked her father for the money he had left her. It meant a new life was possible for them all.

The train chugged on, rocking them in their seats. Florence closed her eyes, feeling drowsy. Then the memories came, of other trains and other landscapes — being lulled to sleep in a pull-down bunk, heading home from school for the holidays. Or hiding, vulnerable and unnerved, locked inside a compartment while angry men on the tracks outside threw rocks, and her new husband proved a disappointment.

The sun flickered behind the tall trees on the embankment, flickered red and gold behind her eyelids as she leaned her head against the juddering window frame. And slowly, languidly, this flickering transformed into the lamp-lit shimmer of Sita's red and gold sari crossing the garden in the purple Agra dusk. But Sita had grown old, her long plait frosted white as it swung across her back. And then there was Ravi, hunched and shrunken, waiting on the veranda. Florence followed the two of them inside and upstairs to her father's room, where he lay and held her hand and gasped the last of his shallow breaths in the trembling, creamy candle-light and the murmur of the radio playing on low.

A moment later, she found herself outside again, walking down the road towards the field where once a circus tent had stood and people had watched a breath-taking spectacle as she'd flown over a rainbow and landed, another person entirely. And now through her tears she saw Sita in her village hut, lying on her bed surrounded by swaying, mourning women whose heads were covered in shining veils, and then Ravi, alone in a tiny apartment with a window that let in the clamour of the bazaar as he finished his dinner and suddenly slumped sideward from the table.

The rhythm of the train continued like a lullaby, and Florence felt a weight materialise beside her: there was her puppy, Jackie, tiny and sharp-eyed and new, covering her snout with her paws. Florence slid her hand forward until she felt once again the softness of those ears, like the fluff on a dandelion clock just before the wind whispers that it's time to float away.

A peacock shrieked, and she looked for Jay, but the peacock kept on shrieking and screeching, and something was tapping at her hand. Florence opened her eyes. Robert was shaking her arm and the train was slowing down, its brakes squealing in protest.

'It's stopping. Are we there?'

But they were still in the countryside, and after a few minutes wait, the train continued on.

Unsettled by her dream, Florence eased herself back into the present. Green fields shot by, lush and bright under the sudden sun. A river twisted by the side of the tracks, a grey heron stalking through the reeds. Then she felt a sense of hope and forward propulsion, and not just that of the train travelling down the tracks.

Resting her head against the rattling glass and looking up, she saw the sky was now a fresh, endless blue. They had reached the outskirts of the city and in the back gardens of the houses, as the train clanked past, women hanging laundry turned their faces heavenward for a moment's peace and warmth. It had turned into a perfect spring day.

Florence reached for Robert's hand and gave it a squeeze. He returned the pressure and left his seat to settle on her lap. 'Will we ever go to India, Mummy?'

Florence stroked his curls, those dark curls that still fell over his eyes, and pressed her cheek against the top of his head. Fragments of the dream returned to her, and it was as if the force of his words, spoken out loud for the first time, made her realise it was possible. If they wanted to, she could return. Anything was possible, really.

'Yes, darling. One day, and perhaps quite soon. There is someone I want you to meet.' Robert looked up at her, a silent question on his face. 'She was like a mother to me.'

'You didn't have a mummy, though, did you? Like I don't have a grandfather or grandmother.'

Florence smiled. 'Actually, yes, I did. Her name was Sita, and she loved me. It's too late for your Grandfather, and I'm sorry about that. But we'll go back and find her, you and I. To thank her properly.'

The train was slowing down now as it drew into the station, whistling long and loud. Florence heaved the cases down from the rack and ushered Robert into the corridor and down the steps. The platform was busy, and they dodged in and out of the bustle of people towards the exit. There she saw someone waving over heads of the crowd. When they got close, Ester called out. 'Over here, dearies.'

Robert ran ahead to Tara, who insisted on taking his case. Florence followed with Ester into the street outside.

'Lovely day for it,' said Ester. 'Here's the car.' She stopped beside a green Morris Eight, took their cases and threw them on to the back seat. 'Squeeze in children.' Tara flung herself inside and Robert did the same. Another first for him, thought Florence. It was his day for locomotives and engines.

'Ready to see what we've done with the place?' Ester started to climb in, then stopped and looked over the roof at Florence. 'Don't suppose you fancy driving, do you?'

Florence hesitated, then remembered: anything was possible, really. She nodded, and Ester threw her the keys.

The next morning she drove down a narrow track, leaving the new riding school and the field of horses to grow smaller in the rear-view mirror. Past the barn where, underneath a heavy layer of tarpaulin, a cannon sat, neutralised by the land she owned, that she now shared with the ones she loved. Getting out to open the gate, she turned for a moment to take in the view. She could see Robert and Tara in the distance climbing bales of straw, and Ester and Andreas carrying buckets across the yard. Then she checked her watch. No time for this now. She mustn't be late today.

Walking through the doors of the works, she reminded herself of all the experience she had, of all the things she had done — on the railways, at the circus, India, the war. A roomful of men wasn't anything she couldn't handle.

She was directed to the end of a corridor where she pushed through swinging doors and took in the scene before her:

tables laid out with parts of engines, another area with frames of levers and dials. Her heart beat faster — it was like a dream come true. A figure detached itself from a group standing at the side of the hall. She smiled and waved.

'Are you ready for this?' Haresh said when he reached her. She held his gaze, steady and strong, ignoring the silence that had descended on the room, the stares of the men at the two of them together.

'Never been readier for anything in my life.'

In the interview room, Hugh Woolf, the Superintendent of the training school, studied her papers, certificates, and letter of application, while another man, Mr Richards, the District Inspector, led the conversation.

'I wonder if you understand, Mrs Greene,' he said, making a pyramid of his fingers beneath his chin, 'how gravely responsible is the task that would be in your hands.'

Florence hoped she looked sufficiently serious. 'I absolutely appreciate the responsibility of the job, Mr Richards. I know from personal experience it can be a matter of life or death.'

Richards looked at Woolf, who leaned in and murmured in his ear. 'Ah, yes,' Richards continued. 'I understand the Indian signalman saved your boy's life.' He pronounced the word Indian as if it were something slightly bitter in his mouth. 'Still, he's a man. Whereas I usually find that among women there's just less of a railway sense.'

'I grew up with railways, sir. I believe I have exactly that sense you're talking about.'

'Oh, I'm sure you do believe it. Just as I'm sure that when you've learned a little of some business, you think you've learned it all. Women, are just, to be short, superficial when it comes to work, and far too impatient of getting a good grounding in the principles.'

'With respect, I think my time at the factory, on the production line, and then in logistics demonstrates the opposite. I am a fast learner, but I certainly don't skimp on the important stuff.'

Richards breathed out heavily through his nose. There was quiet for a moment, then he tried another tack. 'What about textbooks? And regulations, and official language? Do you think you can cope with all of that?'

'Top in my class in mathematics – the textbooks were my preferred reading material. And then my service in the war – rules and regs everywhere. I can't say I ever found the language to be a problem.'

'Of course, there were women working on the railways here during the war,' said Woolf, as much to Richards as to Florence.

Richards looked slightly pained. 'Yes, I know, I know. All doing their bit. And I have nothing but admiration for their commitment, their energy, and their pliability. But that was then.'

The three of them sat in silence, then Richards stood up. 'It's up to you, Woolf. You run the training school. She'll be your liability. But,' and he leaned towards Florence over the desk, 'I shall be inspecting you at the end of your apprenticeship, and if I find the slightest hint of an error, or misunderstanding, or lack of attention to detail, then you'll be out, straight back to your home and your family, quicker than you know. Understand?'

Florence nodded. 'I understand, sir. I promise you I won't let you down.'

'It's him you'll be letting down.' Richards turned and walked towards the door. 'I have a lot more important business to be dealing with than this.'

When Richards had left, Woolf continued to sit there re-

reading her papers. After another couple of minutes he finally pushed them to one side.

'So a talent for mathematics?'

Florence nodded. 'Yes, sir.'

'And cryptography and truck driving in the war?'

'Yes, sir.'

'And your father was a railwayman?'

'Yes, he was. All his life.'

Woolf looked thoughtful. 'Well, that's all good so far. But I have to ask — this stuff about the circus. A human cannonball? You really suppose I'm going to believe that?'

She'd been expecting this. She'd done it deliberately. It was time to provoke, time to get it out there. Why should she hide the one amazing thing that made her different from everybody else?

'Mr Woolf, with respect, why on earth would I put it on my curriculum if it weren't true? I know it's not exactly conventional, but it is relevant. Knowledge of physics, skills in timing, precision — absolute attention to detail. A life or death situation. All qualities and experience I believe would be important in this role.'

Mr Woolf sat silently again for another minute. She wondered if she had made a huge mistake. After all, what woman put human cannonball down as past experience on a job application form? She scanned his face, anxious.

Finally, he said, 'So, this cannon. How exactly does it work?'

Florence smiled. She remembered a conversation in the past, when she had been the one to ask. 'Secrets of the trade, I'm afraid, Mr Woolf. Still, if you ever wanted to see for yourself, you're welcome to visit. It's sitting in our barn. Have a look inside, then give me your theory. You can meet the Great Gombar, too.'

There was a moment when she thought perhaps she had gone too far, and she'd be ordered out of the room, told never to return, but then he burst into laughter. 'Well, Haresh was right. You certainly seem to have some mettle. And you're going to need it working here. You'll be the only woman on the line. It really will be quite a responsibility.'

What had he said? 'So, you mean—?'

'Yes, Mrs Greene. Trainee signalwoman. Terrible hours, shift work, and paid a pittance. Not to mention that most of your co-workers will resent your very presence here. It's yours if you want it.'

Florence struggled to maintain her reserve. 'Thank you. Yes, thank you.'

He stood and held out his hand. 'Jolly good. My secretary will give you the forms to sign. Start next week.' They walked towards the door. 'And as for that cannon, I'll take you up on that offer. Sounds bloody fascinating. I'd love to hear all about it one day.'

Florence managed to contain herself until she was sitting in the car, where she gave a small cheer and drummed her hands on the steering wheel. Then she became aware Haresh was peering in. She rolled down the window.

'Congratulations.'

'All thanks to you,' she said, embarrassed that he'd seen her celebration. 'I never would have got the interview otherwise.'

'I said I would help if I could. I meant it.' He straightened up. 'I have to go. See you next Monday.'

Florence started the car and manoeuvred out of the yard. As she pulled on to the road, she saw him still standing there waving. She pressed her foot down on the gas, and accelerated away, keen and excited to get back to Ester and tell her the good news.

* * *

The door of the signal box was open, and she stood at the top of the steps for a moment on the threshold, watching Haresh as he finished writing in the ledger. He was bent over his desk, but when he saw her, he straightened up and beckoned her inside.

'Please, please. This is your place of work, too. Come in. You'll need to feel comfortable if you are making that journey every day.' He looked at his watch. 'At least the train was on time. Now,' he looked around, 'I have a notebook for you, and a pen. Here.' He handed it to her. 'Your job is to record all the movements I make. And answer the telephone, too. At peak periods we'll be dashing around, pulling levers left, right, and centre. And I'm afraid there's some business that's even less glamorous. Brass needs to be kept polished. Floor needs to be swept. And there's the ... err ... lavatory.' He looked apologetic. 'All part of looking after your own box.'

'I'm not proud. I mucked out three stables this morning.'

Haresh pulled a chair out for her. 'Are you ready to get started? Next locomotive is due through in ten minutes. They should be calling any time now.'

Florence straightened the jacket of her new uniform and picked up the pen. 'I'm all yours.'

Haresh looked up at her, faint creases of gentle humour around his eyes. 'Well, that we can discuss another time. After all, you have twelve weeks with me inside this box. Tell me how you feel when we've finished training.'

Florence laughed. 'I'm sure it will fly by.'

Haresh laughed too. 'That's as may be, but for now, there's a train on its way.'

* * *

The bells ring their secret codes and outside, a mile up the line, a signal arm raises. A crow flies up into the air and caws with displeasure. In the distance, a train appears.

Cramped inside the locomotive cab, a man shovels coal into a firebox, and the heat and smoke of the fire runs down tubes inside the boiler, turning water into steam. The steam flows into a cylinder, and a piston plunges back and forth, and a crankshaft turns, rotating the wheels and powering the engine along. It gathers speed. The signal's all clear. The tracks vibrate and the ground beneath shakes. The iron fiend goes faster now, thunders, roars, devours the distance. Forward it goes, onward on it goes, forward and onward, forward and onward. Propulsion and energy, momentum and pressure, it screams down the line, away from the past and into the future.

In a signal box, a woman watches. Her heart thuds, and her blood quickens as steam engulfs her, and the blast and the clamour, and the world quakes.

And then, as suddenly as it came, it is gone.

Acknowledgements

Many, many thanks to Samantha Brace and Peyton Stableford at Agora for taking this book on and for all their brilliant editing skills and advice. Thank you also to Emma Rogers for designing the beautiful cover.

This novel was born on the MA in Creative Writing at Manchester Writing School, and I am grateful to everyone who read any part of it and offered support and encouragement in those early days. That goes double for Lucie McKnight Hardy, Michael Walters, and our excellent tutor, Nicholas Royle.

Thank you to Cindy Camatsos for reading and re-reading with her keen critical eye, and all the subsequent discussions at Café Calma. Thank you to live artist Liz Clarke, who kindly met me to talk through the imaginative process behind her cannonballista show. Thanks also to Kate McDonald for her unwavering enthusiasm and generosity, particularly during the oddities and adversities of 2020 and 2021. And thanks, too, to all the strong women who keep on keeping on, and especially Natalie Roberts, Caroline Ellis, Katherine High, and Debbie Smith — always a wellspring of support and fortitude.

Above all, I am grateful to my family. Celeste and Steve Gomez for their certainty and those invaluable conversations in the garden about plot and structure. Mum and Dad for their love and constancy and for all the anecdotes about life in India or 1950s Portsmouth. Nanny Frances, who inspired the whole story in the first place. And of course, to Michele, who has always believed I could do this.

Further Reading

For an illuminating and moving account of the personal and the political during India's liberation from British rule, I highly recommend Yasmin Khan's *The Great Partition*.

Two wonderful books on British women in India provided inspiration for Florence's life there as a daughter and wife: *Women of the Raj* by Margaret MacMillan, and *The Dust in the Balance: British Women in India 1905-1945.* Apparently, mock pears fashioned from mashed potato were an actual thing.

Mulk Raj Anand's poignant novel *Untouchable* gives insight into the complexities and tensions of caste and racial divides in a cantonment town.

Finally, a couple of gems I found tucked away on a shelf in the back room of Eastleigh Railway Museum. *War on the Line: The Southern Railway in Wartime* by Bernard Darwin highlights attitudes towards women working on the railways during and after the war, while *Tales of The Old Railwaymen* by Tom Quinn gives insight through personal accounts into the job of signalman in days past. It really was another world entirely.

Love Agora Books?

JOIN OUR BOOK CLUB

If you sign up today, you'll get:

1. A free novel from Agora Books
2. Exclusive insights into our books and authors, and the chance to get copies in advance of publication, and
3. The chance to win exclusive prizes in regular competitions

Interested? It takes less than a minute to sign up. You can get your novel and your first newsletter by signing up at www.agorabooks.co

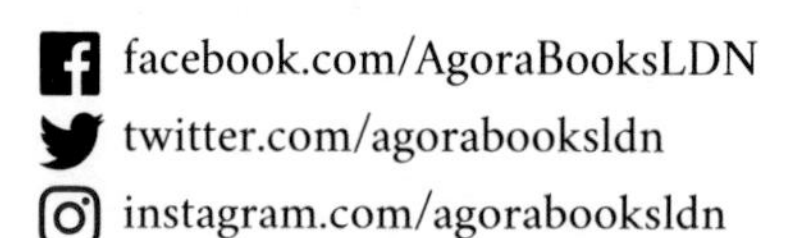

facebook.com/AgoraBooksLDN
twitter.com/agorabooksldn
instagram.com/agorabooksldn